MYSTERY IN THE PALACE OF WESTMINSTER

SARAH LUSTIG

Published by A&A Press, Unit 92893, PO Box 6945, London, W1A 6US

Cover design by Jacqui Crawford
Cover illustration by Katie Melrose Advocate Art Ltd

First published 2022

29 28 27 26 25
10 9 8 7 6 5

ISBN 978 1 7397736 0 1

Printed and bound in Great Britain by Clays Ltd, Elcograf S.p.A

A CIP catalogue record for this book is available from the British Library.

This is a work of fiction. Names, places, events, institutions and incidents are either the products of the author's imagination or used fictitiously. Any resemblance to actual persons, living or dead, or actual events is coincidental and unintentional.

Copyright notice
All rights reserved. No part of this publication may be reproduced, transmitted, stored in an information retrieval system in any form or by any means, graphic, electronic or mechanical, including photocopying, taping and recording, without prior written permission from the copyright owner, except in accordance with the provisions of the Copyright, Designs and Patents Act 1988.

The right of Sarah Lustig to be identified as the author of this work has been asserted by her in accordance with the Copyright, Designs and Patents Act 1988.

Contents

The Palace of Westminster	7
The Speaker's Procession	13
Bedlam in the Lobby	18
An Independent Inquiry	25
The Chief Whip	32
Number Eleven, Downing Street	41
The House of Lords Reform Bill	56
The Lord Speaker	66
Meeting with the Opposition	77
The Serjeant at Arms	84
A New Partner	94
The Lobby Journalist	101
An Uncivil Peerage	112
The Prime Minister's Deputy	119
On the Trail of a Journalist	125
In the Corridors of Power	136
Contraband	149
The Leader of the Opposition	157
Detained	165
The Aides' Revenge	173
Truce	182

Reckoning	192
Gommers	199
The Palace's Secrets	209
Sneaking Past Security	222
In the Bowels of the Palace	234
A Treacherous Thief	241
Justice Through Valour	250
An Unexpected Offer	256
A Game of Tennis	261
Body in the Thames	267
Glossary	268
Acknowledgements	271
About the Author	272

The first rule in politics is that there are no rules.

> Tony Blair

CHAPTER ONE

The Palace of Westminster

Theo Duncan stopped abruptly on his doorstep. He looked along Downing Street to the car his dad was taking him to school in. He had assumed it would be discreet, a nondescript estate, like the one his mum always took when she went out. Instead there was a sleek Jaguar with blue lights and a professional driver waiting for him. Andy, his dad's personal protection officer, waited by the car for them. It was anything but inconspicuous.

'Thought you'd like to arrive in style,' his dad said with a smile, as he followed Theo out of Number Ten, Downing Street.

As soon as his dad appeared, cameras flashed and clicked at them from the other side of the street.

Theo's dad tutted. There was the shadow of a deep frown on his face. It was gone as swiftly as it had appeared.

'Get in the car, Theo.' He fixed his features into a look of friendly professionalism and strode off to meet the reporters.

Theo hurried along the pavement. The palace-like fortress

of the Foreign Office overshadowed the pavement from across the street. It was off-white and dirt-smudged, like clean laundry left out to dry in the rain. Forlorn and forgotten. Wrought-iron gates topped by a crown on a spike barred the entrance archways.

Theo ducked his head into the back seat of the Jaguar and perched uneasily with his backpack on his lap, anxious not to mark the cream leather upholstery. He never thought he would miss his dad's ancient Ford Focus, with its dodgy air conditioning that was hot in summer and cold in winter, and the annoying whining noise it made whenever it reversed. But Theo was starting to see the value of keeping something that was broken. In the Ford Focus, he had never worried about marking the seats – they were stained already.

They still had their old car. But it was sitting unused on the road outside their old house.

Nothing had been the same since his dad had become Prime Minister two years before.

After a few moments, Theo looked through the back window to see what was taking his dad so long. He was still speaking to the assembled journalists, who were hanging on his every word. His long black coat flapped in the wind. He was so tall, he seemed to loom over them, like a lecturer addressing his students. He waved once and closed the wave with his signature move – a clenched fist. Theo had once seen a newspaper article that compared the move to that of an orchestra conductor. Now whenever he saw it, he couldn't help imagining his dad manically waving his arms around his head. Much like that time his sister Harry got a wasp in her hair. He smiled at the memory.

The Palace of Westminster

Andy got in the front passenger side. Theo's dad swept into the back next to him with a flurry of wind and jostling briefcase.

'Ready?' his dad said with enthusiasm.

Theo nodded and tried to smile, but he suspected it looked more like a grimace. He was thinking about what his dad might do when they arrived. His stomach started to twist.

His class was going on a school trip to the Houses of Parliament. When his dad had found out about it, he had leapt at the opportunity to take Theo to work with him. Theo had been counting down the days to the trip with mounting anxiety. He pictured them arriving – his dad waving, his whole class staring – and thought again about just how bad an idea this was.

As their car pulled out of the Downing Street gates, past the police officers guarding the entrance and right onto Whitehall, Theo wished his dad had agreed to let him walk there on his own. It wasn't even that far.

'Are you looking forward to your tour?' his dad asked.

'Yup,' Theo said, nodding while he studied the view from his window. He glimpsed the steel spokes of the London Eye, before it slid out of sight behind an amber-brick Georgian townhouse.

'You'll be able to tell all your classmates that you were christened in the chapel,' his dad said, furiously typing on his phone.

Theo's stomach shrivelled. He wanted to bring that up about as much as he wanted to break into an impromptu breakdance in front of his classmates. He imagined it would get about the same reaction. An unimpressed silence. And

The Palace of Westminster

then the sniggers and outright laughter – at him.

'I wonder if you'll visit it.'

'I dunno, Dad. We're probably just going to see the main bits.'

'The "main bits"?' His dad looked up. '"I dunno"! I brought you up to speak properly, Theo. I hope you're not going to talk to your teacher like that. You know what everything is called – the House of Commons, the House of Lords and—'

'The Strangers' Bar?' Theo interrupted.

His dad put his phone down in his lap. 'You can't mention things like that. You're not supposed to talk about bars at your age. And you know that we can't afford to make any—'

'Mistakes. Yes, I know.' Theo turned back to the view. They were waiting at the traffic lights leading on to Parliament Square.

His dad's phone rang and he sighed as he answered it.

'Yes?'

Theo stared up at Big Ben's clock tower. It looked like the evil, twisted version of a fairy tale castle, with metal spikes thrusting into the sky.

'What all of it?' his dad said into his phone. 'No CCTV in the whole palace? Oh for goodness' sake. What about in the Commons, is the live feed working? Well that's something at least.'

His dad fiddled with the clasp on his Red Box, clipping and unclipping it. The Red Box was a red leather briefcase that contained secret government papers only his dad was meant to see. Theo used to plot ways to look at what was inside it. When he had finally managed to sneak a peek, it had turned out to be full of papers with endless fractions and ratios, and paragraphs of text as long as whole pages. He had never bothered to look again.

'No of course we can't, we have to go ahead with everything as planned. The whips have finally got a majority for this vote, postponing it would be a disaster. Besides, what would we say to the press – admit that the whole system has gone down? It's better if no one knows it's not working. At least then it's a deterrent.'

Theo's ears pricked up at the mention of the whips. They were MPs who worked for his dad. It was their job to make sure every MP voted with the government in debates in Parliament. He had always liked their name, it made him think of whipping people into shape. He hadn't thought their name had anything to do with actual whips – just one of the many weird quirks of government – until his dad told him they kept a real whip in their office. It was a mystery to Theo how they persuaded over three hundred people to all vote the same way. His dad had said, very vague and offhand, that they were persuasive people. Persuasive how? Theo wondered.

The car stopped at the gated entrance of the Houses of Parliament as his dad hung up the phone.

'Bloody builders. I knew something would go wrong. I don't know what they expect me to do about it.' He stared at his dark phone screen as though it might have the answer. On his little finger, a gold ring embossed with their family coat of arms – a hawk in flight, over a naval crown – glinted up at Theo.

Theo's heart didn't sink, so much as nosedive to the floor, like one of his baby sister's toy cars when she dropped them in the bath.

He had thought he might get a ring of his own for his last birthday. But it had come and gone the year before without the ring making an appearance. Now his fifteenth birthday was only two months away and he didn't have any hope of being given it this time.

It was a family tradition. It was supposed to be a reward for an act of particular bravery – the family motto was Justice through Valour. His dad had been given his by his father on his thirteenth birthday after he shot a stag on the family estate. Theo had only tried shooting on his grandpa's land in Scotland once. He had been so terrified that he might actually hurt an animal that he deliberately shot off in the wrong direction. His dad had taken the shotgun from him with a grim expression and never given it back.

The year before Theo had thought he might get the ring because he had been doing particularly well in school – he had got full marks in every spelling test for months. But when his birthday passed and no ring had arrived, he had started to accept what he had suspected deep down for some time: that passing spelling tests was not worthy of the reward. His dad didn't think he deserved it. He must be doing something wrong; he just didn't know what.

The car pulled through the gates into the Houses of Parliament courtyard and came to a stop.

'Ready, champ?' his dad said with a smile.

Theo suppressed a gurgle of anxiety and opened the car door.

CHAPTER TWO

The Speaker's Procession

'Hurry up, everyone.' Mr Gatimu herded Theo and his classmates into St Stephen's Hall. 'We don't want to miss the Speaker's Procession.'

He raised his voice to be heard over the noise of banging and a buzz saw. A man wearing a hard hat lumbered past, a toolbox swinging from his burly arm.

Theo's arrival had been just as excruciating as he had imagined it would be. His classmates had stopped all conversation to gawp in silence as he got out of the government vehicle. While his dad shook hands with his teacher, Mr Gatimu, he had felt as unremarkable as a goat in a zoo during the lions' feeding time. Mr Gatimu, at least, had acted normally. The first time his head teacher had met his dad, Theo had cringed inwardly as she flicked her hair and giggled nervously. He was grateful that Mr Gatimu had kept his cool. But after his dad left, his classmates had turned their precision-laser attention on him. He had tucked his head down and tried to ignore the stares.

Theo trudged along the aged stone tiles of St Stephen's

Hall, past aged marble statues wearing Roman togas, long enough to be draped over an arm. One in a long judge's wig seemed to scold him with a stern pointed index finger.

Paintings on the left-hand walls depicted chaotic, medieval battles in stark primary colours. Those on the right were ordered and calm. He recognised Queen Elizabeth I and was that Christopher Columbus with her? These seemed to show monarchs and ambassadors – political negotiations, Theo concluded. It felt odd to paint the battles with the peace treaties. Who wanted to remember the fight? Surely it was better, Theo thought, just to celebrate the truce.

He felt eyes on him. He turned to see the new girl, Samira Jhor, looking at him. She had started a few weeks ago, unusually, at the beginning of the summer term. She was a lot shorter than him and looked up at him with dark brown eyes. Her long dark hair was shot through with artificial cherry-red streaks and her thumbs poked through frayed holes in her jumper sleeves, showing chipped nail polish. It was black today. Theo had also seen purple and teal green. She didn't look away as Theo stared. He became embarrassed and turned back to the paintings.

They moved on into a vast octagonal chamber. There were police officers clustered in the doorways, tourists loitering nearby and, to the right, a handful of men and women dressed in formal work wear.

The buzz saw stopped. It left a gaping silence in its wake, making the grand space feel as sacred as a crypt.

The vaulted ceiling soared high. He squinted against the glittering of the ceiling's gold gilt, the great gold chandelier. The floor was black and gold – a chequerboard pattern that reminded Theo of a chessboard. Everything was bright and dark at the same time, a weird clashing mixture of gloomy and glowing. Stone statues guarded vast gothic windows. Each one was wearing a crown. He didn't get it. This was supposed to be the home of democracy. So what was with the obsession with kings and queens?

'Shut it!' Mr Gatimu shout-whispered. He had the shadow of stubble against his brown skin and his black buzz cut was growing long and fluffy. He looked harmless. But he had a particular stare that told you he knew exactly what you were thinking. If you were lying about your lost homework. Or if you thought you might know the answer to a question but didn't want to risk answering in case you were wrong and you looked stupid.

When the students fell quiet, Mr Gatimu explained in a hushed voice that they were in Central Lobby. To the left was the House of Commons and to the right, the House of Lords.

Theo's head swung between them. He noticed that those clustered at the entrance to the House of Lords were grouped around one old man. Theo recognised him, he was sure he had seen his face recently, but he couldn't place where. He was wearing a black cloak and white cravat, just like his mum's court cloak, but without the wig. The others seemed to be questioning him and the man had his hands out as if he was telling them to calm down.

Mr Gatimu was still speaking. 'Who can guess what these mosaics represent?' He pointed up at the nearest one. There were four – one over each doorway – each showing three figures. He looked around slowly at the students.

Theo tried not to stand out, which was difficult, because he was at least a head taller than any of his classmates. He pulled his head in towards his body like a snail going into its shell and avoided Mr Gatimu's eye.

'Theo—' His shoulders dropped – 'can you guess?'

Theo tried to reposition his backpack on his shoulders, his sweaty palms slipping against the straps. He didn't have a clue. He searched the mosaics. He spotted the Scottish flag, then the English flag. If he had to guess, he would say they were something to do with the four countries of the UK. He thought of what his dad had said earlier. 'We can't afford to make mistakes.' He didn't want to guess.

Theo swallowed nervously. 'Erm, I don't know, sir.'

'Just have a try,' Mr Gatimu persisted. His stare was morphing from mild to penetrating.

Theo could feel his colour rising.

'Sorry, sir.' He shrugged.

Mr Gatimu blinked and looked away. Theo breathed a sigh of relief.

'They represent the four nations that make up Great Britain,' Mr Gatimu continued.

Theo had been right.

'Quiet, everyone,' Mr Gatimu called as the noise of the class rose, 'just a minute now.'

The tourists were looking towards the opposite doorway and Theo turned to stare also. The noise died away and just audible was the echo of a rhythmic patter, like the first drops of rain dripping on a window.

'Hats off, strangers,' a police officer called so loudly, Theo jumped.

The tourists quickly removed their hats.

The procession rounded the corner into view. At the front was a man in a black tailcoat and white gloves. He

The Speaker's Procession

was wearing those silly short trousers that ended just below the knee, like the men in historical dramas often wore. The ones his sister Harry always swooned over. His shoes were like that too – black with a shiny silver buckle. His expression was very solemn. He looked like someone who had got locked out of his house in his dressing gown and was trying very hard to act like he had meant to do it.

The man who followed the first was wearing the same outfit, but it wasn't so noticeable on him. Because on his shoulder he was carrying an enormous gold club with a crown on the end of it. Theo wondered whether it was solid gold, and how much it weighed. Despite the weight, the man looked serene, at ease. With the shining gold at the back of his head, he looked like an African king, gazing over his subjects. Theo felt a sense of quiet awe. The same spell seemed to have come over the rest of the crowd too, who had all stopped whispering. He wouldn't have been surprised if they had all kneeled as the procession moved past.

There was a strange sound, like tin cans rolling down a deserted street. Theo looked around and saw the tourists, strangely ordinary in their branded puffer coats.

Just as he felt the spell of unreality was shimmering away into nothingness, there were a few loud pops.

And the room started to fill with smoke.

CHAPTER THREE

Bedlam in the Lobby

The smoke rose quickly. It billowed upwards, swallowing whole people in a single gulp. Theo couldn't see his own body below his waist.

The smoke clawed at his throat and eyes. It tasted bitter and metallic. Was it poisonous? He clamped his eyes shut and tried to hold his breath.

There was yelping. Swearing and shouting. He was buffeted by bags and, was that, flailing limbs?

A hand grabbed his wrist in a vice-like grip. Surprised, he let out the breath he was holding.

He thought of the kidnap training his dad had been offered, and refused, for his children. Had someone come for him?

His heart beating fast, he wrenched his arm away as hard as he could. A girl squealed. With a stab of guilt, he wondered who he had just shaken off.

But there was no time to think of that. Someone might be after him.

He backed away one inch at a time, his arms out ready

to ward off any would-be attackers. He could hear a scuffle to his left. It sounded like his school when the bell rang for the end of the day – like hundreds of students pushing and scrambling through tiny hallways, all barging each other aside. He imagined a group of burly, armed men among them. Shoving people to the ground. Shouting at them to move.

Only he hadn't imagined that. Somebody really was shouting.

He knocked into something or someone and dropped his coat. Just leave it, he thought. Not worth it.

Someone shoved him and he toppled over.

Crash. A sharp jab.

All the air in his lungs escaped, like a popped balloon. He coughed on the smoke, choking.

He stayed on the ground, trying and failing to open his streaming eyes. What was happening? He thought of terrorists, but no bomb had gone off. There hadn't been a blast. But then what was all that smoke?

His bruises started to throb. His heavy backpack had come down hard on his back, jamming his hips into the ground. Above him, the shouts had turned to squeals, like a swarm of birds squawking desperately to one another. He tried to focus on the undamaged parts of his body. The tiles under his fingers were smooth and not altogether cold. They reminded him of the tiles on the terrace at their house in the south of France. They were softer than he would have expected, worn down by time, and warmer.

After a moment, he realised the air wasn't so thick here and he could breathe more easily.

Tentatively, Theo opened his eyes and looked around. The smoke was thinning. There was a clear gap under it, just enough to see police-regulation boots braced for action.

A prone figure appeared through the smog. It was the man who had been holding the golden club. He was lying sprawled on his stomach, unmoving, his arms splayed out in front of him. He needed help. There was someone wearing a pair of grubby trainers beside him and Theo hoped they had come to help him. But the shoes backed away from him swiftly and disappeared in the fog.

Should he go to him? It might be a trap. But if someone was coming for him, they would never find him in the confusion.

Theo levered himself onto his knees and made to crawl towards the man.

Something jerked him backwards. Rubber squeaked against tile as a police officer crashed past in front of him. He had been about to put his hands down there.

He looked back. Through the smoke, Samira peered at him with wide eyes. She was crouched low, her hand braced against the wall. In her other hand she had hold of him by the toggle of his backpack.

'Thanks,' he tried to say, but the end of the word was lost in a cough.

He waited for her to let go of his toggle, but she held on. 'Need to get to him,' he rasped, pointing to the man on the floor. The sounds didn't quite form proper words, but she seemed to understand him.

She shook her head.

Frustrated, Theo tried to yank back his toggle.

'Nobody move,' someone boomed. 'Stay calm.'

Samira dropped the toggle and crossed her arms with an expression that said, *See*.

Theo gave up and crawled back to perch against the wall with her.

The smoke was clearing upwards now, revealing several pairs of knees close by. Some he recognised as belonging to his classmates; others to a team of police officers who were streaming in from the doorway they had come through.

As the smoke dissipated he saw his classmates huddled together, some crouched, some standing; Mr Gatimu standing in front them with his arms outstretched, like a dam holding back a flood; the team of police approaching cautiously; the old man in the cloak advancing from the corridor he must have retreated down; the scattered members of the procession, now disbanded; and the man, still lying on the floor.

'The mace is gone,' one man said. He had been part of the procession. Theo recognised him vaguely and wondered if he had seen him on TV. 'Oh my god, it's gone.'

He was talking about the golden club. Theo couldn't see it anywhere.

Whispers whooshed around the echoing space. Theo and Samira slowly got to their feet.

'Everybody stay calm,' the same voice from before repeated and Theo saw that it belonged to the man at the head of the team of police officers. He checked for a pulse on the man on the floor and then spoke into a walkie-talkie.

The police officer's words tore through the fog of quiet and everyone started speaking at the same time. The chatter reverberated off the stone walls, looping over and back as though the lobby was passing the message along to the rest of the building.

People were arriving now, streaming in from the other

entrances to the lobby. Some were dressed in the same costume as those in the procession. Most looked prepared for a dull day at the office.

Out front, ahead of the others, was a short woman in her fifties – Ruth Morris, the Leader of the Opposition. There was a deep-red flush in her otherwise pale-crepe cheeks and her chin-length mousey curls fell into her face. In her burnt-orange blazer and cream linen trousers she stood out as if she were the only colour character in a black and white movie.

Nobody followed the police through the doorway behind Theo.

Someone was pushing their way to the front of the newcomers. It was his dad. Felix Humphries shoved between people to follow closely behind him. As usual, Felix was clutching several folders to his rotund stomach. Theo knew that underneath them, the bottom buttons on his shirt would be straining. He was speaking directly into his dad's ear. Despite the chaos, Felix's stiff white hair – what little he had left of it – was plastered firmly across his head.

His dad didn't seem to have spotted him, although he was frantically searching the faces of Theo's classmates. Theo didn't want to wave, so he craned his head towards his dad's field of vision.

His dad's gaze settled on someone with a deep frown. It was a young woman Theo didn't recognise. She had wispy strawberry blonde hair, held back from her face by a knotted headband, showing piercings all the way up her ear. She didn't quite look as confused as everyone else. In fact, Theo thought that she looked a bit excited. He turned back to his dad. His mouth was fixed in a disapproving line.

Bedlam in the Lobby

As though he felt Theo's eyes on him, his dad suddenly looked straight at him. His face cleared in relief just for a moment. Then he was furiously mouthing something, but Theo couldn't tell what. He didn't know what his dad wanted him to do.

The police officers formed a barrier with outstretched arms, preventing any more new arrivals from entering the lobby.

A police officer with a kind face took charge of their school group. 'We're going to have to take statements from everyone here,' she said, raising her voice to be heard over the din of the echoing gabble.

Mr Gatimu said something to her, but Theo was distracted by the arrival of paramedics. They rushed to the unconscious man's side. Only the very particular tone of his teacher could have drawn his eyes away from them.

'Right, we all need to get into groups,' Mr Gatimu said, 'and then you're each going to go with an officer to give them a statement.' He counted Theo into a group with Samira and they were assigned a police officer, who introduced himself as PC Shah. He told them sharply to follow him closely. He led them towards the opposite doorway, further into the palace, right past Theo's dad.

'Theo, Theo,' his dad said. The crowd parted to allow his dad through. It was like what happened when you tried to put two opposite magnet ends together and they repelled each other. His dad had a magnetic field around him that strangers could not enter.

Theo felt the eyes of everyone present searching, like lighthouse beacons, for the person his dad was speaking to. They hadn't fallen on him yet; he dreaded the moment

Bedlam in the Lobby

when they did. He could always tell when they found him disappointing. People thought that the Prime Minister's son should stand out in a crowd, should have some charisma. He could almost hear their disappointment at his unremarkable appearance.

Apart from being freakishly tall for his age, he knew he was forgettable. Ordinary brown hair, blue eyes, but not interesting blue, pale and watery. Besides his height, he didn't even particularly look like his dad. No one who saw them side by side would guess they were related if they didn't already know.

The police officer looked as if he was going to tell him off when Theo hesitated, waiting for his dad to get to him. But his mouth dropped open in surprise when he saw who it was.

'Theo, are you all right?' his dad said. He had a wild look in his eye that unnerved Theo. He had never seen his dad look so rattled.

'I'm fine, Dad.'

'Stay with that officer and I'll send someone to get you,' he called, as Theo continued out with his group. 'Stay with that officer!' Over his dad's shoulder, he could just make out the paramedics still bent over the unconscious man on the floor.

A red-haired man appeared at his dad's elbow. He was the only person not wearing a suit jacket. The sleeves of his white shirt were rolled up and he had sweat at his brow. He spoke urgently to Theo's dad, who finally looked away, his attention diverted from his son.

They passed through a set of swing doors and were cut off from the commotion of the lobby.

CHAPTER FOUR

An Independent Inquiry

'And did you see anything while you was on the floor?' PC Shah said with a marked sigh.

Theo rubbed his sweating palms on his trousers. PC Shah had taken them to a meeting room, where he had set himself up in a corner and brought them over one by one for questioning. Theo felt like a suspect in an old detective novel. The dark wood panelling made it look as if they were in a historical country house, a bit like his grandpa's at Glencoe. Technically it was his uncle's house now, since his grandpa had died six months before. But in Theo's mind it would always be his grandpa's. He concentrated on PC Shah's chair, its casters refusing to roll on the carpet.

PC Shah had first asked Theo for his details and huffed when Theo gave his address, as though he thought Theo was having him on, despite having seen him with his dad. Theo tried not to seem annoyed. Although he didn't think he was in any trouble, he had been present during a crime. This was exactly the sort of mistake his dad was always warning him not to make. He couldn't risk making it worse.

'Erm, I saw a man lying on the floor. The man who was holding that big golden club thing.'

'It's a mace.' PC Shah didn't look up from his notes.

'Right. And I saw a pair of feet next to him. Someone wearing trainers.'

PC Shah looked up with interest. 'And then what?'

'Then they just walked away.'

'Which way?'

'I don't know,' Theo said. 'It was hard to tell in all the smoke.'

PC Shah turned back to his notes, his interest gone. 'What did the trainers look like?'

'Grubby, old…' Theo couldn't think of anything else to say.

'Colour?' PC Shah prompted. 'Brand?'

'Oh right, yeah. They were Adidas trainers.' Why hadn't he thought of that first? 'And white, except kind of grey because they were old.' Theo wanted to be as specific as possible, but somehow the more he said the more garbled his answers became. Under pressure, he never managed to say what he meant. He often wondered if the wiring was wrong between his brain and his mouth.

'White but kind of grey?' PC Shah said, one eyebrow raised.

'Yes.' Theo didn't try to elaborate. He would only mess it up. He wiped his hands on his trousers again, as surreptitiously as he could, because PC Shah was watching him closely.

He sent Theo back to sit with the others and then ignored them, while he spoke into his walkie-talkie.

They waited.

An Independent Inquiry

None of the others spoke to Theo. He didn't fit in at Anderson School. His dad and his dad's dad and all the men in his family as far back as he could remember had gone to Montgomery School – Gommers, as his dad affectionately called it. He had grown up on tales of his dad's school days. He had been weaned on stories of the students' pranks played on the masters, dreaded the school's signature punishment – a run to the boathouse and back during break time – had daydreamed about tasting his first alcoholic drink in the social bar (the 'sosh'). And he had accepted that he would have to wear the mortifying tailcoat and straw boater that made up the school uniform. Before he was ten years old, he had already lived all his teen years in his imagination, following neatly in his dad's footsteps.

When he had started at Anderson, he had felt as unprepared, and useless, as a poet conscripted into nursing in a war-torn hospital. Early on, he had raised his hand to answer every question in class. He hadn't expected his classmates to laugh behind their hands when he got answers wrong. He was in an unfamiliar setting, without an example to follow. Because the closest he had ever got to the anticipated acceptance at Gommers was a visit to watch a rugby match between current and past students.

Theo wasn't allowed to go to Montgomery. He had to go to Anderson School, for 'political reasons', his parents had said.

That morning a leaflet had arrived for Theo's dad from his old school, inviting him to an alumni event. It was printed on glossy card with a photo of the beautiful school building – more like a National Trust property – splashed across the front page. Theo had folded it neatly in half,

An Independent Inquiry

creating a splintered crease right down the middle of the school building, and tucked it out of sight under one of his mum's catalogues.

Sometimes he wished his life was different, that his dad hadn't become a politician. He wished that he had gone to Gommers, like he should have, and been just another anonymous student. Somewhere where he fitted in. Belonged.

As the others whispered to one another, Theo replayed everything that had happened during the theft in his head. He kept trying to remember if he had seen someone wearing those trainers. One of the tourists maybe? Were they there when the smoke had cleared? He thought he had seen them. But his memories were jumbled up like the pieces of a jigsaw puzzle and he couldn't make them fit back together.

His coat! He felt a stab of panic. He hadn't picked it up after he dropped it. His mum was going to be annoyed.

'Shh,' Samira said. Two of the others, who had been whispering, went quiet. Samira was trying to listen in on PC Shah, who was speaking into the walkie-talkie again. Theo strained to hear too and he thought he heard him say something about trainers.

PC Shah came over to them.

'We don't need nothing more from you now. Your parents are coming to pick you up. Except you,' he said, pointing to Theo. 'Apparently something big was supposed to happen today and your dad's too busy to get away. Your dad's sending someone to get you.' Theo wondered why his mum wasn't coming, but said nothing.

The others eyed him with open curiosity and, not for the first time, Theo wished he wasn't the one who was always singled out. None of them minded about the attention.

An Independent Inquiry

Some of them had obviously enjoyed being questioned. Why couldn't it be one of them?

Theo watched and waited while another police officer came to pick up each of the other students in turn until only he and Samira were left. PC Shah was having what sounded like a frustrated conversation with someone on his walkie-talkie.

'Your mum's here,' he said, nodding at Samira, 'but there's no one to take you to her, so you're coming with me. You too,' he told Theo. 'I'm not to leave you on your own.' He seemed annoyed about this and Theo had the urge to apologise, even though it wasn't his fault.

Theo scooped up his bag and trudged out behind the others. In the corridors, people were shooting between rooms like pinballs propelled through a pinball machine. This part of the palace wasn't nearly so grand as the entrance they had come through earlier. The corridors were narrow and dark, like a servant's staircase. The stone walls were old, but they could have been one hundred or five hundred years old for all Theo could tell.

Samira dropped back next to him. 'What was that about trainers?'

'I saw a pair of trainers by that man on the floor.' Again, he realised the message had been scrambled. 'I mean, not just the trainers, trainers with feet in them.' Theo stopped talking, feeling stupid. Why didn't he say, *someone wearing trainers*? He had made it sound like they were a pair of phantom feet walking around on their own, like Thing from the Addams Family.

'Keep up,' PC Shah said, holding a door open for them. Theo jogged to get through it.

An Independent Inquiry

They walked out into the open air, past a car turntable. The officer who had shepherded them about earlier was coming towards them with another woman. It was clear the woman was Samira's mum. Her hair was shorter and curlier, without the red streaks, but their faces were similar. She was wearing a plain black trouser suit that contrasted starkly with her vivid hot-pink scarf. Her forehead was creased in a deep frown.

'Thank god you're all right, I've been worried sick.' She clasped Samira in a tight hug.

'God, Mum, I'm fine.' Samira extracted herself and repositioned her squashed hair. 'It's no big deal.'

'Like my colleague told you, Mrs Jhor,' PC Shah said.

'It's Miss Sohal actually,' she replied, but she quickly turned her attention back to her daughter. 'It is a big deal. It's been all over the news, your father has been ringing me every ten minutes. I don't want you mixed up in all this.'

'It's not my fault I was here.'

'Well, good. You see that it stays that way. You are not to get involved, do you understand me, Samira?'

Samira pulled at one of the many keyrings hanging from her backpack zip. Her hair fell over her face so that it was hidden from her mum. Theo got a full view of her, though. He saw the glint of defiance in her eye, the look of mischief.

Her mouth turned up in a serene smile as she waved goodbye to him. He had the distinct impression that she had enjoyed being told off. He found himself waving back and smiling just a little too late, when she was already walking away from him. He dropped his hand. For a moment, he had been so impressed by her gumption, he had forgotten to disapprove of it.

An Independent Inquiry

'Come on,' PC Shah said, 'your dad said to leave you with someone in the Whip's Office.'

CHAPTER FIVE

The Chief Whip

Theo followed PC Shah back inside. He led them back to the corridor where the theft had happened, but they were turned away by a police officer at the entrance. Before they turned away, Theo caught sight of people in forensics overalls taking photographs of the scene. Sighing in annoyance, PC Shah took them back the way they had come.

They turned left and right. Right and right again. All the corridors were identical. Narrow and dark, worn carpet underfoot snaking ahead of them, leading them on without leaving any clues for the route back. Theo hoped his dad would collect him from here. He could never find his way out on his own.

Finally, they arrived at an ancient wooden door with a plaque that read, 'Office of the Chief Whip'. PC Shah knocked and someone inside called for them to enter.

The room reminded Theo of the sorry rejects discarded in the lost property bin at school. They might be vintage, but they had been misused by all their previous owners. This room felt the same. Like the one they had been in earlier, this one was wood-panelled and dark; it had no windows. The furniture was imposing antique wood, but it was piled with subsiding stacks of papers, scattered pens, crumpled crisp packets and cans of drink.

'Ah, Theo, come in,' a man behind a desk said. It was the red-haired man Theo had seen with his dad after the theft. 'Thank you, Constable.'

PC Shah left and Theo was alone with the man.

He was younger than most MPs, probably in his thirties. His hair was ruffled, as though he had been running his hands through it. Like earlier, he wasn't wearing a jacket – it was slung over the back of his chair. Behind his head, a corkboard was plastered with newspaper clippings – some about politics, but mostly they were about Chelsea Football Club matches. He smiled encouragingly at Theo.

Closing a Red Box on his desk – one identical to Theo's dad's – he got up and came around to shake Theo's hand. He knocked a freestanding whiteboard that was placed awkwardly in the centre of the room, and swore. It had tallies listed under the headings 'Aye' and 'No'. It was too close to call the majority from a cursory glance.

'I'm Rupert Spencer. I work for your father as his Chief Whip,' he said with a friendly smile. Theo tried not to stare. This was the man whose job it was to persuade everyone to vote with the government.

He was well dressed in a pale-blue shirt and suit trousers, but although the shirt was fresh, the trousers were rumpled as though he might have been in them a long time. As he shook Theo's hand, Theo noticed that he was wearing a gold ring on his little finger, just like his dad's.

'I'm afraid your father's rather tied up at the moment,'

he went on. 'You don't mind waiting in here do you? It's a mess, I know and it's just the two of us. The others are running around trying to work out what the hell is going on.'

'I don't mind,' Theo said, which he meant. He preferred the quiet of this room to the possibility of lots of people ogling him.

Theo looked around for somewhere to sit. There were plenty of chairs, but all of them were occupied by stuff – files, papers, a paint-stained t-shirt.

Seeing his uncertainty, Rupert said, 'You can have this desk.' He pointed to the one next to his. 'It's where we dump all our detritus, but it's technically spare.'

Approaching it, Theo found a sports bag under the t-shirt on the chair.

'Sorry, you can move that.' Rupert returned to his own seat. 'It's purely decorative, never get time to go to the gym anyway,' he said with a smile.

Theo moved the bag gingerly to the floor. Rupert must have been telling the truth about never going to the gym because it felt as light as if it were empty. He sat down with his own bag on his lap. With the sports bag at his feet and a discarded old monitor in the corner, there wasn't much space to put his bag down.

'I think it might be quite a while before someone can pick you up. Your mum has gone to collect your sister from school and your dad... Well.'

Theo couldn't help frowning. 'Why has Mum gone to pick up Harry? She's all right, isn't she?'

'Oh yes, she's fine, but there was some worry... To be honest, we thought it might be a terrorist attack. They wanted to make sure your family was safe.'

The Chief Whip

Rupert's friendly expression had been replaced by concern. He was watching Theo as though he expected him to say something, so Theo felt he should.

'But it was just that club,' with relief he remembered what PC Shah had called it, 'that mace. Wasn't it?'

'That appears to be the case.'

Theo wanted to say that it seemed like a lot of fuss for one mace, but he resisted. He had noticed that things that seemed trivial to him – like baffling newspaper articles and dull TV interviews – were very important to his dad. He had learnt not to question these things. The questions often had long and hard-to-follow answers.

Rupert rested his chin on his clasped hands. He seemed to guess what Theo was thinking. 'Theo, do you know why the mace is so important?'

Theo thought it might be part of the crown jewels, but he didn't want to guess and look like an idiot if he was wrong, so he shook his head.

Rupert got up and perched on the side of the desk.

'The mace represents the monarch in the House of Commons, the Queen, you see? Every day the mace is brought into the House of Commons and it stays there while MPs debate new laws. And it's taken away and locked up at the end of the day. The House of Commons can't meet and debate new laws if the mace isn't there.'

'Why not?'

'Because the Queen must be represented in Parliament, we act under her authority.' When he saw Theo's puzzled expression he went on, 'Those are the rules. We can't make any laws without it.'

Theo thought for a moment. It didn't sound like an ideal

The Chief Whip

situation, but there must be a solution, a contingency plan. 'Don't you have a spare one you could use?'

Rupert laughed and for a moment Theo was worried he had said something stupid. 'Exactly right, Theo, that would be prudent! But no, we don't.'

'So you can't make any new laws now?'

'That's right.'

Theo sat back in his chair. 'You mean, there's all those MPs able to work and the building is still here, but because you don't have that one mace, everything has to stop?'

'Yes.'

'That's ridiculous,' Theo said without thinking. He felt strangely comfortable with Rupert. He didn't feel like he was judging him.

'Many people would disagree. The delicate understanding between monarchy and government is the fine balance on which our constitution rests.'

Theo thought about what it would mean if the government couldn't make any laws. For a second he thought his dad might have more time at home again. But the idea was squashed like a bug under the weight of the one that followed it. His dad would never be at home. The government was in crisis and Theo knew what that meant. Working twenty-four-seven. Meals snatched at odd hours, often when Theo was already in bed. He might not see his dad for weeks. Months.

Theo unzipped his bag to take out one of his books. He supposed he might as well do his History homework while he was waiting. It wasn't due in until next week, but he didn't have anything else to do.

He opened his textbook, but he kept thinking about the

The Chief Whip

mace. He had assumed that someone wanted it because it was valuable. It looked like solid gold, it must be worth a lot. But what if they actually wanted to stop new laws from being passed? Theo thought of the law Mr Gatimu had told them about in Citizenship class, the one the government was trying to pass in a vote in Parliament, the one his dad had mentioned countless times.

'You were going to vote on the House of Lords Reform Bill today, weren't you?' Theo said.

Rupert looked up in surprise. 'Yes. What made you think of that?'

'Do you think,' Theo paused and looked at the book in his lap. He was going to suggest something outlandish and wondered whether it was really a good idea to say it out loud. He decided he probably wouldn't see Rupert again, so it didn't matter too much if he thought he was silly. 'Do you think someone took the mace because they wanted to stop the vote?'

Rupert seemed to consider him with sharper intensity. 'Yes I do, Theo, that's very perceptive of you. I don't think it's a coincidence that the theft happened today, on the eve of one of the most important votes in the history of the British constitution.' His eyes flickered to the whiteboard with the tally on it and quickly away. 'The government was due to win that vote. But now...'

Theo mustered his resolve. He had a feeling the Bill would change the law so that some members of the House of Lords were elected. He couldn't remember any of the details. He knew he was supposed to know all about the Bill, his dad droned on about it enough. He could almost hear his dad's voice saying, *You know all of this, Theo, haven't*

The Chief Whip

you been listening? Luckily, his dad wasn't here and for the first time, he was interested in what the vote was about.

'I can't remember what the Bill says...' Theo said, letting his sentence trail off.

'You know about the difference between the House of Commons and the House of Lords, don't you?' He didn't wait for Theo to explain that he had learnt about it in Citizenship and Theo didn't want to interrupt, so he let Rupert go on. 'The House of Commons is the chamber of elected Members of Parliament, chosen by the people. They amend and vote on any new laws, which then go to the House of Lords to vote on. The House of Lords used to be the unelected hereditary lords of the land, such as dukes and earls. Now they're mostly appointed by the government, the Prime Minister in fact. Some of them are appointed by a special selection committee. A few are representatives of the church – bishops. A lot of them used to be MPs or they are very experienced people in particular areas of business.'

Theo nodded.

'The new Bill is going to change that. It will drastically reduce the number of Lords selected by the government and increase the number selected by the committee. It will also mean that some Lords are elected. It's quite radical. This Bill will change the face of British politics.'

'And some people don't want that to happen?'

'Some people believe that the British political system is steeped in rich tradition and making changes like this would violate the fabric of our culture.'

'Is that what you think?'

'Absolutely not. This crime is an affront to the great British democracy.' He sounded like he was regurgitating

The Chief Whip

a speech he had learnt for a TV interview. Theo supposed they would all be preparing their soundbites now. 'And my party places high importance on the rule of law.' Rupert seemed to remember himself and he let the persona drop. 'It's my job to think like the opposition.'

'Well who are these people? There must be groups – people who say they don't want the Bill to go through. Shouldn't they be the ones being questioned?' Theo thought of PC Shah questioning his classmates. The police were looking in the wrong place.

'I don't think this was done by an outside group. Not many people can get into the Houses of Parliament. Think of all the security you went through to get into the building.'

'Err, I didn't. I came in with my dad.' Theo shuffled in his seat. He hated having special treatment. Most of his classmates hated him having it too.

'Oh well, there's metal detectors, x-ray machines. It's as tight as airport security.'

'Do you mean, you think it was someone who works here?'

Rupert hesitated. 'Perhaps.' He seemed to regret his answer.

'That makes it even easier, there must be a record of people's speeches in Parliament. You just need to look back at those. See what MPs have said about the Bill.'

'It's just not that simple,' Rupert said with a trace of brittleness. 'Theo, in politics, as in life actually, it's not always possible to tell what people really believe. People in politics don't always argue the opinions they really agree with, deep down.'

The Chief Whip

'Why not? That's their job isn't it?' He was getting annoyed now, the feeling swelling in his chest. He didn't know where it was coming from.

'For a variety of reasons. They might agree with government policy in order to secure a government promotion. They might be reluctant to disagree with their constituents – the people who voted for them – in case they don't vote them in again. Issues as contentious as this tend to bring out people's true beliefs, but you can't be certain.'

Theo scowled. 'MPs shouldn't lie about their opinions just for the sake of their careers. That's completely wrong.' Too late he realised he shouldn't say that to Rupert – he might have lied to save his career in the past. He didn't want to seem judgemental.

'I agree. It's utterly wrong. I think everyone should act with their conscience,' he said it quietly, but there was a strange power in his words. Theo could feel the weight of the conviction behind them. 'It's dishonest not to, isn't it?'

Theo frowned. 'But you have to persuade people to vote with the government. Doesn't that mean you have to tell people not to vote based on their own opinions?'

'It's much worse than that,' Rupert said, the heaviness suddenly lifting. 'I have to actually change their minds.' He winked. Theo wasn't certain whether he was joking or not.

He was itching to ask Rupert how he did it, but Rupert's phone rang and he answered it.

He tried to turn his attention back to his History homework, but he couldn't concentrate. He wondered what would become of the Reform Bill now. Maybe they would find the mace and it would all be over by tomorrow. What was his dad going to do if they didn't?

CHAPTER SIX

Number Eleven, Downing Street

It was late by the time their government car pulled back onto Parliament Square. He had waited for hours in the Whips' Office for his dad to collect him. But he had barely said anything to Theo, before shuffling him quickly into the vehicle that waited to take them home.

As they pulled out of the palace gates, photographers crowded around the car, their cameras clanking against the glass as they pressed up to the windows. The angle of the car meant they were forced to his dad's side. He subtly shifted his position so that he was blocking the view of Theo and Theo's view of the photographers. Theo could still hear them though, shouting through the glass.

'Turn up the radio,' his dad told Andy, his personal protection officer.

A frantic piece of classical music was just ending, reaching a crescendo. It made Theo's heart hammer against his chest as the car sped up, leaving the photographers behind. He looked out of the back at the last stragglers dropping back, hands on their knees, cameras swinging at their necks.

His dad's phone rang once, before he answered it. 'Yes?'

He listened in silence, his face turned away from Theo, towards the window.

'Well where the bloody hell is Chris? I need my deputy. You get him on the phone. Now.'

The music on the radio faded out as his dad rang off, muttering under his breath. He didn't look up, but punched furiously at the keypad.

'And now, the latest on today's theft of the parliamentary mace,' a woman's voice said.

Theo noticed that his dad stopped typing, but he didn't look up.

'Tonight, the Prime Minister will chair a meeting of CO-BRA in the wake of the theft of the parliamentary mace from inside the Palace of Westminster itself. Parliament was in chaos today as a vote that had the potential to change the face of British politics was called off. One person was injured during the theft, the palace's Serjeant at Arms, Bob Piggott, who is understood to be in a stable condition in hospital. Police are searching the palace and are appealing for witnesses who have any information regarding the theft to come forward. It is understood that the Prime Minister's son, Theodore Duncan, was at the palace during—'

'Turn it off,' his dad ordered.

'And his daughter, Harriet—' The radio cut out.

His dad was looking up from his phone now, no longer pretending not to listen.

'Is he all right?' Theo asked.

'What?' his dad said a little sharply. His face softened. 'Who?'

'Bob Piggott. They said he's in hospital.'

Number Eleven, Downing Street

'He's going to be fine. It was just a bump on the head.'

Theo thought of Bob sprawled on the lobby floor, unconscious still when he had left. It didn't seem like just a bump.

He caught a glimpse of the black stone block Second World War memorial – the hats and coats of the nation's greatest heroes hung on it expectantly, as though their owners had just stepped out to the shops – before the car pulled through the Downing Street gates, past the police officers guarding the entrance. The Georgian houses on one side of the street looked like the embodiment of prime ministers past lined up on parade, in their regimental black box shirts, with white window ledges for dickie bows.

Stepping through Downing Street's great black door was like stepping into the past. A grandfather clock ticked tiredly in the corner, as though it had been going for centuries and was patiently waiting for someone to say it could retire. On the other side of the room, a shining fireplace made it look like the living room it must once have been. The illusion was broken by the appearance of a gaggle of parliamentary aides, who were staring at their phone screens as they waited for his dad.

'Tell Mum I'll be up later,' his dad said as he joined his assistants on the staircase.

'Dad!' Theo called. His dad stopped. 'I can't remember the way.' He felt his cheeks warm. He hated to ask for help. He knew he should be able to manage on his own. But he never came through Number Ten or used the main front door. It was a popular myth that the Prime Minister lived in Number Ten, Downing Street – they actually lived next door, in a flat above Number Eleven. It was possible to get to it through Number Ten, but Theo couldn't remember how.

His dad sighed and nodded to one of the assistants – a young woman. She gestured for Theo to follow her.

They dogged his dad's footsteps on the stairs. Despite their closeness, Theo couldn't make out what his dad was saying, he was speaking so quietly and quickly to the young man hanging at his elbow. Theo tried to shake off the feeling that he shouldn't be here. The walls were lined with portraits of former Prime Ministers and Theo peered at them sidelong as he passed. They all stared back and he had the growing sensation that they didn't think he should be there either.

He was relieved when they reached the first floor and turned off. His dad went the opposite direction and he watched his retreating back, hunched and tense.

The woman continued on and Theo started to mentally note the directions she took. Right, then up the small set of stairs... They reached the door to the flat and he tried to keep it all in his head as he said goodbye to the assistant. He would write it all down later and keep the route on him until he knew it off by heart, so that he never had to ask for help again.

He let himself in.

'Mum?' he called as he slung his school bag off his back. He could hear the noise of washing up coming from the kitchen and he suspected his mum hadn't heard him.

His sister had though. Harry appeared suddenly in the hallway. She had his little sister, Milly, resting on one hip and a face like a tsunami wave that was about to crash over his head. That didn't mean much though, he didn't think he had seen his sister smile since... He couldn't remember when.

'Feo!' Milly gurgled and smiled a toothless grin. She stretched her arms out to him and Harry let him take her. At least someone was pleased to see him.

'You were there when it all happened,' Harry said, in an alarmingly accusatory tone. Sometimes she looked uncannily like his mum – light ginger hair and sharp blue eyes. They also both had the same fair skin, as translucent as tracing paper, which sizzled within moments in the sun. It was funny how two such similar faces could look so different. His mum looked like the Maid Marian of Theo's imagination – all flowing hair and kindliness. His sister looked like an invading Viking, come to pillage the locals.

'In Parliament you mean?'

'Yes, Parliament. Where else, you imbecile?' She liked finding ever more obscure insults for him; she obviously thought his lack of intelligence to understand the insult was an insult in itself. 'I hope you didn't get in everyone's way. Why they let you stay there all this time is beyond me. Obviously you should have been sent home straight away.' There was a vicious glint in her eye.

Thankfully Theo was saved from having to defend himself by his mum's appearance in the hallway. She had her mobile wedged between her ear and her shoulder, her hair was pushed roughly out of the way, some of it dripping. The yellow marigolds on her hands dripped onto the carpet.

'*Maman, Theo est là. Oui. À plus.*' She pressed the button to end the call with a wet finger and dropped the phone into the front pouch of her apron – like a kangaroo protecting its baby.

'Come here,' she said, smothering Theo, along with Milly in his arms, in a wet hug. Harry tutted and flounced away to her room.

'Mum,' Theo complained over her shoulder. He was taller than her now, by a couple of inches. If he kept growing at this rate, soon he would be six foot. One day he might even be as tall as his dad. He patted his mum's back awkwardly.

She released him, took Milly from his arms and swept him through the living room towards the kitchen. He stared. Milly's toys were scattered across the floor. An old-fashioned toy phone in garish red and white plastic was hanging by its cord from the antique card table. School books cascaded from the worn velvet chesterfield sofa. A skirt and jacket had been slung over the cracked leather armchair in the corner, looking like their person had melted away. Someone had knocked the brass over-reach lamp askew. It usually hung over the sofa, but was now hanging backwards over the bookcase behind, illuminating the out-dated hardbacks his parents had been hoarding for decades. There was an uneasy equality in their house – the antiques were treated as carelessly as Milly's free magazine toys.

Theo grimaced. It was always messy in here, but not that messy. It looked like a giant had gone through, upending everything in its path.

Larry, a tabby cat, looked sharply at Theo from his guard post on the windowsill, revealing a tortoiseshell triangle on his white chest. He was Downing Street's cat – he belonged to the building rather than the family. Or perhaps the building belonged to him. He must have sensed that food was soon to be served, because he leapt down and followed Theo into the kitchen.

Number Eleven, Downing Street

'We've eaten already, but I've saved you some cottage pie,' his mum said.

Still in her wet gloves, she grabbed a Tupperware box and thrust it into the microwave. She jiggled Milly, who had started to grizzle because she wasn't getting enough attention, on her hip. She waved at Theo to indicate that he should take a seat at the kitchen table. Usually his parents insisted on eating dinner as a family in the dining room off the other side of the kitchen. The kitchen table was for hurried breakfasts. And now, apparently, emergency dinners.

Theo pulled out a chair to find a thick manila envelope on it.

'What's this?' he said as he moved it to the table and sat down.

'Oh that. That's the Admiral's research into the history of the house and its architect.' The Admiral was the family nickname for his grandpa. Only his grandchildren had ever called him Grandpa. Everyone else still knew him by his naval title, even his children. 'Uncle Charlie posted it down to Dad. I don't think he'll have any time to look at it now.'

'Can I look at it?'

'Of course. He would have loved you to have it.'

Theo took out the wodge of papers and thumbed through the top few. They were handwritten. He traced his grandpa's familiar handwriting with his fingertips.

'Is it all handwritten?' he asked.

His mum nodded. 'You know what he was like. Wouldn't touch a computer.'

Grandpa had been hoping to get his research published in a book. Theo couldn't imagine a publisher would take it like this. Somehow that only made the papers more precious, because only he really understood the value of them.

He pulled a salad bowl towards his plate. He couldn't say he would choose it given the option, but now there was food in front of him he realised he was starving. He piled salad on to his plate, picking up as many tomatoes as he could get. Even Larry seemed to want a piece; he was twining himself around Theo's legs under the table, being uncharacteristically friendly.

Theo stopped when he realised his mum was watching him. She had a funny look on her face, like she might be really angry at him. 'What? I thought this was for dinner too?'

His mum laughed and to his horror a couple of tears slid down her cheeks. She was still laughing though. What was going on? Was she happy or sad?

'It's all right, darling, eat up.' She wiped her eyes on her apron as best she could.

Theo began to eat his salad, just for something to do. His appetite had evaporated – the crying and the fact that his mum was still staring had put him off.

'Are you OK?' his mum said and there was a dangerous wobble in her voice again.

'I'm fine, Mum.'

She nodded and Theo thought there might be more tears coming, but thankfully the microwave pinged. She collected herself and turned to take out his food.

Theo went to bed with his grandpa's research and a cup of ginseng tea his mum had made for him. It had the comforting effect that he knew she had intended. It reminded him of her and of home.

He took a fresh pair of folded red tartan pyjamas – the

Admiral's idea of a joke Christmas present – from his drawer and pulled them on. There was nothing to see through his telescope tonight. There were clouds like thick clods of dust blocking out the sky.

He got under the duvet covers and took his grandpa's research out of its envelope. The pile was as thick as a writing pad. He glanced over the first page. He read just enough to see that Grandpa had been researching an architect called Charles Barry, who had worked on their Scottish house. He couldn't face reading any more. His grandpa's handwriting was too real. And familiar.

Theo put the pile carefully on the floor next to his bed and took his phone from his bedside table. He wasn't meant to have it in his bedroom at night, but his mum was so distracted she had forgotten to take it. On Twitter he found a link to a very good article about the security measures used in the Houses of Parliament. In fact, it was almost too good. If the mace hadn't been stolen already, someone might use that article to plan how to take it. Although he couldn't see how anyone had managed it, which was the same conclusion they had come to in the article.

Every exit from the palace had metal detectors and police guards. Police also patrolled the perimeters, so if someone had thrown it over the railings then it would have been spotted. The article made quite a lot out of the fact that government ministers could take anything in or out of the building in their ministerial Red Boxes – they weren't searched. The article didn't mention that they were only the size of a briefcase. Not much use for hiding a great big mace.

He read a wild theory about the mace having been

thrown into the Thames from the Houses of Parliament terrace. It had already been debunked because there had been an event taking place on the terrace. The people attending it would have seen it if a balaclava-clad thief had run out and lobbed a massive mace over the wall.

He refreshed Twitter and found a breaking story. The CCTV in the Houses of Parliament had gone down that morning and his dad had known. So that was what his dad had been talking about in the car. Theo didn't want to read the replies to the post. He knew there would be comments about his dad, some of them vicious. He logged out and wiped his internet history. He didn't use the app because he wasn't allowed to have an account. His parents didn't trust him not to post something that could get them into trouble. But he never posted anything. He just liked to read what other people were saying.

The front door clicked and Theo switched off his screen.

'How was it?' his mum whispered in the hallway.

'Carnage. Everyone's running around like headless chickens. I'm sitting in the middle of it all wondering what the...' His dad's voice trailed off as they moved further into the flat.

Theo lifted his covers silently and crept towards the door. He turned his door handle achingly slowly and opened it just a crack. He could hear his parents talking in the living room.

'I'm surprised they've let him out of hospital so soon, he's had a nasty bump.'

Theo guessed they were talking about Bob Piggott. He had looked him up online, but there was very little information about him. Just that he had moved from Jamaica to the UK in the late sixties and had worked in the palace ever since. Theo had found himself refreshing the news page every few minutes to see if there was any update on Bob's condition. He had read about his release from hospital and his subsequent visit to Downing Street to meet with his dad.

'Frankly I'm glad, because we need him. I've told him to get his office in order. They're responsible for the security, they need to bloody well sort this out.'

His mum said something that sounded like, 'He needs time to recuperate.'

'I've told him, we've got to halt all the works now,' his dad said. 'The workmen have been interviewed and sent home. None of them will admit to cutting the wires to the CCTV, but then who would? They know we don't have any evidence. No fingerprints because they were all wearing protective gloves. No CCTV because that part of the building is ancient. That's why we were renovating it in the first place. God, I've got a massive headache.'

Theo's mum said something he couldn't catch.

'It's possible. They've found where it was cut and it has definitely been cut, it wasn't gnawed by rats. But who can tell whether it was cut on purpose or whether someone cut a wire by accident?'

'What do you think?' his mum said. She seemed to be shifting around, so Theo only caught snippets of her voice.

His dad sighed so heavily, Theo could distinctly hear it. 'I don't know. I'm just not sure.' There was silence for a moment, then suddenly, 'What I don't understand is how they've got it out of the building.'

'Is it definitely not in the building?'

Number Eleven, Downing Street

'Police have been searching it top to bottom, they're still going. It's a vast place. The mace weighs nearly eight kilograms. It's not the sort of thing someone could dash out with. They would have to lug it out, it would be noticeable. Somebody should have seen the thief leaving with it, but nobody saw anything. It can't have just vanished.'

'It hasn't just...'

Theo opened the door a little wider so that he could get his ear in the gap. It squeaked against its hinges. The voices in the living room stopped. Theo held his breath, ready to pull the door closed.

'Somebody took it,' his mum continued. 'Someone who didn't want your vote to pass. I think it's still in the building, Will. I think someone in the building took it and they're keeping it hidden.'

'You think it's the Opposition?'

'Or it could be the liberals. You said yourself the coalition is fragile.'

'The liberals are the ones who want this bloody Bill to go through. It was Chris's manifesto promise. I wish I had never agreed to it.'

'It could be someone in your own party. Some of those dinosaurs...'

'Don't, Nicole. I can't argue with you now. I need a good night's sleep.'

Theo heard them get up. He tiptoed as fast as he could back to his bed. A door closed on his parents' bickering voices.

He couldn't believe it. His mum thought someone from the coalition might have stolen the mace.

His dad hadn't managed to win a clear victory at his

election. His party had come closest to a majority in the House of Commons, but they didn't quite have it. And neither did any other party. They called it a hung parliament. After he saw what it did to his dad, Theo came to think of it as hung, drawn and quartered. He didn't like to think about the weekend after the election, during which his dad had tried to negotiate a coalition agreement with another smaller party.

They had all spent election night in his dad's Surrey constituency; Theo in his childhood bedroom. His dad had gone out to see the vote count and hadn't come back for two days. The next morning the children had gone back up to their Chelsea house with their mum and to school as normal. That had been excruciating. The other children had stared even more than usual.

In the evening, Theo waited at home to see if his dad was going to come back, listening in on his mum's phone conversations. She seemed to know what he was up to though, because she limited all her replies to 'yes', 'no' and a quick 'love you' before she hung up.

On Saturday morning he discovered that his dad had returned in the middle of the night, when he came down in the morning looking as if he hadn't slept for a week. It was the forced jollity that Theo couldn't stand. His dad tried to smile and joke with them like normal, but he was strained. Whenever his smile dropped there were pronounced lines around his eyes and his mouth disappeared into a thin line.

He had drunk two coffees in quick succession, tossing them back while they were still searing hot, while Theo's mum fluttered around him like a bee around a flower. He had promptly swept back out. He came and went all weekend.

His phone never left his hand. He never seemed to blink.

Theo spent the weekend in a state of heightened alert. Would they move to Downing Street – yet another upheaval? Would his dad become even more important, have even more work, become even more distant? Or would the coalition talks fail? In which case his dad would likely lose his position as leader of his party. He didn't know which was worse: losing his dad to his job or getting him back as a broken man. And he would be broken if he failed in all his ambitions. Theo had seen what an election loss looked like.

Finally, on Monday morning before school, Theo had seen on the news that his dad had made an alliance to create a formal coalition. He had given a press conference with Chris Elliot, the leader of the other party, who was to become his deputy.

It was a victory, but it was hard-won. Theo's stomach still tightened with anxiety whenever he thought of the moment afterwards, when they had stood waving and smiling for the cameras on the doorstep of Number Ten. He had felt like a soldier returning victorious from war. Inside he felt hollow, empty.

He had thought the two coalition parties had an understanding. They had made an agreement to work together. His dad got on really well with Chris. He often ate dinner with them. What would it mean for the coalition, for his dad, if the other party were really working against him?

Under the duvet, he curled into a ball to warm up. His eyes traced his homework timetable propped up on his desk without really noticing it.

He thought about Bob Piggott. He was in trouble. And

Theo didn't think it was his fault. He was the victim, the only casualty of the theft.

His dad, Bob. They needed to find the mace. And he wanted to help.

He imagined himself unveiling the thief, handing him in to the police. Suddenly he had a vision of himself opening a small box, containing a ring – the family signet ring.

He turned over in bed. How could he possibly think he could find the mace? The police must be looking for it. And all the security at the Palace of Westminster. If they couldn't find it, how could he?

But then, he thought, it couldn't hurt to try. No one would have to know. If he didn't find it, no one would ever know he had tried, know that he had failed. He just had to go about it secretly.

Theo lay awake for a long time, his eyes fixed on the ceiling.

CHAPTER SEVEN

The House of Lords Reform Bill

Theo yawned over his lunch tray.

He had been up the night before thinking about how to begin his investigation. It was all he had thought about all week, ever since the theft. He had decided that the best place to start was the Palace of Westminster itself. If he could go where the public weren't normally allowed, see people behind closed doors, he might pick up some clues. That meant somehow getting in. He would need someone's help for that. Someone who could be relied on not to mention it to his dad.

This was where his plans always ended, because he didn't know anyone he trusted enough to help. But that morning his dad had said that Parliament was going into recess the next day and would be closed for a week. In the absence of the mace, Parliament couldn't sit, so there was no point in keeping it open. His dad had decided to close it to buy himself time. If Theo didn't go now, he might not get another opportunity. He had reached an impasse. Either he asked someone for help or he might as well give up on the investigation now. He didn't know what to do.

He watched Josh and Wilson laughing together. Josh was doing an impression of a footballer missing a header, his short black dreads wafting around his head. Typically, his shirt was untucked and his school tie hung loose around his neck.

Seeing Theo's serious face, Josh said, not unkindly, 'All right, Sport?' He liked to take the mickey because he thought Theo was posh. Theo didn't mind when Josh did it.

'Yeah, I'm all right.'

Josh nodded, his smile unwavering. 'Fair does.'

Josh turned back to Wilson. This was one of the things Theo liked about Josh. Josh knew when to leave him be. That hadn't extended to the morning after the theft though. Josh hadn't been on the school trip with him because he wasn't taking Citizenship. When Theo had got into his form room the next morning, Josh had demanded to know all the important details. Had the police shot anyone? Had anyone made a heroic but ultimately doomed attempt at escape? His interest disappeared when Theo explained that he had spent most of the time lying on the floor trying not to get squashed.

Theo spotted Harry through the throngs of students, sometimes six of them to tiny round laminated tables. She was sitting with two of her friends on the other side of the cafeteria, in front of the uPVC French windows on to the playground. He decided to take the plunge.

'I'll be right back,' he told the others and made his way over to her.

She didn't immediately look up when he arrived. Not until her table went awkwardly silent.

The House of Lords Reform Bill

'Yes?'

'I think I might stay late in the library after school today,' Theo said. 'I mean, I haven't decided yet. But I might.'

'I'm not waiting for you,' Harry replied. 'I want to be home in time to watch *Celebrity Cook Off*.'

He had been worried she might say something like that. The only reason Theo and Harry were allowed to walk to and from school without personal protection officers was because they were supposed to stick together. And watch out for one another. That was the deal Harry had struck with their parents when their dad became Prime Minister. Theo hadn't cared much at the time, but he had learnt to be grateful for it since.

He would need permission from his mum to walk home alone.

The bell rang for class and Theo jostled through the crowds back to his table. Josh wouldn't get up to go to class until the last possible moment, but since he had Geography and Theo had Citizenship, Theo didn't feel like he had to wait for him. He said goodbye and headed across the playground back to the main school building.

The giant sundial over the school's door was unreadable on a cloudy day like this. It might have been useful in 1774, which was when the inscription said that the school had been built. But it wasn't now. The whole school reminded him of an overclouded sky on a sunny day. Behind all the murk and the grey, something bright and beautiful tried to break through. He could never make it out.

He dawdled through the antique red-brick main entrance for as long as possible. Then he pushed through the door into the new block.

The House of Lords Reform Bill

In this case, new meant not old enough to look historical and interesting, but still old enough that paint was flaking away from the dirty magnolia walls and for the floor to be scarred by scuff marks. The new block was like an old t-shirt that you kept for playing rugby in. Best treated badly so that no one thought you actually liked it. That was probably why students kept scrawling graffiti on the walls. And why the teachers had stopped bothering to paint over it.

He leapt on to the stairs. They were like concrete breeze blocks. Stark and brutal. On the second floor he turned onto the humanities corridor, his shoes squeaking against the sticky linoleum.

He pushed through the door into his Citizenship classroom. He was the first one there. Good. That meant he got his pick of seats. He took one in the middle row, at the very end, next to the window. It was the most inconspicuous spot in the room. Not close to the front, where he might inadvertently look eager to participate in the lesson, not at the back where it might seem like he was trying to stay out of it.

He doodled idly on the inside front cover of his notebook while the other students filtered in.

The door swung open with a crash.

Theo was jolted out of his daze.

It was Mr Gatimu, an open rucksack slung carelessly over one shoulder. He was clean shaven now and alarmingly bright and enthusiastic.

'Good afternoon, everyone!' He smiled around at them all, his row of perfect white teeth gleaming. Theo knew he saw their indifference and their post-lunch drowsiness. But it seemed to fire him up even more. He read out the register

The House of Lords Reform Bill

like he was announcing each of them had won a lottery.

The classroom door shot open with another crash. It was Samira.

'Late again,' Mr Gatimu said, his buoyancy slipping for the first time.

'Sorry, sir. I was in detention, I didn't have enough time to eat my lunch.'

'What was the detention for this time?'

'Answering back,' Samira said, taking a seat at the very back of the class.

Mr Gatimu's eyebrows twitched and Theo could swear his lips hitched up in a smile, but it was gone as swiftly as it appeared.

'I thought we would do something slightly different today.' Mr Gatimu put away his pen and register. There was a collective groan. 'Why do you automatically assume different is bad? Maybe it's good different.'

'You're right, sir. There can't be anything worse than our usual lessons,' Ben Dryden heckled from the back of the class.

The other students snorted to themselves. Mr Gatimu would always let them get away with a little bit of cheek, as long as it didn't get out of control. They had learnt to toe that line well.

'Then you might even enjoy yourself,' Mr Gatimu retorted. 'We're going to take a little detour away from the topic of the first past the post system. Instead we're going to talk about the House of Lords Reform Bill.'

As the rest of the class slumped lower, Theo sat up straighter.

'After the theft of the mace, the vote on the Bill was

The House of Lords Reform Bill

postponed. So I thought we would learn a bit more about it today. Who can tell me what the Reform Bill sets out to change?'

Theo didn't put his hand up. Rupert had explained it to him only a few days before, but he couldn't be sure he remembered it all. He wasn't going to risk it. Nobody else raised their hand either. But just as Mr Gatimu was about to speak, a small hand slithered into the air at the back of the room.

'Yes, Samira.' Mr Gatimu failed to keep the surprise out of his voice.

'It's going to change the law so that the lords can be elected.'

'That's right. At least some of them would be. If the government can go ahead with the vote on the Bill. And win it, of course.'

'Do you think they will win it, sir?' Samira asked, not bothering to raise her hand.

Mr Gatimu rubbed his jaw in thought. 'It's hard to say. It's government policy but...' He pounced suddenly on his bag, rifled through one of its pockets and turned towards the whiteboard with a board marker in his hand.

'Firstly, you need to understand about the coalition,' he said. He drew a big blue circle on the board, then jabbed it with the marker nib. 'This is the governing party – the largest. But they need more than three hundred and twenty-five seats in the Commons to win a vote and—'

'Why?' Ben cut in.

'Because there's six hundred and fifty seats in total,' Mr Gatimu answered. No one was ever told off for asking questions in his class, even if they did interrupt him. 'The

The House of Lords Reform Bill

government need at least half to win any vote, otherwise all the other parties can get together, gang up on them and vote them down. Now, they didn't have enough seats for a majority, so…' Mr Gatimu rifled through his bag again. He pulled out two more markers – green and red. 'It'll have to do,' he muttered to himself. 'Just imagine this is yellow,' he said, waving the green marker at them. He drew another, smaller circle in green on the board. 'The governing party joined together with another, smaller party to form the coalition. Between the two of them,' he drew a third, medium-sized circle on the board in red, 'they have enough seats to vote down the opposition party.'

A collective quiet had fallen over the class. Mr Gatimu was one of the few teachers who had this effect on all of them.

'Now, what's interesting about the House of Lords Reform Bill is that the governing party aren't really into it. It's not their thing. They're traditionalists and this would be the most revolutionary change in Britain's political history since the Civil War deposed the monarchy.'

'So why are they doing it?' Megan Phillips asked from the front row.

'Because it's a flagship policy of the party they are in coalition with. The liberals believe in rational government and there's nothing more irrational than an unelected house in a so-called democracy. The government agreed to do it as part of the coalition talks. They need this, to keep the coalition together. So they can be sure they'll get these votes.' He jabbed the green circle. 'But they don't know how many of these votes they'll get.' He tapped at the blue circle, like a woodpecker whittling a hole in a tree trunk. 'And these are the important votes, because they need this voting power.'

'Who cares, sir?' Ben drawled.

'*I* care and you should too. We all should. We believe we live in a democracy, but there's eight hundred unelected peers sitting in Parliament voting on our laws.' Mr Gatimu grew animated. 'Some of them, most of them, don't bother to show up to vote. They squander that privilege. They've been handed it on a plate by a former Prime Minister and they use it like a title. Like it's just an excuse to get everyone to call them Lord Fauntleroy. When it's so much more than that. It's a voice. It's a privilege and a responsibility.'

Theo was on the edge of his seat. He realised this was exactly what he had wanted to know. Why it mattered. He wanted to keep talking about it, but he could already see Mr Gatimu trying to climb back down from his anger.

Slowly, hesitantly, Theo raised his hand.

'Yes, Theo?' Mr Gatimu seemed even more surprised than when Samira had raised her hand.

'Sir, do you think… Is it possible that someone took the mace to stop the vote, to stop the government winning?'

The silence in the room was deafening. Theo kept his eyes trained on Mr Gatimu so he didn't have to see the others all staring at him.

Mr Gatimu hesitated, assessing Theo. 'It is possible, yes.'

'A vigilante!' Ben said. 'Cool.'

'It's not cool.' The words were out of Theo's mouth before he could stop them. 'You can't just steal the mace because you disagree with a law the government are proposing. That's wrong.' He felt the same as when Rupert had told him that MPs didn't always vote with their conscience. A bubble was expanding in his chest, filling him up, squeezing out every other feeling.

'Ben raises an interesting point,' Mr Gatimu said, before Ben could get worked up at Theo. 'How far is it acceptable to go to defend your beliefs? Does the end justify the means?'

Theo thought that he would like to be someone who fought for his beliefs. Someone who went on protests and marches, who signed petitions. Of course he couldn't do any of that. Not while his dad was Prime Minister. He couldn't ever be seen to disagree with him.

'Is it acceptable to break the law?' Mr Gatimu went on. Theo didn't quite manage to hide his scowl of disapproval and Mr Gatimu caught it. 'The suffragettes did when they were campaigning for votes for women. Was that wrong? Theo?' he pressed, his eyes on him.

'That's different,' he mumbled. The bubble of anger was shrinking, his embarrassment returning.

'In what way?'

Theo looked to the whiteboard behind Mr Gatimu as if it might have the answers. Was it different? It felt different because the suffragettes had been right. History had shown that.

As if he had read Theo's mind, Mr Gatimu said, 'It's easy to forgive those we agree with and condemn those we don't.'

When the class ended, Theo had made up his mind. They weren't supposed to use their phones in the corridors, but with all the students squashed in together, it was difficult for teachers to spot them.

Theo took out his phone. He sent a message to his mum asking permission to walk home on his own.

The House of Lords Reform Bill

He paused. He thought about who he could ask to get him into the Palace of Westminster. He thought Bob Piggott could do it. He was head of security; he must be able to get Theo in. But as head of security, Theo was sure he would also tell his dad that he had been there. Besides, Bob didn't know him. Would he even believe Theo when he explained who his dad was? That option was out. He could only think of one other.

He sent an email to Rupert Spencer asking if he could give him a tour of the palace after school.

CHAPTER EIGHT

The Lord Speaker

It turned out to be an effort to persuade his mum not to send a protection officer to pick him up. After several texts back and forth between lessons, he had invented a school friend who would walk with him most of the way home. It was a risky lie, but he didn't feel like he had much choice. Rupert had emailed him back and agreed to the tour. He couldn't miss this chance. If he was found out, he would say the friend backed out at the last minute.

At the end of school, Theo went to the toilets to sort out his clothes. He would stand out less if he wasn't wearing school uniform. He hadn't brought anything else to change into, so he made do with removing his blazer, jumper and school tie. Without them he was wearing black trousers and a white shirt, like most men wandering around Westminster. He was so tall, he almost looked like a grown man, apart from his perfectly smooth face. If only he could remember to stand up straight, he didn't think many people would clock him as a student. There was always the risk that someone would recognise him and his dad would find out he had been at the palace. He would have to say he was researching an essay. He wiped his sweating palms on his trousers.

On Victoria Street, he passed cars and buses queued up in a traffic jam. Soon he crossed Parliament Square, making not for the well-known Parliament building, but its lesser-known sibling, Portcullis House, which was an unassuming office building above Westminster tube station.

As Theo approached the entrance to Portcullis House, he heard running behind him.

'Hey!' someone shouted behind him.

He turned around to find Samira catching up to him, out of breath.

'I waved at you from the bus, but you didn't see me,' she said between puffs.

'What are you doing here?' he said.

'I could ask you the same.'

Theo fought the heat rising in his cheeks. 'Working on my Citizenship project.'

'Me too.'

Theo suspected she was just saying that because he had, but he didn't dare challenge her. Was she there to investigate the missing mace too? Her mum had thought she would try to get involved and here she was. She didn't look like she was there for something as serious as investigating a crime or even for school work. She had changed out of her school uniform. The hems of her long black trousers were ripped, the torn ends trailing on the ground. Her long-sleeved black top was pulled down over her hands with holes for her thumbs to poke through, just like her school jumper. A silver chain necklace swung down almost to her stomach. She had scooped her hair into a loose ponytail. A piercing through the top of her ear was now visible, but her red streaks were mostly hidden. She looked like she should be at a gig.

'Well?' she said.

'What?'

'Come on,' she replied with an impatient sigh.

The whole wall of the building was glass, with a revolving glass door. Theo caught sight of his reflection in the window and stood up taller. He glanced at Samira as she pushed into the revolving door, wondering how he was going to get rid of her. Without thinking, he followed behind her into the revolving door and they got caught in the same tiny cubicle. Samira scowled at him over her shoulder then pushed on the door. It didn't move. Theo leant over the top of her and pushed. He was so close that the hair in her ponytail tickled his chin. They scuttled around quickly as the door gave and propelled them forwards.

They stumbled out with a clatter. Samira turned deliberately to glower at him. He shrugged in what he hoped was an apologetic manner.

A security guard waited for them at the end of an airport-style security scanner. They loaded their bags into trays and pushed them on to the conveyor belt towards the scanner.

'So what are you really up to it?' Samira asked quietly.

'Nothing.'

'If you say so.'

Theo bristled. He was on the point of asking her what *she* was up to, but she went on ahead, out of whispering range.

The Lord Speaker

As Samira went through a metal detector, Theo searched behind the wall of glass separating them from the main hall. It was a glass-covered piazza. Light from the glass ceiling bathed the people congregated below, their heads bent together, talking intently. It streamed through the trees that lined the middle of the space, creating dappled shadows on the creamy stone floor. It looked like a Mediterranean town square.

Rupert waved at him from the other side – he was on time. Like the last time, he wasn't wearing a jacket. Theo suspected this was part of his look. It was a 'man of the people' look, unlike his dad's, who was always formal, to suggest leadership and competence.

After he had explained to the woman on security who he was meeting, she gave them each a tag to hang around their necks and directed them through a turnstile in the glass wall. The security guard had assumed that Samira was with him and Theo wondered with mounting anxiety whether he was now lumbered with her.

Theo went through the turnstile first. As soon as he passed through the glass wall, the noise of chatter hit him. It reminded him of going into an echoing swimming pool filled with screaming children.

'Hi, thanks,' Theo said as he reached Rupert. 'This is Samira,' he said, as she came up behind him.

'It's Sammy actually,' she said.

'Pleasure,' Rupert replied. 'Are you coming on the tour as well?'

'No,' Theo said as Samira said, 'Yes.'

'I've got somewhere to be first. I'm meeting someone.' She started to hurry away. 'I'll catch up with you later.'

The Lord Speaker

Rupert was clearly taken aback.

Theo watched her with a deep scowl. Who could she possibly be meeting? He didn't appreciate her piggybacking off his plans. On the far side of the piazza, Samira had come to a stop. She was talking to someone. With a start, Theo realised it was Ruth Morris.

He looked quickly at Rupert. He was watching Samira too. Rupert's brow was furrowed in a way that could have been either annoyed or thoughtful. Theo hoped he wasn't cross that she was meeting with one of his rivals.

'Sorry about that,' Theo said. 'Just someone from school.' He didn't want Rupert to think she was with him.

Rupert set off towards a mini escalator that led underground, a little too brisk for even Theo's long legs to keep up. 'She better be quick. With Parliament closing tomorrow, I don't have much time tonight.'

The escalator led into an underground tiled walkway. Theo felt like he was in the Underground, until the ground sloped up and into the light.

'Thanks for doing this and for agreeing not to tell my dad. I want it to be a surprise.'

'Of course, I understand, Theo.' Rupert paused for a moment. 'I know what it's like to grow up with a politician for a father.'

'Your dad was an MP?'

'Yes,' Rupert said, rubbing self-consciously at his ear. 'They can have... exacting standards.'

Theo's chest felt tight and he couldn't find anything to say.

'Sometimes it's easier not to tell them what you're up to.'

Rupert smiled reassuringly and patted him on the shoulder. Theo knew he didn't have to say anything. He had the feeling that Rupert did understand. Some of the pressure in his chest released at the thought that he really wouldn't tell his dad. He realised he had been worried that Rupert would quietly let his dad know what he was up to, in that way that adults sometimes had of only pretending to keep your secrets. Somehow now he felt he could trust Rupert not to tell.

Rupert pointed out certain areas and architectural features to Theo as they walked and Theo made noises of appreciation. He wasn't really listening though. He was trying to memorise their route. He needed to learn his way around if he was going to have any hope of working out where the thief had taken the mace.

They crossed an open courtyard – which Rupert told him was called New Palace Yard – and passed into the main Houses of Parliament building. After several identical corridors that Theo couldn't get straight in his head, they arrived in the Central Lobby. Theo had a sudden memory of the theft, the smoke in his lungs. He felt disorientated.

He was coming from the opposite door from last time – the door the procession had come through. He walked slowly down the corridor leading into the lobby. Like its opposite, it was lined with statues. The only one of a woman stood out among the many men. The procession had walked this way and he had watched them from the other side of the chamber.

'It's an incredible place,' Rupert said, seeming to perceive Theo's wonder. 'It stretches for miles underground too. They're still discovering bits of it – Victorian engine rooms and what not. They found one under a room they're renovating on the other side of the building.'

Theo gazed around, wondering for the first time where the smoke could possibly have come from. He guessed they were those military gas canisters. He had seen them in dramas on TV. Had someone thrown them from above? He couldn't see where they would have come from. The windows stretched high above people's heads and they didn't look the sort to open. None were broken. He looked back down the corridor. There were no doors, just impregnable ancient stone walls.

It must have been someone already inside the room who had slipped the canisters from their pocket.

Theo's eye was caught by a familiar figure lumbering towards them – Felix Humphries. Instinctively, Theo turned his back on him, towards the statue of the woman, pretending to study it. It was too much to hope that another of his dad's employees wouldn't tell him that they had seen Theo in the palace.

'Spencer! What are you doing here?' Felix said rather curtly.

Rupert replied, 'I could ask you the same question.'

Felix affected not to hear him. 'Did you get my note? The Prime Minister wants a list of all the people who could swing either way in the vote on the House of Lords Reform Bill.'

'I wonder that he didn't ask me himself.'

'This request comes from the Prime Minister.' Theo detected a hint of irritability in Felix's voice. 'You know I only work on his behalf.'

'What does he want the list for?'

Felix took a moment to respond. Theo was tempted to

turn around and see what he looked like, his voice gave so little away. Was he angry? Did he look guilty? He couldn't really afford the risk of being noticed just to check.

'Does it matter?'

'MPs tell me their voting plans in confidence,' Rupert said. 'I'm not giving up their names without good reason.'

Theo breathed in sharply. He had never heard anyone refuse Felix Humphries or, by extension, his dad. He felt an absurd sense of pride and victory in Rupert for standing up to them.

'We don't need good reason; we don't need any reason. Ours is not to reason why. Or have you forgotten that you work on behalf of the Prime Minister too?'

'I do. But the difference is, I have principles and I don't stoop below them.'

'This won't be the last you hear on this matter.'

Theo heard Felix shuffling away. He passed Theo and Theo watched his retreating back as he left. He turned back to Rupert with a renewed sense of respect for him.

'Come on then,' Rupert said, as though nothing had happened. He strode off through the lobby and Theo had to trot to catch up to him. 'Is your friend going to join us?' Rupert asked him, stopping abruptly.

'Erm, I don't know,' Theo said, wondering himself.

'I was going to take you to the private gallery above the House of Lords, but we'll have to use the public one. Your friend won't be able to get into the private one without me.'

He led Theo down a discreet hallway, nodding to several attendants on the way. That led on to a staircase that seemed to be in a tower. It twisted around on itself for several floors before they reached the top. They had to give their bags to another attendant who manned a sort of cloakroom, with walls covered in large pigeonholes into which he placed each one.

'I think it will be fairly busy in there today,' Rupert whispered as they followed a narrow corridor on to the gallery.

The gallery ran, high up, around the walls of the House of Lords. Several rows of pews sloped steeply down in front of them. Stained-glass windows cast a murky light on the chamber. Underneath, people were packed on to red leather benches like Pez sweets in a dispenser, ready to pop off the end. The black and white-clad officials sitting on the central pouffes resembled king penguins overseeing their flocks. They were dwarfed by a giant altar and an imposing throne, both made of gold, on the back wall.

Theo could hear everything that was being said below, but it sounded amplified.

'Where's the sound coming from?' Theo whispered to Rupert. No one else in the gallery was speaking.

'Speakers,' Rupert said, pointing out the microphones that hung from the ceiling. He indicated an empty row and they slid into the seats.

There was a very heated debate going on. A man sitting just in front of the gold altar stood up and called them all to order. Theo realised with a start that it was the old man he had seen in the lobby on the morning of the theft. He still had that niggling feeling that he had seen him somewhere before. This time he couldn't be sure that his brain wasn't just dredging up the last time he had seen him. But he had felt it before too. Despite his age, the man had a booming voice that rang clearly over the other noises of the chamber. Theo noticed something gold glinting behind his seat.

The Lord Speaker

'But that's a mace!' he said, louder than he meant to.

'That's the Lords' mace, the Commons and the Lords have one each,' Rupert whispered.

'Why can't the Commons use that one then?'

'It's been suggested, but the Lords aren't very happy about it, as you can see.'

As he said this a loud jeer went up in the chamber and many voices joined it. Soon the noise drowned out every other sound. The woman who had been speaking sat back in her seat, while the man sitting with the mace tried to recall the House to order.

'Come on,' Rupert said and he led the way back out.

They collected their belongings from the attendant and made their way back downstairs.

'Who was that man with the mace?' Theo asked.

'He's called the Lord Speaker, his name is Trevor Thompson. It's his job to keep order in the House. There's also a Speaker of the House of Commons.'

'Is he one of the people who doesn't want the House of Commons to use the Lords' mace?' An idea was forming in Theo's head.

'Yes he is. But he isn't very happy about the House of Lords Reform Bill, so it's no real surprise he doesn't want the Commons to sit.' Rupert stopped with one foot on the stair below. 'Theo, you won't mention that to anyone, will you? I shouldn't really have said so much.'

'Of course not,' Theo said eagerly. His suspicions were confirmed. Who would want to stop the House of Lords Reform Bill more than the Lords themselves? He had his first suspect.

'Thank you.' Rupert smiled warmly at him. 'Good man.'

The Lord Speaker

When they walked back out into Central Lobby, to Theo's annoyance, they found Samira coming towards them.

'Ah, here you are,' Rupert said a little stiffly. He was still annoyed about Samira leaving them, Theo thought.

'Have I missed the tour?' Samira said.

'Yes, I'm afraid I've run out of time now,' Rupert replied, looking at his watch. 'There's a lot to get through before Parliament shuts down, so I really must get on.'

'It's all right, I can take Samira to the gallery. We can go up to the public gallery,' Theo said, inspired by his own quick thinking.

'Yes,' Rupert said slowly, 'yes, all right.'

He gave them directions for the main exit and left without a backward glance.

Theo waited for him to get out of earshot, before turning to Samira.

'What do you think you're doing?'

'I was going to ask you the same question! Are you going to tell me what you're up to now or do I have to go back and ask that man what you've been talking about?'

'All right!' Theo said. He didn't think she meant it, but he didn't want to risk it. 'Come on.'

He led the way out of the lobby.

CHAPTER NINE

Meeting with the Opposition

Instead of going back up to the gallery, Theo led them to the main entrance, retracing their footsteps from the day of the theft. He took them to the café that was attached to Westminster Hall. It felt like a chapel, with stone archways over the doors and a low ceiling.

Samira chose the table in the furthest corner of the room, while Theo bought a mint tea for himself, and a mocha and a sausage roll for Samira. She snatched up the sausage roll and bit into it as soon as Theo had set it down. He tried not to stare, but his dismay must have been obvious on his face.

'What?' she said. 'I'm not allowed meat at home. We're vegetarians.'

Theo drank his tea in silence as Samira polished off the sausage roll. She slowed down as she came to the end of it. She seemed to be looking at him more closely now, considering something.

'I came here to ask Ruth about the theft of the mace,' she said suddenly.

Meeting with the Opposition

'Really?'

'Yep.' She sipped her mocha, warming her hands on the cup. Her nail polish – chipped – was dark red today, matching her hair. 'Is that what you were doing here too? Looking for clues?'

Theo stared down into his cup. He didn't want to share his plan with Samira. She was always in detention. She had a dangerous disregard for the rules. He didn't want her getting him into trouble, it was too risky. And she might tell someone what he was doing.

'Didn't your mum tell you not to get involved?'

Samira lifted her chin and said, 'It's not up to her.' Her eyes were glittering with defiance. 'Does your dad know you're here?'

Theo shifted uncomfortably in his seat.

'Thought not. Don't you want to know what I found out from Ruth?'

Theo had to concede that he did. He was never going to be able to question her himself. She knew who he was and wasn't likely to speak to him.

'How did you get that meeting with her anyway?' Theo asked, stalling for time.

'My mum's a member of the party. She's done voluntary campaign work for them for years. We used to live in Ruth's constituency, so she knows her quite well. I got Ruth's number off her phone and called her.'

With every word, Theo felt an increasing stab of panic. He had never spoken to a member of the opposition before, not properly. There had been dinners and events with his dad, for his work. But he had never made friends with one. He was absolutely certain this was one of the mistakes

Meeting with the Opposition

his dad kept telling him not to make. He thought of making an excuse and leaving, but Samira carried on talking and it seemed rude to interrupt.

'Anyway, I think what you said in Citizenship was right.' Theo felt his cheeks warm. 'Someone took the mace because they didn't want the vote on the House of Lords Reform Bill to go ahead. So I asked Ruth's opinion about it. She said that her party agreed with the Bill in principle, but not the details, which was why her party had planned to vote against it. They disagreed with the proportion of elected members versus selected. Only thirty per cent were going to be elected and Ruth said she thought it wasn't good enough. She wanted it to be more.'

Theo sipped his tea as he listened. This was all very promising. It definitely sounded like someone in Ruth's party wouldn't want the government to win the vote. Maybe a member of the opposition had decided to steal the mace when it seemed possible the government might win.

'What gave you the idea that the theft was about the Reform Bill?' Samira said.

Theo couldn't refuse to answer her when she was sharing all her information with him. He explained what Rupert had told him the first time they met and who Rupert was.

'I haven't got to the best bit of my story yet,' Samira said when she had listened to everything he had to say.

'Go on.'

'At first I wasn't planning to ask Ruth for an alibi, because I didn't think she would steal the mace.'

'Why not?' Theo couldn't help interrupting.

'Just, I've known her for years. I didn't think it was the sort of thing she would do. But, once she said all that about how she disagreed with the Bill, I thought I better ask what she was doing on the morning the mace was stolen, just to be sure. And she went all funny. She really didn't want to answer me. Then she got very suspicious about why I was asking. I went on about how I was there and I saw it happen and wasn't it scary to try to distract her, but she wasn't having any of it.' Samira drank the last dregs of her mocha. 'She told me she was busy and basically said I had to leave.'

'Oh,' Theo said, feeling deflated. 'Well, we saw her immediately after the mace was stolen. She came in with my dad. She can't have had time to get the mace away.'

'She might have stashed it somewhere and gone back for it later. I'm telling you, she was really shifty about where she was. She's definitely hiding something.'

Theo didn't say anything. She hadn't found out whether Ruth had an alibi. All of the evidence about her motive would be useless without knowing if she had an alibi.

'But, I did find out something very useful,' she said, leaning forward.

Theo waited for her to go on, but she didn't. She was waiting for him to ask.

Feeling impatient Theo said, 'What?'

'I saw a walking stick in her office,' she said with wide eyes. She sat back with a satisfied smile.

'Erm, right…' Theo didn't know what she was talking about. He wondered whether he was being thick and not getting something really obvious, or whether she wasn't making any sense.

She wiped the inside rim of her cup and licked her finger.

'Don't you see?' She became impassioned. 'She must have injured herself during the theft! Think about it. I've

Meeting with the Opposition

never seen her use a walking stick, have you?'

He thought back. 'No, but...'

'There you go. She isn't going to use it in public, is she? People would get suspicious.'

'That could be it.' He went on gently, 'Or maybe someone else left it there by accident?'

'Oh no, she got all anxious and squirmy –' she wriggled in her seat as though she were mimicking Ruth – 'when she caught me looking at it.'

Theo considered this. It seemed quite a leap from walking stick to injury sustained during high-profile robbery. But Samira was so pleased with her discovery and after all, it was an idea – one that they couldn't yet disprove.

She seemed to sense his doubt. 'Look, maybe it wasn't her. But she's hiding something about that morning and it could be a clue. I think it's important.'

Theo nodded, if only to humour her.

'What about you? What did you find out?'

Theo still wasn't convinced they should be working together. But he felt he owed her, now that she had told him what she had found out. He reasoned that one information sharing session couldn't hurt. He told her about Trevor Thompson and how Rupert had confirmed his suspicion that Lord Thompson also had a motive.

Samira nodded enthusiastically to everything he said. 'We should start a suspect list. Have you got any paper?'

'Good idea.' Theo took out his pad and pen. He wrote down Ruth Morris and Lord Thompson and what little they knew about them. It was a short list. 'Can you think of anyone else?' he asked Samira.

'You're more likely to know suspects than I am.'

Meeting with the Opposition

'Right,' Theo said. He remembered his parents' conversation about Chris Elliot and added his name to the list.

'Why him?' Samira asked, peering over the page.

'Just brainstorming.'

He couldn't tell her about the conversation he had overheard. There was no knowing who she might tell.

'I suppose Felix Humphries was there after the theft. Seems a bit far-fetched,' Theo said.

'Why? Who's he?'

'My dad's Private Secretary. He works for the civil service. They're politically neutral so I can't see him being involved.'

'He must have opinions though.'

'Why?' Theo asked.

'Doesn't everyone? Write him down anyway.' Samira pointed at the list. 'We can't afford to be picky right now.'

Although he didn't see much point in it, Theo wrote him down.

'There were lots of people there right after it happened,' Samira said. 'Your dad was there.'

'We're not putting him on the list,' Theo said a bit too quickly. There was a moment of silence, just long enough to feel distinctly uncomfortable. 'I think that's enough for now.'

Samira nodded as if nothing strange had passed between them. As he put the list back in his bag, she jumped out of her seat.

'Right, let's go then,' she said, collecting her bag from the floor.

'Hold on, Samira, I thought I might look around a bit more before I go.' Theo felt his cheeks reddening.

Meeting with the Opposition

'I told you. It's Sammy,' she said with a scowl. 'And we are. We're going back up to the gallery. I want to see Lord Thompson too.'

CHAPTER TEN

The Serjeant at Arms

When they got back up to the gallery, Theo pointed out Lord Thompson to Sammy and settled himself back in his seat to watch. The wooden bench had an uncomfortably straight back and there was no space to stretch out his legs. But there was something mesmerising about the sound of the debate. Despite the jeering and heckling, it felt choreographed. Each member waited for the Lord Speaker to call on them to speak. Then they called each other things like 'My honourable friend'. They sounded like they had walked out of the pages of *The Three Musketeers*.

'Come on,' Sammy said, disturbing his thoughts. She was already out of her seat.

'Where are you going?' Theo hurried after her. It was difficult to shuffle his long legs along the narrow row.

'Hurry up,' she said.

He clattered out and apologised to the people around him who were tutting and shaking their heads.

In the corridor, Sammy said, 'We don't want to lose him, come on.' She darted around the corner.

They collected their bags, then Sammy ran down the stairs.

'Lose who?' Theo gasped.

'Lord Thompson. Didn't you see him leave? We're going to question him.'

Theo overtook Sammy in two strides. 'Are you serious?'

He stopped in front of her, but she dodged easily out of the way.

'How else will we find out his alibi?'

'He isn't going to tell us!' Theo jogged awkwardly after her. She was small, but she was quick. 'Look what happened when you asked Ruth.'

'We've got to try. What have we got to lose?'

He didn't have an answer. He had a strong feeling that this was another mistake. Sammy didn't understand. She didn't have to worry about being written about in the newspapers. Her dad wouldn't lose his job if she put just one toe over the wrong, invisible line.

'I'm not doing it,' Theo said.

'Fine, I'll do it without you.' Sammy flicked her hair over her shoulder at him and looked about for Lord Thompson.

They were back in the Central Lobby. Lord Thompson was making his way out and Sammy dived after him. Theo hung back.

'Lord Thompson, can I ask you about the Reform Bill?' Sammy said. Theo couldn't help admiring her guts.

'Who are you?' Lord Thompson said, peering closely at her.

A police officer approached them. 'I'm going to have to ask you to step back, miss,' he said.

Theo swore under his breath. He couldn't leave her to

get into trouble. He hurried towards her.

'I'm Theo Duncan, sir,' he said to Lord Thompson. He saw the spark of recognition in Lord Thompson's eyes; he knew Theo's name. 'Me and my friend Samira are researching the Reform Bill for a project at school.'

'Oh, I see. It's all right, officer.' Lord Thompson waited for the officer to leave.

Theo breathed a sigh of relief too soon.

Lord Thompson gave him an imperious glare. 'This isn't the way to go about things. Accosting people in hallways, shouting at them. Does your father know you're here?'

Theo looked at his shoes.

'We're very sorry about the shouting and the costing,' Sammy said quickly. 'We just want to know what you think of the House of Lords Reform Bill.'

'I gathered that. You might have had better luck if you had gone about it properly.' He swished his cloak and Theo thought of how his mum sometimes did that when she was wearing hers. It was funny how a uniform could make a person feel powerful. He could tell it was having that effect on Lord Thompson as he stalked off.

'That didn't go very well,' Sammy said thoughtfully.

'It's *a*ccosting, not costing.'

'I wondered why he was talking about costing. What's accosting then?'

A heavy hand fell on Theo's shoulder and he jumped.

'Hello there,' a deep voice said behind him.

Theo turned slowly.

It was Bob Piggott. Serjeant at Arms. Head of security at the Palace of Westminster.

The Serjeant at Arms

*

'Come with me,' Bob said, with a slight Caribbean lilt.

Theo glanced anxiously at Sammy as they followed Bob out of the lobby. Bob walked casually ahead of them. He didn't seem to be marching them out of the building. But then where was he taking them? Theo silently wished he wasn't taking them to his dad.

Theo studied the back of Bob's head and wondered what he was thinking. He still had a dressing over the spot where Theo assumed he had been knocked out. He wanted to ask him what he remembered of the theft. He didn't have the nerve.

They approached the door out to New Palace Yard, which they had taken on the day of the theft. Theo expected Bob to go through it, but he carried on past it. Instead they turned right, further into the belly of the building.

They passed a few harried-looking people coming the other way. A couple seemed to notice them and frown. Bob kept up his steady pace, ignoring them all. He walked with authority and people seemed to accept that whatever he was doing, he must have good reason for it. Even those who frowned at them, didn't stop to ask questions. Slowly Theo realised that this was what respect looked like. He didn't see that often at school. He remembered thinking Bob looked like a king on the day of the theft and realised that was what he had been feeling. This was a person who commanded respect.

They turned into a corridor that was littered with tools and paint tins. Theo peered through an open door that led into a room draped with dust sheets. This must be the section of the building being renovated. There was no noise of works now though.

'This way,' Bob said and Theo hurried to keep up.

He took them down a narrow corridor. There were several doors leading off it, all of them closed. The door plaques showed they were the offices of the palace security. So Bob had brought them to the security offices. With a sinking feeling, Theo thought that they must be in serious trouble.

As they reached the door at the end of the corridor, one of the doors behind them opened. A woman came out of it, someone Theo recognised. It was the woman with all the ear piercings, the one he had seen his dad staring at on the morning of the theft.

She looked startled, her eyes wide. After a second, she shrugged slightly, smiled thinly to Bob and walked quickly back the way they had come.

'Who was that?' Sammy asked. Again, Theo admired her courage.

'Journalist,' Bob said, opening his office door. 'Don't be minding her.' He stood to one side to let them in.

Theo and Sammy filed inside. The room was a simple office, indistinguishable from the few others Theo had seen in the palace – a cross between an academic's study and a medieval dungeon. The ancient stone walls were lined with burgeoning bookcases; the bare stone floor only partly covered by a threadbare, faded maroon rug. Huge architectural plans – larger than A3 – covered Bob's desk. The window behind the desk had a beautiful view over the river, towards Lambeth Palace on the other side. As Theo squeezed inside he spotted an empty glass case on the wall. It looked like a museum case, with a heavy, old-fashioned padlock on the front.

'That's where it usually lives,' Bob said, seeing the direction of Theo's gaze. There was no need to ask what he meant. The spectre of the mace hung in the air. 'Come, look.'

They clustered around the case. Theo could see Sammy was as nervous as he was. What on earth did Bob want with them?

'Every day I lock the mace in there, then I lock my office. T'aint nobody who knows where I keep the keys. You see that lock.' He pointed to the door they had just come through. 'Unbreakable. Nobody is getting through that door without the key.' Theo saw now that its wood exterior was a façade, encasing a solid metal interior only visible to them because the door was open. 'Somebody knew that. That's why they took the mace from the corridor.'

Theo didn't know what to say. They didn't seem to be in trouble, but he still wasn't quite sure what was going on.

'Do you remember what happened?' Sammy asked in a hallowed voice. 'In the corridor.'

Bob regarded them shrewdly. 'What do you want to know for? You think you gonna solve it, find the mace? Is that why you're here?'

Theo tried to fight his rising colour, but it was no use. He might as well own up to it. 'Well, yes,' he said. Sammy whipped around in surprise, but Theo ploughed on. 'I want to help my dad.'

'That's good,' Bob said, 'honourable. It's not gonna be easy though. Might even be dangerous.'

'You mean, you're not going to try to stop us?'

'Could I, even if I tried?'

'No,' Sammy said. 'Theo's not going to give up and I'm incorrigible, my nanaji says.'

Bob barked a surprised laugh and Theo went bright red. How did Sammy know he felt compelled to find the thief?

'I thought so. My kids were the same. You try to stop them, they just gonna hide what they're up to.' Bob's smile faded while he considered them. 'That's when everything goes wrong. So you come to me if you need anything, you understand me?'

'We promise,' Sammy said.

'Hmm,' Bob rumbled. 'The lines were cut you know, for the CCTV.' Theo nodded enthusiastically. 'Not accidentally, you understand. Someone did it deliberately. We're looking for someone who knew my routines, knew about the renovations. Someone inside this building.'

Theo didn't miss the fact that Bob had said 'we'.

'You understand what that means?' Bob seemed to be addressing Theo in particular. His expression was very grave. Most of the time he had a twinkle in his eye, but it wasn't there now. He usually looked deceptively young, but Theo felt suddenly conscious of his age – the lines on his forehead, the white in his eyebrows. He had the sense that something important was being left unsaid, something Bob was worried about.

He said, 'Those tourists, who were there during the theft, were they just tourists?'

'Yes,' Bob replied, his eyes crinkling in a wry smile. 'Ordinary tourists from Italy. I think we can safely cross them off the list.'

'What do you remember from the theft?' Sammy pressed.

'Not much. Last thing I remember is the bump to me head.' He touched the spot. 'Someone with a bit of strength behind them, I can say that at least.'

'Did you see anything, a face or even just their feet?' Theo said, thinking of the grubby trainers.

'I couldn't see anyting in all that smoke. No, all I'm sure of is that they came from behind me.'

'Behind you?' Sammy repeated.

Thinking of Lord Thompson, who was definitely in front of Bob when the smoke went off, Theo said, 'You might have turned around, though, in the commotion.'

'Oh no, I was rooted to that spot, holding that mace like my own baby. I knew... somehow I knew they were coming for it.'

Theo felt a ripple of uncertainty. Perhaps that meant it wasn't Lord Thompson. Or maybe he had just gone round behind Bob to sneak up on him. He wouldn't want to come at him from the front and risk being seen.

Bob went back to the door. 'I'm trusting you two to conduct your investigations quietly now. No more disturbing the lords or the members. I wouldn't want to be forced to tell your father you were here.'

Sammy and Theo nodded appreciatively, while Bob silenced their thanks. 'It won't hurt,' he went on, 'to be very discreet. Someone doesn't want that mace found. I don't want them getting wind that you're looking for it.'

He told them he would see them back out of the building and they followed him obediently back down the corridors, this time with a sense of relief.

As they reached the corridor leading to the lobby, they saw Rupert coming from the opposite direction. He was distracted and didn't notice them at first, running his hand through his ruffled hair.

Theo waved to him as he passed and Rupert stopped.

'There you are,' Rupert said. 'I was wondering what had happened to you.'

'I thought you would have been in your office now,' Bob said, 'giving the last instructions to your team before the recess.'

'I came to find the children,' Rupert said.

'We're OK,' Theo said. 'Mr Piggott is going to see us out.'

'Good, good.' Rupert still seemed distracted and had to be prompted by Bob to turn in the right direction for his office.

With a final wave to Bob, Sammy and Theo walked across New Palace Yard towards the security lodge to drop off their visitor passes.

'There goes the Lord Thompson theory,' Sammy said as soon as they were out of the palace gates.

'Why?' Theo asked.

'Because Bob said whoever did it was really strong. Thompson doesn't look very strong.'

'Neither does Ruth Morris.'

'Because she's a woman?' Sammy scowled.

'Anyway, I don't think we should rule anyone out yet. Maybe it was more than one person or whoever was responsible masterminded the whole thing and paid someone else to carry out the attack.'

'There was something weird though. When Bob said it must be someone inside the building and then asked if you understood what that meant. He looked at you really intensely. I didn't get that.'

'I think he was saying that it might be someone who works for my dad.'

They both looked back at the palace. It wasn't dark yet, but the blue was seeping out of the sky, like someone had taken an ink eraser to it. It made the great hulk of the palace stand out, tarnished gold against ash grey.

Theo thought of the significance of Bob's warning – that someone who worked for his dad might have taken the mace. He remembered his mother's worry about Chris Elliot. He didn't like to think of the consequences if it turned out the thief was someone his dad trusted.

CHAPTER ELEVEN

A New Partner

The bell rang for the end of class as Theo was still writing up in his notes on the British voting system. He finished his sentence while his classmates were all packing their bags.

'Homework on my desk before you leave,' Mr Gatimu said.

Theo's heart juddered. He had forgotten to do it. He had been so distracted, he had completely forgotten about it. He could distinctly remember the last time he had failed to hand in a piece of homework on time. It was three years before, but the memory was vivid with the shame he had felt when he had to tell his teacher that he had left his work on the printer at home. It was almost as bad as when his dad called the school to confirm that he really had done his homework, to get Theo out of detention. It was one of the reasons none of his classmates liked him. They thought he had special treatment. Except Josh, who had thought it was brilliant. Theo would rather have done the detention than get singled out.

He shuffled his papers slowly into his bag. In front of

A New Partner

him students were filing past Mr Gatimu's desk, depositing dog-eared pages on a pile.

Out of the corner of his eye, Theo spotted Sammy, also lingering near the back of the classroom. She looked at him and bit her lip. He guessed she hadn't done her homework either.

Theo packed as slowly as possible. The room was nearly empty.

Sammy strode in front of him. 'Sir, I'm sorry I didn't have time to do the essay this week. My mum wasn't well and I had to help her last night.'

'Do you have a note from her?'

'I forgot to ask. I had other things on my mind.'

Theo waited behind Sammy. She didn't seem phased by getting into trouble and she was a good liar. If he hadn't seen her onto her bus home late yesterday evening, even he would have believed she spent the evening at home looking after her mum.

'You know you need a note,' Mr Gatimu said with a sigh. 'Detention with me next Thursday.' He scribbled out a detention slip for her. She slipped it into her bag without another word. 'Right. Theo?' He held out his hand to take Theo's work.

'Err...' Theo was suddenly really conscious of Sammy still in the room. She was fiddling with the zip on her bag in the doorway. 'I must have left it at home, sir.'

Mr Gatimu drew his hand away slowly. He watched Theo for a few excruciating moments of silence. Theo could feel him really looking at him, like he was a book that Mr Gatimu was reading and there had just been a twist in the story that Mr Gatimu hadn't seen coming and he was readjusting

A New Partner

his opinion of the author. Theo felt vulnerable, exposed.

'Detention on Thursday,' Mr Gatimu finally said.

Theo snatched the detention slip and hurried out of the room. Sammy was waiting for him just outside.

'Shall we walk down to the gym together?' she said.

Shaking off his discomfort, Theo remembered that they had tennis together. Sammy had never spoken to him at school before.

At the start of the school year they had been given a choice about which sport they would like to do. With some encouragement from his dad, Theo had chosen rowing in the first term. It hadn't turned out well. He didn't like having to squeeze his unwieldy legs into the tiny canoe. Then they had to do capsize drill in the Thames. One dunk in that ice-cold murk had been more than enough for him. When the new term had started he had switched to tennis, which was at least on dry ground. The only downside was that Josh had stuck with rowing, so he had no partner for tennis. In most classes he had ended up with Michael Kyriaku, who couldn't hit a ball. He spent most of his time waiting for Michael to serve.

Thinking he wouldn't mind a change of partner for at least one class, Theo agreed to meet Sammy outside before heading off to the boys' changing room.

When Theo got outside in his shorts and aertex, Sammy bounced over to him. He saw Michael's face fall when they strode off to a net together and felt a stab of guilt.

Sammy decided to serve first and sent a ball soaring over the net towards Theo. He dashed forward to reach it and hit it back.

'We need to decide what we're going to do next,' Sammy

A New Partner

said after she had hit the ball back to him.

Theo waited till it had collided with his racket and said, 'About what?'

'Our investigation,' Sammy said, without attempting to parry Theo's ball.

Theo watched it roll off with disappointment. That was getting quite good. He didn't think he and Michael had ever kept a ball in the air that long.

'We need to find out more about Ruth Morris. I definitely think she's hiding something. And I think we should find out who that woman was who we saw coming out of the security office.'

The mention of the Leader of the Opposition made Theo nervous. How did Sammy intend to find out more about her? He hoped she meant by reading about her from a distance – a long distance. He couldn't be seen by Ruth, who would certainly recognise him. What if she told his dad what he was doing?

Their teacher called to them to ask why they weren't playing. 'Sorry, miss!' Sammy called back.

She ran to get the ball and served it back to Theo. 'Earth to Theo. Are you listening?'

'Yeah.' Deciding to shelve the issue of Ruth Morris for now, he said, 'Do you mean the journalist?'

'Obviously. It shouldn't take long for us to find her online.' Sammy ran to return the ball to Theo.

'I think we should focus on Trevor Thompson. I mean, do some research on his background,' he added, before Sammy got ideas about trying to corner him again.

It was getting easier to return Sammy's shots. She had a tendency to send them off to his right, so he could just

A New Partner

stand in one place and volley them back to her.

'Good plan. How about you come to mine after school,' Sammy said.

Theo hit the ball back softly. It bounced, giving Sammy more time to get to it.

'Really?' Josh was the only other school friend who had ever invited him over. A funny feeling passed through him, like he was standing at the edge of a cliff about to jump and he might fall or he might fly straight into the sky.

'Yeah, we can treat it like a school project. Research, write up some notes. Then draw up a plan of action to look into our leads. You could have dinner with me and my mum.'

'I'll have to text my mum and check with her,' Theo said, but a warm feeling was spreading from his stomach to the rest of his body. Did Sammy want to be friends?

Sammy served the ball and this time Theo could see exactly where to hit it from. He lobbed it back in the opposite direction from where she was standing. Sammy ran to get it and missed.

She stopped with her hands on her hips, catching her breath. 'You're good at this. Do you play at home?'

'Nope. Shall I serve this time?' He ran to get the ball.

'You should take it up.'

'Don't have time. I have rugby on the weekends.'

'And you like that more?' Sammy hit the ball back without enthusiasm.

Theo let it putter away. It was hardly worth trying to hit that one.

He played rugby every Saturday morning. His dad had suggested he take it up and now he made a point of nev-

A New Partner

er missing Theo's matches. Which was really inconvenient because his dad was always there to see him mess up. Theo would have preferred not to have an audience for his ritual humiliation. But there always was an audience – people who took an interest in his triumphs and failures (mostly his failures), whether they knew him or not.

One week one of the dads had been filming on his phone when Theo managed to trip over his own foot. This wasn't uncommon. His legs had got so long, he found it difficult to keep track of them. But this time he knocked over the other team's player, who had the ball, which rolled out of his arms and across the line into goal. The other player launched himself on the ball and scored a try. Theo was mortified.

It was even more mortifying when the video of the incident had gone online. For a whole day at school, everywhere he went people pretended to nosedive in front of him and then fell about in fits of laughter. When he got home and told his mum about it, her face had gone stonily blank – a sure sign that she was fuming. That evening the video had disappeared from social media and the next day at school everyone avoided him. When Theo said hello to the boy whose dad had taken the video, he had squealed and run off. And that was the last time they ever spoke.

'I wouldn't mind giving it up, but my dad wouldn't want me to.'

'Why not?'

'It's a bit of a family tradition, rugby. My dad did it at school.'

'Doesn't mean you have to like it,' Sammy said. 'Come on, you serve again.'

Theo had almost forgotten the game. He trotted off

A New Partner

to pick up the ball with his mind elsewhere. He wondered what his dad would say if he asked to give up rugby. His stomach clenched at the thought of it.

As he took up his spot in front of Sammy and threw the ball up to hit it, he watched it slowly fall back towards him. He brought up his racket and hit the ball as hard as he could across the court. It felt good. Powerful and easy. The ball went where he wanted it to go without him having to think about it. If he could give up rugby for this, he would do it without a second thought.

Sammy ducked. 'Hey, that could have hit me in the face!'

'Sorry!' He watched the ball roll into the bushes at the edge of the playground and with it any hope of choosing a sport that his dad would let him drop rugby for.

CHAPTER TWELVE

The Lobby Journalist

Theo's mum had agreed to let him go to Sammy's after school, on the condition that a personal protection officer came to pick him up at the end of the evening. Theo thought that was getting off lightly. It turned out it was Harry who was the problem. He found her at lunchtime in the cafeteria and explained that he wouldn't be walking home with her.

'Again?' she had said, her voice arch. 'Why?'

'I'm going to my friend's for dinner.'

Harry narrowed her eyes at him. 'What friend?'

Theo cast around for a sign of Sammy, but he couldn't see her. She was probably in another detention. In the end, he told his sister to take it up with their mum if she didn't believe him. She flounced off to join her table of friends, annoyed at him about something. He didn't know what. He thought she would be glad not to have to walk home with him.

Theo and Sammy got the bus together down to Forest Hill – part of London Theo had never been to before. As they walked from the bus stop to Sammy's, Theo examined everything they passed with interest. There were several takeaway places selling 'Best Fried Chicken' and 'Pizza to GO'. They turned off onto a residential street where the houses were large and detached.

While they walked, Theo asked Sammy why she had moved schools in the middle of the year.

'We used to live in Brighton. But when my parents got divorced, my mum decided to move back to London. Her family lives in Croydon.'

'What about your dad?'

'He stayed in Brighton.'

Theo wanted to ask more, but didn't want to pry. 'So you had to move schools.'

Sammy only nodded.

Theo thought it must have been difficult for Sammy moving schools. He knew what it felt like.

When he was eight his dad had been promoted to the Shadow Cabinet, working directly for his party's leader, and decided to move the family into London. Before that they had lived in his constituency, in Surrey. Theo had liked his school there and had lots of friends.

Everything had changed when they moved to Chelsea. All of the children at his new school had friends already. They all knew his dad worked for the government and that seemed to be interesting to them, whereas none of his friends before had cared. For the first couple of weeks they had pestered him with questions, like had he met the Queen and did he live in a really big house. When his mum invited a few of them round for tea afterwards it had turned out they did think his house was big. It was all they had talked about at school the next day and Theo found himself feeling embarrassed about it. He didn't want to invite anyone over again after that.

He had counted down the days until he would be moving on to secondary school. Then he had found out he wouldn't be going to Montgomery like he had hoped. And no one he knew from primary school went on to Anderson School with him. On his first day, he had known no one. Eventually he had fallen in with Josh, who he could sit with at lunch and break time and that had made life a lot easier. But he never really felt like he fit in with anyone else.

Theo asked Sammy about her old school and her friends. As he had guessed, she had a lot of friends at her last school and she had had to leave them all behind. She didn't seem to be worried about making new friends. Unlike Theo, she was one of those people who could eat lunch on her own without looking like a loner. Still, he suspected that she might like to have some new friends. He thought about inviting her to sit with him and Josh. But what if she didn't want to? He decided to wait and see if the topic came up.

They turned into a street of semi-detached houses. They all looked blandly uniform, with neat rectangles of grass for front gardens, only broken up by the occasional tree or hedge.

Sammy turned into number forty-two. The wood stain around the windows was faded, but it had a window box in front of the ground floor window which was bursting with coral-pink flowers. It was the sort of ordinary house that a child might draw a picture of. Square body, square windows and a triangle for a roof. It looked like a home.

Sammy let them in with her key. 'Mum won't be home

for a bit yet,' she said, slipping off her shoes in the hallway. Theo did the same.

There were only a couple of coats on the hooks by the door, nothing like the overflowing coat rack at home. There was nothing else in the hallway but a small chest of drawers under the coat rack. No toys on the floor. No post lying around un-opened. Everything exactly in its place. He wished his home was this neat.

Sammy put her shoes in a drawer in the chest and told Theo to leave his there, before bounding up the stairs two at a time.

Four large cardboard boxes were piled at the top of the stairs. They had labels written on them in marker pen, saying, 'PHOTO ALBUMS' and 'STORE CUPBOARD'. Theo glimpsed a bathroom straight ahead before they turned into a bedroom.

Sammy's bedroom was a lot smaller than his, although he thought it might look a bit bigger if it wasn't quite so messy. Clothes in bold colours – crimson, black, purple – spilled out of open drawers on to the floor. Open magazines thrust out from under the bed. It was as though everything had been tried once and either discarded or everything else shoved aside to find a slither of space for something new. There was no desk, just a laptop perched on top of a chest of drawers, next to a pile of school workbooks. The violet bed sheets were in a tangle at the bottom of the single bed.

Sammy flopped on to the bed and Theo looked around for somewhere he could sit.

'Take the beanbag,' Sammy said and Theo did a double take. He hadn't noticed it under the pile of trousers and school shirts.

Gingerly Theo lifted a pair of trousers from the pile. A bra was revealed underneath. He went bright red.

'Just shove it all on the floor.' Sammy got up from the bed, took the whole pile in her arms and dumped it in the corner of the room. 'Sorry, Mum doesn't tidy up in here because she says it's my responsibility.' Theo couldn't blame her.

He sunk into the beanbag. Sammy grabbed the laptop and plonked herself on the bed again. Some of her workbooks slipped off the drawers and Theo bent to pick them up.

'Leave them!' Sammy said with alarm.

Theo drew his hand back, suddenly interested in what was inside them. He could make out scrawled handwriting on the inside cover of one that had come open, but not what it said.

As she started up the laptop, which seemed to be rather old and slow, Theo thought about the argument his parents had had the night before. He had only caught snatches of it. Enough to know that it was about his dad working long hours. The last time they had argued like that was during the election. He thought they had got past it, but this problem with the mace had brought back old issues.

'What's wrong?' Sammy said.

'Nothing. Why do you think something's wrong?'

'You're all brooding and silent. I mean more silent than usual.'

'I'm fine,' Theo said.

Sammy picked at her nail polish while she waited for the internet to load.

'Right.' She tapped at the keyboard. 'First, I think we

should look up that woman who was coming out of the security office. That was definitely fishy.'

'Erin Connelly,' Theo said. He went to sit next to Sammy on the bed. 'I found her online earlier.' He made it sound simple, but he had spent all his time between lessons on his phone, looking at journalists online until he found her face.

Sammy typed her name into the search bar as Theo spelled it for her. A long list of articles appeared on the screen. Sammy clicked on the first one that mentioned the House of Lords. Theo read it over her shoulder.

'"An outdated, out-of-touch institution that is completely divorced from the real world,"' Theo read out.

'"The Prime Minister's reforms don't go far enough,"' Sammy continued. '"There is no place for an unelected body in our great democracy. The House of Lords shouldn't be reformed, it should be abolished." Too right. And it looks like we've got another serious suspect.'

'You don't think we should abolish the House of Lords, do you?'

'Yeah, she's totally right. It's practically prehistoric. Who are these people anyway? Old cronies of past prime ministers.'

Theo didn't know what to say. He didn't really appreciate Sammy calling his dad's friends and colleagues 'old cronies'. But he didn't want to contradict her and risk falling out with her either.

'There's several more here,' Sammy said, scrolling through a list of similar articles. 'She's been on one about this for a while. Let's find out a bit more about who she is.'

She typed Erin's name into the search bar and this time selected the Wikipedia entry under her name.

She read out, "'Erin Connelly was born in Belfast in 1984 to parents Eileen and Thomas…'" blah blah blah. Ahh, here's something about the articles she's written. "She was an active supporter of the Road Safety Bill in 2011," blah, blah, blah. Here! "She is a known advocate…'" She sounded out the last word awkwardly.

'Advocate, like lawyer,' Theo supplied. 'It means she supports it.'

'Good word. "…a known advocate of parliamentary reform. At the last election she argued strongly for the need to include House of Lords reform in party manifestos. Since the election, she has been a fierce supporter of the abolition of the House of Lords." Bingo!' Sammy pointed excitedly at her screen. 'It all fits. It must be her.'

'True…' Theo said. 'But I don't know. Lobbying government and writing articles is one thing. Stealing the mace…'

'She's Irish, she could be part of the IRA or have links to them. Maybe they put her up to it.'

'Just because she's Irish that doesn't make her part of an Irish terrorist organisation. That's like saying all Muslims are part of Al-Qaeda.' Theo stopped, his ears warming again. Perhaps he had gone too far.

'Or like saying all Indians are Muslim. You know my family is Sikh?' Theo didn't know that but he nodded to indicate he understood. 'All right, maybe not the IRA, but it definitely could be her.'

'But you said you thought it could be Ruth Morris.'

'Yeah, I still think that. It could be more than one person. Besides I'm keeping an open mind.'

Theo frowned. 'I need to write this up.'

He took out his list and ran his finger down the suspects'

names. He had to accept it was a possibility that Ruth Morris could have hidden the mace and returned quickly to the lobby. He had a strong feeling about Trevor Thompson. He had a clear motive and if Ruth could move the mace and get back in a flash, Trevor could too.

He added Erin's name to the list and noted down her motive.

'Let's try Trevor Thompson,' he said. 'He was really keen not to answer any questions. I wonder what he's hiding.'

Sammy went to his Wikipedia page and they read through it silently for a moment.

'What does this mean?' Sammy said. 'It says he's part of the Montgomery Pack of politicians.'

'That's where I saw his face!' Theo said. 'It was in a leaflet from my dad's old school – Montgomery. Thompson's giving a speech there.'

Sammy clicked on the link. 'Several people from that school went into politics, apparently a few of them from the same school year. He's one of them.'

'This is interesting,' Theo said, reaching across Sammy to point at the screen. 'It says here that they're all very traditional. "Their group is marked by their right-wing ideas, particularly a strong belief in the sanctity of the family and the rule of law." The rule of law… I think that means they would be likely to want to preserve the House of Lords.'

Suddenly the bedroom door opened. Sammy's mum stood in the doorway, looking somewhat flustered.

'Didn't you hear me calling you?' she said.

'No,' Sammy replied.

'Well, I'm not surprised with the door closed. You must leave it open, Samira.' She pushed it open against the wall.

'Hello Theo, it's nice to see you again. I'm sorry Samira hasn't properly welcomed you. Samira, why have you not made your bed?' She went around the room, picking up clothes. 'And have you offered your guest a drink?'

'No,' Sammy said again.

'Well?' her mother said, her eyebrows raised.

'I'm all right, Miss Sohal,' Theo said.

'Samira.' There was a dangerous edge to her voice.

'Theo, would you like a drink?' Sammy said in a monotone.

'No, thank you.'

'Well, you must have something to eat. You must be hungry after your long day at school. Come downstairs with me. I'm making chapatis,' she said, ushering them out of the room. 'And call me Karminder.'

Later that evening, Sammy waited with Theo in the living room for his lift to arrive. He had almost forgotten about their investigation. He had really enjoyed his evening with Sammy. For all her complaints about their vegetarian diet, her mum was a really good cook. After the chapatis, she had made them veggie lasagne – not out of a jar like his mum did, but properly, with all the fresh ingredients. He could hear the chink of cutlery as she cleared up in the kitchen.

'I think Trevor Thompson could be in on it,' Sammy said. She had her feet pulled up underneath her on the sofa. Behind her, Theo had a full view of the street, since they hadn't got round to putting up their curtains yet (which Karminder had earnestly apologised for, until Sammy protested that she was being embarrassing). A well-worn bureau in the window recess was covered in cards congratulating them on their new home and, in the centre, one large photo of what he was supposed was Sammy's family.

'What, as well as Erin Connelly and Ruth Morris?'

'Probably not. But I definitely think at least one of them was involved. We know they all have a motive.'

'Connelly because she wants to abolish the House of Lords and Thompson because he wants to keep it?' Theo said.

'Exactly.'

'Right,' Theo said, his brain spinning.

'We know Morris had the opportunity and very likely an injury from the theft. We know she's hiding something about the morning of the theft, but we don't know what. She definitely has a motive. We need to find out more on Connelly and Thompson.'

'It's going to be very difficult to get anything on Thompson. I don't think we're going to get anywhere near him. Unless…' Theo thought for a moment. 'Maybe I could persuade my dad to take me to that alumni event at his school, the one where Thompson is speaking. Then I could, I don't know, try to speak to him again.'

'That's great,' Sammy said, as the doorbell rang. She jumped off the sofa and Theo followed slowly behind. 'I've got an idea about Connelly, but I need to do some more research. Morris is easy. The local party are having a meeting next week and Morris is going to be there. My mum's going, so we can go with her.'

Before Theo could reply, she opened the front door. Andy was waiting for him on the doorstep.

'I'll be out in one minute,' Theo said, gesturing to his shoes, still on the floor rather than his feet.

'Right you are,' Andy replied and walked back down the front path.

Theo checked that he was gone and then pushed the door until it was nearly closed again. He drew breath to speak, but Karminder appeared in the kitchen doorway, a tea towel in hand.

'Are you off now, Theo?'

'Yes, thanks for having me and for dinner.'

'You're welcome any time,' she said, before turning back to the sink.

'You're suggesting I should go to a party meeting of the opposition to my dad's government,' Theo whispered to Sammy, as he struggled to get his shoes on with sweating palms.

'Yeah, why not?'

Theo stared at her blankly. 'Sammy, I can't go with you, you'll have to go without me.'

The front door opened again. 'Hurry up, Theo. The car's blocking the street.'

'Sorry.' Theo pulled on his remaining shoe without bothering to tie the laces.

'Wednesday night,' Sammy said, as he followed Andy out. 'Make sure you clear it with your parents.'

Theo only gaped at her, as Sammy waved happily to him from the doorstep.

What on earth was he going to say to his dad?

CHAPTER THIRTEEN

An Uncivil Peerage

The next morning, Theo returned to Downing Street after an exhausting rugby match. His team had won by a whisker. Nothing to do with his efforts, he couldn't take credit for it. But his mum had insisted that he tell his dad the good news. It was one of those rare occasions when he had missed Theo's game. He was so busy trying to resolve the problems created by the House of Commons not being able to sit, he couldn't afford to take time off.

Theo was still wearing his dirty rugby clothes as he wandered the corridors of Number Ten towards his dad's office. The spikes of his boots clacked along the marble floors. He passed open doors behind which phones were ringing and people talking.

Rupert Spencer emerged from one of them.

'Theo, just back from rugby? I hope you thrashed them,' he said.

'Well, sort of,' Theo said.

'That's the spirit. Are you going in to see your dad?'

Theo nodded.

An Uncivil Peerage

'Better get those muddy shoes off before you walk on his carpet. Don't want to upset housekeeping.' Rupert's phone rang. He nodded to Theo to indicate he needed to take it, then he answered the call in a jovial manner. 'Charles! So good to hear from you…'

He strode off down the corridor, booming into his phone as though he was trying to communicate through a tin can on a string.

Theo looked down at his boots. They were a bit of a state. He walked further up the corridor to sit on the bottom step of a set of stairs. As he untied his shoelaces he heard fervent whispering coming from above him.

'You should have come to me. I could have got you a majority. But there's still time. We can swing this while they scramble to find the mace. By the time they get it back, we'll have turned the vote against them. Give me one name to work on.'

Theo leant back slowly to see who was above him. He could only make out the back of someone's head. They were leaning against the banister on the floor above. They moved as if to turn around. Theo dodged out of sight.

'You need me.' Theo recognised the voice, but couldn't place it.

He looked at the window onto the staircase and could just make out the reflection of someone short and very round, now standing in profile. It was Felix Humphries, his dad's Permanent Secretary.

'Get me that peerage and I'll get you the majority for the vote. Speak to the PM this week.' Felix hung up.

He shuffled away while Theo was still sitting with one shoe on, one shoe off.

What on earth did that all mean? Who could Felix have been speaking to? It sounded like he was offering to fix a vote. Could he have been talking about the Reform Bill? Was it possible he was actually talking to the person who stole the mace?

He remembered the conversation he had overheard between Felix and Rupert at the Palace of Westminster the day Rupert took him round. Felix had been asking for a list of people who could swing either way in the vote. And hadn't Rupert implied that he didn't know why the Prime Minister hadn't asked him for it? Maybe this was why. Maybe his dad didn't know Felix was trying to get that list.

The door to his dad's office opened at the end of the corridor. Theo pulled off his other shoe and jumped to his feet. Three of his dad's advisors scuttled out, their heads together and Theo knocked on the open door.

'Dad?'

'Come in,' his dad said. He was standing in front of his desk. He smiled at his son, but his expression was strained.

Theo hesitated as he entered the room. He had felt nervous in here ever since the first time he had come in and sat on the nearest chair, only to be shouted at by three people simultaneously. It turned out it had once been Winston Churchill's chair. His dad had brought it in when he made the room his office. Theo hadn't been the only one to make the mistake and it had soon been removed to a safer location. He still felt embarrassed about the mishap.

Now there were two leather armchairs facing his dad's imposing dark wood desk. Theo didn't dare sit in one of them. Especially with the portraits of admirals, generals and marshals past staring down at him from the walls.

An Uncivil Peerage

'How was rugby?' his dad said.

Theo, whose mind was still elsewhere, tried to remember why he had come to see his dad. 'Oh yeah, good. We won.'

Just for a second, his dad's smile faltered and he looked stricken. Theo was suddenly worried he had upset him. Didn't his dad want him to win? He stood awkwardly clutching his rugby boots away from his shirt, while he waited for his dad to reply.

'That's brilliant!' his dad said, smiling again and grasping his shoulder. 'Well done. I wish I could have seen it.'

Theo felt guilty. He had obviously given his dad the impression that he was responsible for their win, that this was his victory. He knew he shouldn't have made such a big deal out of it by coming down to tell him. But if he hadn't come down, he wouldn't have overheard Felix's conversation.

'Dad, what's a peerage?'

His dad's forehead creased. 'A peerage is when you make someone a lord or lady. Why do you ask?'

'I just heard someone talking about it.' That wasn't a lie. He preferred not to lie; he wasn't very good at it. 'So if someone became a lord or lady, would they get to sit in the House of Lords?'

'Yes, of course,' his dad said, returning to his chair and sifting through the papers in front of him.

'Who usually gets a peerage then? Would a civil servant get one?'

'Absolutely. The top civil servants are almost guaranteed a peerage. Prime Ministers give it to them when they retire, it's practically part of their retirement package. Of course all that will have to change. If we can actually get this Bill through.' He put his head in his hands. He looked up again suddenly, with curiosity. 'Where's this sudden interest come from?'

'Just trying to understand your work. Actually I'm doing a lot of work on the parliamentary system in my Citizenship class.'

His dad seemed satisfied with that answer and smiled at him over one of his documents.

'That's great, Theo.' He shouted through to the connecting office, 'Can someone get in here and remind me who's going to be on this next call?'

A young man in a suit marched in through the connecting door. 'Apart from the Tee-shaw, you'll have—' he began.

'No, no,' Theo's dad said. 'It's Tee-shahk.'

'Tee-shah,' the young man said hesitantly.

His dad bowed his head.

Theo felt the young man's pain. His dad was a language lover, fluent in French and Italian, with a smattering of Mandarin, Spanish and even a dash of Latin. He prided himself on speaking like a native and loved nothing more than to pick up local phrases. Theo remembered one summer in the south of France when he had become positively gleeful explaining to his children that a French phrase meaning literally 'to fall among the apples' actually meant to faint. His dad wasn't going to let this go.

'Tee-shahk,' Theo repeated to help the man.

'Very good,' his dad said to Theo. 'There you go, Ali, my son can say it. Do you even know what the Tee-shahk is?' he asked Theo.

'He's the Prime Minister of Ireland,' Ali explained before Theo had to admit he didn't. 'He'll be on the phone for you in one minute, Prime Minister.'

'Right. Now bugger off, Theo. I can't have you showing up my staff with your superior powers of dialect.'

'Dad, I just wanted to quickly ask you something. I saw your invitation to that event at your old school. Can we go to it?'

'Really?' Theo had timed the request well, because despite the fact that his dad was obviously baffled, he didn't have enough time to properly question him. 'Of course, if you want to.' With his hand already on the phone receiver, he said, 'When is it?'

'Next Saturday.'

His dad nodded and waved him off.

As he walked back through the building to the flat, he looked up the Irish Prime Minister on his phone and discovered 'Tee-shahk' was written 'Taoiseach'. He almost regretted finding out. It was easier to remember how to pronounce it when he didn't know how it was spelled.

After lunch, Theo went around the flat picking up any copies of *Bullseye* he could find. The magazine specialised in politics, but always found a way to make it funny. There were several lying around the house because of his dad's subscription. Recently they had been piling up unopened on the hallway table. Theo hauled the stash into his room and sifted through it looking for anything he could find about Felix Humphries and, failing that, peerages.

There was nothing on Humphries. *Bullseye* wrote reams on MPs and even private business owners who had got themselves into trouble. But there was very little about civil servants.

Theo sat back with a sigh. He reflected on what he knew.

An Uncivil Peerage

He knew that Felix wanted a peerage and was asking – no, demanding – that someone get him one. And what had his dad said? That the Reform Bill would mean no more peerages for civil servants. That seemed like a strong motive for Felix to try to prevent the Bill making it into law. He strongly suspected that that was exactly what Felix had been talking about on the phone. Theo was convinced he had been speaking to the thief.

He pulled out his list of suspects and underlined Felix's name.

CHAPTER FOURTEEN

The Prime Minister's Deputy

Theo was stacking the dishwasher when the doorbell rang. The remnants of their Sunday roast dinner were still scattered across the dining room table. Milly was strapped into her high chair, where she could cause the least trouble. But she was banging her fork against her tray table to make sure no one forgot her.

'That will be Chris,' Theo's dad said. He abandoned the dish of leftovers he was putting together and answered the door.

Chris came back into the dining room with him, accepting the offer of whisky from his dad. He plucked a roast potato out of the leftovers dish and popped it in his mouth. 'Yum,' he said through his mouthful to Theo, who was collecting the dirty glasses. 'Great potatoes, Nicole.'

'Will cooks them actually. The gravy is mine.' She gestured to the gravy boat on the table as she took the chicken carcass into the kitchen.

Chris took another potato and dunked it into the gravy. 'Delicious!'

'Stop flirting with my wife,' Theo's dad said light-heartedly as he handed Chris the glass of whisky he had just poured him. 'We've got a constitutional crisis to resolve.'

'Don't I know it.' Chris pulled up a chair.

Theo had finished packing away the dishwasher, but he didn't want to be sent to the living room, where he would hear nothing of their conversation.

'I'll help with the washing-up, Mum.'

'Really?' she said, as Harry looked around sharply. 'Thank you, darling.'

Theo started to fill the sink with hot water. He could feel Harry's eyes on his back, but after a moment he heard her stomp out. She came back with Milly in tow and almost flattened Larry underfoot as she clomped through to the living room.

With the water running, Theo couldn't hear his dad's conversation. He waited impatiently for the sink to fill, squirting too much washing-up liquid into the water. His mum kissed him on the cheek, then took her glass of wine into the next room. As soon as she was gone, Larry sprung on to the worktop and settled himself on the windowsill behind the sink. Theo turned off the tap.

'We can't keep Parliament in recess for more than a week,' his dad was saying.

'If we don't find the mace, we'll have to, Will. We can't reopen without it,' Chris said.

'We've got to. Think of the papers if we don't. Lazy, incompetent, work-shy, that's what they'll say about us.'

'Work-shy! It's not like we chose this.'

The pan Theo was washing up knocked against the side of the sink. He stopped to listen properly.

'That's what they'll say, Chris, and you know it.' There was silence for a moment, then his dad went on, 'We have to reopen after a week, whether we've found the mace or not.'

Someone got up and walked back into the kitchen. Theo quickly resumed his scrubbing as his mum came back in for her bottle of wine. She stopped, seeming to watch his work.

'How though? The House of Commons can't sit without the mace.'

'We'll use the Lords' mace.'

Theo's mum turned back to the dining room. She was listening as closely as he was.

'Is that legal?' Chris asked.

'I've checked with the Attorney General and she thinks we can do it.'

Theo's mum went back into the dining room. She said, 'Are you sure?'

'The AG says we can do it,' his dad repeated with an edge of annoyance.

'Thompson won't like it,' Chris said.

'He'll be a thorn in our side,' his dad agreed. 'We can deal with him.'

There was another long silence. Worried that they might question what he was up to, Theo filled it with the sounds of dishes clanking and water splashing. He sloshed water all down the front of his t-shirt. Larry regarded him coolly, his tail flicking.

'I don't know, Will. Are you sure this is worth it?'

'What do you mean?' his dad said.

'The House of Lords reform. Parliament is divided. The Lords are up in arms and there will be total outrage when they hear we're going to use their mace. The rebellion in your party is getting stronger. They could turn against you any day, oust you as leader and the coalition would come crashing down.'

Theo's mum said, 'I'm sure it won't come to that.'

'No, Chris is right,' his dad said. 'The party is fragile. I don't know how long I can hold it together. But if we drop this, we look weak, as if we don't have control of our own people. The public don't re-elect weak leaders. So choose your poison. If we back down now, we will be out in three years. If we keep going, we may or may not be out in a few weeks. But if we can make it through this, we'll be home and dry. Think of how we will be remembered if we succeed where so many have failed before us.'

'You don't know the public won't vote for us again at the next election.'

Theo had finished the washing-up. He picked up a tea towel and started to dry everything in the drying rack.

'We made a commitment to this, Chris. Don't back out on me now.'

The other room was very quiet again. All Theo could hear was the squeak of his tea towel against the wine glass he was drying.

'How's your sister?' his mum said.

'Why do you ask?' Chris replied, his voice sharp.

'Will said you were in Clapham on the morning of the theft.'

'She's the same.' The power had gone out of Chris's voice. 'The same.'

'I'm sorry,' his mum said. 'Don't give up, you'll get through this.'

'Are you telling me not to give up on my sister or the Bill?'

'Both.'

Theo picked up a roasting tray from the drying rack, but not carefully enough. Several other items toppled into the space it left, making a loud clang. Larry shot off the windowsill, clattering past the mess of dishes as he made his escape.

His mum hurried through from the other room.

'Leave that, Theo, you've done enough.'

'It's all right, I don't mind.'

'No, come on. You've got homework to finish.' His mum took the tray and the tea towel from his hands.

With nothing left to do, Theo went back to his room. His mum was right, he had Maths homework due in the next day, but he didn't feel like doing it.

He flopped on his bed and stared at the ceiling. It sounded like the coalition was even more fragile than he had first thought. Chris and his dad disagreed about getting the Lords Reform Bill through. They disagreed about when to reopen Parliament. Chris was worried they might get kicked out of government in the next few weeks.

What would happen to Theo then? He supposed they would all go back to the house in Chelsea. He would have to give up this room, this flat. He looked around him. It was his room. He had got used to it.

He turned on his side and found himself looking at the stack of *Bullseye* magazines he had collected the day before. At least he had discovered something useful. Chris had been in Clapham during the theft, so he couldn't possibly be the thief. Unless he had an accomplice. He thought of

Felix's conversation the day before. Could he have been on the phone to Chris? Maybe Chris planned to bring down the government, get elected in his dad's place. He could definitely offer Felix a peerage then.

It seemed like a long shot for Felix to risk so much on. And if it was Chris and Felix, Theo would definitely back Chris over Felix as the one more capable of lifting the mace. But he was the one with an alibi. Perhaps it was a decoy. Perhaps he had been in the palace all along. He thought of his dad on the phone in the car coming back from the palace, demanding to know where Chris was. They couldn't find him then. Could they be sure they knew where he had been now?

Theo took out his list of suspects and drew a line between Chris and Felix.

There was no harm in being thorough.

CHAPTER FIFTEEN

On the Trail of a Journalist

Theo pushed his way out of the throng of students rushing out of the school doors. Usually he didn't like to join the crush, but Sammy had told him to meet her promptly at the end of school. He kept a wary eye out for his sister. He had told her he was going to the library to do some homework. It was unlikely she would be out of school this early. He usually had to wait ages for her. She always disappeared into the bathrooms with her friends at the end of the day. But he didn't want to be caught out.

Sammy was standing just beyond the school gates. Theo wondered how she had got there so quickly.

'Hurry up,' she said as soon as he got within earshot and she strode off down the road.

Theo ran to catch up. 'What's the rush? She won't get out of work for a few hours.'

At lunch they had made a plan to go to Erin's office after school. Sammy had looked her up at home over the weekend and found out her office was within walking distance of the school.

'Journalists come and go, Theo. It's not a desk job. She might not even be in the office today.'

'So this could all be a waste of time?'

'Don't worry, it'll be worth it. Trust me.'

He wasn't sure that he did. At lunch, he had told her about the conversations he had overheard at the weekend. She had taken up the idea that Chris might have stolen the mace with enthusiasm. Theo pointed out that he had an alibi. But she had countered that neither Erin, Ruth nor Trevor could have got Felix a peerage. Only someone with substantial influence over his dad could and that fact pointed squarely at Chris. Theo had to admit it was true. He still suspected that Trevor, who must be able to pull strings to get someone a peerage, was working with Felix. But Sammy was so excited about his discoveries that Theo didn't have the heart to deny her anything.

'I think we should look into Felix,' Sammy said.

Theo started. Had she known what he was thinking about? 'What do you mean?'

'I've been thinking and I think you might be right. That phone call was really suspicious. It can't hurt to investigate him a bit more.'

The idea made him nervous. Felix was a bit too close to home – literally, he had an office in Downing Street. What if his dad found out what they were up to? 'We would have to be really careful. We could get into a lot of trouble.'

'You'll have to be really careful.' Sammy looked pointedly at him. 'You'll have to do the investigating. I can't. I'm not allowed in Downing Street.'

Theo panicked. Had her mum told her she wasn't allowed round to his house? Maybe she wasn't allowed to go over because he was a boy.

'Sorry, I didn't think. I didn't realise it would be a problem for you.'

'Well, obviously. I bet there's a whole massive security check process to go through.'

Theo almost laughed, he was so relieved. 'Oh that.'

'Obviously that. What did you think I meant?'

'Nothing,' Theo said quickly. 'Anyway, that's fine.' He hadn't actually invited anyone to the flat before. Harry had her friends round all the time and he didn't think she had done any security checks. 'I better check with my mum though, just to make sure…'

His stomach twisted. He had accidentally agreed to investigate Felix with her. What on earth was she planning?

Sammy put her arm out in front of him to stop him from going any further.

'There she is,' she said, pointing up ahead.

Erin was coming out of a vast glass office building that thrust proudly onto the pavement, like the prow of a great ship. She didn't notice them. She walked purposefully to the traffic lights and pressed the button.

Theo hung back to let her get ahead, but Sammy yanked on his jumper sleeve. 'Come on, let's catch her up.'

'Hold on,' Theo said. 'You said we were just going to check her out. We can do that from here.'

'I didn't think we would actually see her. Now she's here, we should ask her if she has an alibi.' Her voice got smaller as she took in Theo's thunderous expression.

'We can't… can't…' Theo spluttered.

Erin looked over her shoulder, straight towards them.

Theo backed down a side street. 'She nearly saw us,' he

wheezed, panic making his chest tighten. He motioned for Sammy to follow him.

'Theo, we can't pass up this opportunity!' Sammy followed him, while keeping an eye over her shoulder at Erin.

'Do you know what my dad would say if he found out I was doing *any* of this? What if she wrote about us in the newspaper?'

'I'm sure she has better things to write about than two slightly curious teenagers.'

Not if one of those teenagers happened to be the Prime Minister's son, Theo thought, but he didn't want to voice it in case Sammy thought he was being pompous. 'You told me we were going to check her out. That's it. You didn't say you wanted to speak to her. You lied to me.'

'Yeah, all right,' Sammy said, her voice rising. 'I didn't want to tell you that we were going to speak to her because you never would have agreed to it. We're not going to find out whether she has an alibi by lurking around street corners.'

'But obviously if we ask her, she's just going to come out and tell us,' Theo said, his voice heavy with sarcasm.

'We're wasting time,' Sammy said. She checked around the corner again. 'Look, she's gone now. Great. We've missed our opportunity.'

Theo came out of the street to look too. She was gone. He was filled with relief. He wasn't going to get into trouble for nothing.

He turned back to Sammy. She wasn't looking at him. She was staring at the ground, clenching her teeth as if battling an invisible pain. She wiped furiously at the corner of her eye with her sleeve. To his horror, it came away wet.

'Look, it doesn't matter. We can come back tomorrow.'

On the Trail of a Journalist

'It's fine,' Sammy said, still not looking at him.

Theo had a niggling feeling, as if something wasn't right. He realised it was guilt. It was his fault she was upset. 'I'm sorry I said you lied. I didn't mean it like that.'

Sammy didn't reply. She rubbed at her eyes again with her sleeve.

Over her shoulder, Theo spied Erin coming out of a corner shop. She turned to walk down the street, away from them. His stomach dropped. He didn't want to do it, but somehow it felt like the right thing to do.

'She's back,' he said. Sammy whipped around.

She turned slowly back to him, a question in her face.

If ever there was a moment to tell Sammy he wasn't up for this, it was now. He didn't want to interrogate a journalist. He didn't want to go to the opposition meeting. And he didn't want to investigate Felix, whatever that meant. He should just tell her they had gone too far and he was out.

He thought about the family ring. The hope of being given it felt like a mirage. He had no idea how he would solve the case. If he didn't do all the things Sammy was suggesting, he had no ideas of his own. If it was up to him, he probably would have done some research in the library and that would have been the end of it. He couldn't have got this far without her.

He didn't like her plans, but perhaps they were the only way.

'We follow her, that's it,' Theo said, with as much resolve as he could muster.

'No talking to the journalist, agreed.'

'Hurry up then, we better not lose her,' he said.

Sammy smiled weakly at him, then set off quickly down the street.

Erin was moving fast. She looked back at her office once, before ducking down a quiet side street.

'What's she looking for?' Theo said to Sammy.

'No idea.'

They followed her at a safe distance down several twisting streets. Theo was glad he had a map on his phone. They would never find their way back without it.

At the corner of another road, they paused to watch which way she went. She pulled open the door to a grimy pub and disappeared inside. The sign over the front was faded and peeling.

'We'll never get in,' Sammy said, 'not in our school uniform.'

'And it looks small. She'll see us if we go in.' There was one of London's excuses for a park across the street, with a deserted set of swings and a couple of benches. 'Come on, let's wait there for her to come out.'

'Are you sure?' Sammy said.

'We're here now. We might as well.'

The swings had a good view of the pub's entrance, so they took one each. They reckoned they were mostly hidden behind the park's perimeter hedge. They could just make out the top of the pub door on the other side of it. Any time it opened, Sammy stood up to get a good look at who was coming out. Although Theo was taller, they agreed that Erin might recognise him, so it was better for Sammy to do it.

It was a cloudy day and for once Theo was glad of his thick school blazer. Sitting on the exposed swing, in that barren park, the wind soon sent a chill through him. He buried his hands in his pockets and put his blazer collar up. He could do nothing to protect his frozen face.

'How do you think the thief caused all that smoke?' Sammy said, out of nowhere.

'Gas canisters, you know those military ones.'

'Yes, but how did they get them in the building? How did they get them past security?'

Theo thought in silence for a minute. 'Maybe one of the builders brought them in. I doubt all their equipment goes through metal detectors.'

'Hmm,' Sammy said. 'I read this article that said ministers can bring anything in in their Red Boxes, they're not checked. Is that true?'

'Yes, but only ministers have them. You're not suggesting…?'

'Chris is a minister. He could have done it.'

'I guess…' Theo preferred the theory that one of the builders had done it.

Sammy pushed off the ground, swinging gently backwards and forwards. 'Who are our main suspects now?'

'Felix, obviously.'

'Definitely, that conversation you overheard… He must be involved somehow.'

Theo nodded. 'Lord Thompson. We can't rule him out because he won't talk to us.'

'Ruth,' Sammy supplied. 'We can't rule her out yet. I still think that walking stick in her office is important. And Chris.'

'I'm not sure about Chris. It sounds like he has an alibi.'

'But we don't know if anyone has checked it, so we can't

cross him off yet. And that just leaves her.' Sammy nodded towards the pub.

'Do you really think she did it?' Theo asked.

'I don't know,' Sammy said. 'I haven't got a clue to be honest. We just know she has a motive.'

'But you always seem so certain.'

'I'm certain one of them did it. I don't know which one.'

They heard the door open and Sammy jumped to her feet. 'False alarm.' The swing's metal chain rattled forlornly as she sat back down. 'Again. God, there's just loads of old men coming out of this pub. It looks scuzzy. Why would she want to come here?'

'Maybe because she's not likely to bump into anyone she knows.'

Sammy turned to him looking impressed. 'You know, you're quite clever when you actually start speaking.'

Theo felt his ears warming. 'You make it sound like I never say anything.'

'You don't much, or not much in class anyway. That's how I knew you were interested in the mace, the day we met in the Palace of Westminster. That Citizenship lesson was the first time I ever heard you voluntarily speak in class.'

Theo scuffed at the ground under his foot. The grass had been worn away by countless others who had sat there, forming a moat of dry earth around the swing.

'I don't like getting things wrong.'

Sammy nodded slowly. 'I get that.' There was an embarrassed silence. Theo felt a bit exposed. 'Who do you think took the mace?'

'You know what I think.'

'No I don't, not really.'

Theo thought for a moment. 'I think Trevor Thompson has something to do with it. And Felix. I don't trust him.'

'That would make sense,' Sammy said.

'Well, sort of. I can't really see either of them running off with that great, big mace and then reappearing seconds later as if nothing happened. They wouldn't be strong enough or fast enough. Maybe you're right about Erin. She certainly walks fast and she's a lot younger than them.'

'Maybe it was Erin and Felix, like you said.'

'But then who offered him a peerage? You were right. Erin can't get it for him.'

'No,' Sammy said and the conversation trailed away into silence.

Theo wondered if she was also thinking about their earlier disagreement. He didn't really know if she had forgiven him. He wished he hadn't said that she had lied to him. It might have been true, but it had sounded so accusatory. He had also been surprised by the strength of her reaction. She had seemed more angry than sad, but then she had definitely been fighting back tears. He had thought nothing fazed her. Perhaps she cared more than she liked people to know.

'I really am sorry I said that you lied,' Theo said.

Sammy smiled weakly again. She picked at the chipped rubber seat of the swing.

'That's not why I was upset. I mean, that wasn't great, but I'm not that much of a delicate snowflake.'

Theo noticed the forced contempt with which she said it. Displays of vulnerability obviously ranked very low in her book. Even though she always encouraged him when he was nervous.

'What was it then?' Theo asked.

'Nothing, it was nothing,' Sammy said, pushing her hair out of her face and looking away.

There was a long silence. There was obviously something, but Theo didn't want to press her, if she didn't want to tell him.

'I might like to be a journalist, one day,' Sammy said this as if she was daring him to contradict her. The fire was back in her eyes.

Theo thought of her confidence speaking to people she didn't know, how good she was at questioning people. 'You'd be a great journalist.'

She seemed satisfied with that and he felt as if some invisible barrier that had been between them since their argument had come down. He realised she had had her guard up. She seemed to have relaxed now.

'Is that why you wanted to be involved with this investigation?'

'Partly,' Sammy said.

The pub door swung open again and Sammy jumped up to look. She ducked down again straight away.

'It's her,' she whispered.

Theo rose slowly from his seat until he could just see over the hedge. Erin was standing by the pub doorway. She was kissing someone.

Sammy's head appeared at Theo's shoulder. 'Who's that?'

Erin and the man broke apart. Theo and Sammy ducked as the couple turned separate directions and started to walk away.

Theo stood again before the man walked out of sight. Not bothering to hide now, he craned his head to get a good look at him. The man looked over his shoulder, back at Erin, and Theo saw his full face.

He sat slowly back down on the swing.

Sammy was still jumping from toe to toe, trying to get a good look.

'I know who that was,' Theo said.

'What? Who?'

'He works for Bob Piggott. She's having a relationship with someone who works in the security office.'

CHAPTER SIXTEEN

In the Corridors of Power

The following day, Theo hung back at the end of History to wait for Sammy. His mum had agreed that she could come over for dinner that evening and confirmed – with a smile – that a security check wasn't necessary.

He was starting to have that slightly twitchy, never quite comfortable, feeling. They were going to walk home with Harry. Sammy was going to meet his family at dinner. Then they planned to spy on Felix. His palms began to sweat at the thought of it all.

He wondered how vicious his sister was going to be. She was fine with most people, with the exception of Theo and his friends. When she had met Josh, she had barely acknowledged him. Josh found this funny and went out of his way to be extra polite to Harry by formally wishing her good day or lavishly apologising if she knocked him in the corridor. Theo didn't think that Sammy would take it so lightly.

Theo met Sammy outside the classroom door. He noticed that she was wearing a new jumper. There were no holes in this one.

'Nice jumper,' he said as they pushed through the crush on the stairs.

'Very funny,' she replied, even though he wasn't joking. 'My mum made me wear it. She doesn't want me to show her up in front of your parents.'

Theo laughed nervously. Her mum was probably right. He looked at the streaks in her hair and wondered, with alarm, if she had any tattoos. He shook off the thought. She couldn't have; she was too young.

At the school gates, they stopped to wait for Harry. Theo watched the school door anxiously. Sammy was saying something about how rude her English teacher had been in class that day when she said she hadn't read their set text, *Lord of the Flies*. This caught Theo's attention.

'But you have read it,' Theo said. He had seen her reading it the day before. Despite the fact that she was near the end and looked engrossed, when he went over she had shut the book hastily and stuffed it in her bag. 'You were reading it yesterday at lunch.'

Sammy looked uncomfortable. 'I wasn't going to tell her that.'

'It would have got you out of trouble.'

'The point is, we shouldn't have to read it. It's sexist. There isn't a single girl in it.'

Theo didn't understand. If she had read it, why risk getting into trouble by pretending she hadn't?

'I think Golding meant it to be like that,' Theo said. 'I'm sure he said at some point that if there had been girls on the island then none of the story would ever have happened.'

'Too right. It's obviously about the patriarchy and how self-destructive it is. But that doesn't make it OK that we're studying it. Between that and *Macbeth*, all we're learning about is white male violence. They're both about power struggles. There are other themes we could study.'

Theo was bowled over. He had never heard her speak so eloquently about their school work. Why on earth did she refuse to do her homework, constantly getting herself into trouble, if she was capable of making points like that?

The school door opened and Harry came out, waving goodbye to one of her friends. Her eyes widened for a moment when she saw Theo and Sammy. Then a sinister smile slipped from her eyes to her mouth.

Theo swallowed.

'Harry, this is Sammy. Sammy, Harry.'

'It's so nice to meet you,' Harry said with the sort of genuine warmth Theo rarely saw in her these days. It unnerved him. This might be worse than her being rude. 'What were you two so wrapped up in talking about?'

'*Lords of the Flies*,' Theo said, suspecting a trap.

'Theo doesn't think it's sexist,' Sammy said.

'I didn't say that.'

Harry spoke over him. 'Of course it is. If it's meant to be an allegory for the whole of society, why isn't there a single girl on the island?'

'Exactly!' Sammy said. 'As if only a group of boys would try to set up a mini democracy. I bet if Golding had put girls on the island, he would have had them cooking the boys' dinners. He's not exactly an advocate of women's rights, is he?'

Harry and Sammy continued the conversation as they wandered past shops and anonymous office blocks on the streets towards Downing Street. Theo said nothing.

In the Corridors of Power

'So were you at the library together yesterday after school?' Harry said.

'Yup,' Theo replied.

'Only I stayed to do some homework and I didn't see either of you.' Harry's voice was light, but he knew she was secretly rejoicing over her victory.

Theo felt a lurch of panic. She might tell their parents he was lying about where he was going.

'We decided to sit outside instead,' Sammy said, without a trace of nerves.

'Didn't you get cold?' Harry pressed.

'No,' Sammy said and it had a finality that shut down the conversation.

Theo wondered whether they had got away with it. He glanced sideways at Harry. She didn't look smug, just thoughtful. He silently thanked Sammy's quick thinking and convincing lies.

As they turned onto Birdcage Walk, running alongside St James's Park, the scenery changed. The buildings along here were grand and imposing, where those on the streets before had been drab and forgettable. Theo could see Sammy staring up at them – the backs of magnificent Georgian houses. When they turned onto Horse Guards Road, Sammy said, 'Wow' and for the first time in a long time, Theo felt a bit of pride in showing a friend his home. They passed the back of the Treasury and the Foreign Office, both incredible buildings, not like offices at all. There were statues peering down from their plinths on the walls and columns framing the vast windows. Theo thought of the Parthenon in Greece, an ancient temple to Athena.

They reached the back entrance to Downing Street. Black

railings sealed it off, but there were no tourists swarming around, unlike the Whitehall entrance. The police officer in the hut recognised him and Harry, and let them through with a smile.

They went to the back door and Harry let them in with her key. By this time, conversation between them had trailed off and he had the feeling that Sammy might be nervous.

'I know it seems weird, but actually we're just a normal family,' Harry said.

Theo felt indescribably grateful to her. He tried to convey this with a look and for once his sister seemed to look at him with sympathy, instead of open hostility.

'Right.' Sammy didn't sound convinced.

They climbed the stairs to the flat and let themselves in. Theo called to his mum. She called back from the kitchen and Theo gestured for Sammy to follow him through.

His mum was watching a stir fry on the hob, while Milly assaulted some carrot sticks in her high chair.

'Who's this then?' his mum said, her forehead creased.

'This is Sammy.' Theo felt suddenly alarmed. Had his mum forgotten the day? 'You remember, I told you she was coming over?'

'Of course, it's lovely to meet you, Sammy.' Theo could see his mum was surprised. Perhaps her dyed hair had gone down even worse than he had imagined it would. He didn't think his mum would be this perturbed. His dad maybe. But not his mum. 'Harry, would you show Sammy to the bathroom to wash up before dinner?'

'Come on,' Harry said, looking jolly.

'You said she was a boy,' his mum hissed as soon as Sammy was out of the room.

'No I didn't.'

'Yes, you did.'

'Mum, why would I say she was a boy, when she's obviously a girl?'

Milly looked between them with a very serious expression. Even she had guessed that something unusual was happening. Theo wished she could explain it to him. She might understand it better than he did.

His mum looked flustered. 'Never mind. You've just surprised me, that's all.'

'What difference does it make?'

His mum turned back to her cooking and didn't answer the question.

Sammy came back and Theo had the distinct impression she knew something was up. Harry had only just insisted that his family was totally normal and now they were behaving like weirdos.

'Girl,' Milly gurgled happily, looking right at Sammy.

Theo thought he might die of embarrassment. 'This is Sammy,' he managed.

'Thammy,' Milly repeated, with a near-toothless smile. At least someone was friendly, Theo thought.

They still had a few minutes before dinner, so Theo took Sammy to show her his room. His mum embarrassed him before they left by telling him to keep the door open. With a feeling of mounting discomfort, he realised why she thought it made such a difference whether Sammy was a boy or a girl.

Sammy stopped in the doorway of Theo's room. 'Huh.'

'What?'

'It's not very you, is it?' Sammy said, taking the seat by

the desk. 'It's so neat. It looks like a middle-aged accountant's bedroom.'

'Hey!'

'Actually, maybe that is you.'

Theo chucked his pillow at her.

Dinner went better than Theo had hoped, after the disastrous beginning. His mum was nice to Sammy and even Harry made an effort. Sammy seemed to get on with everyone and she complimented his mum's cooking, so his mum was in a very good mood at the end of it. She was in such a good mood, he decided now would be a good time to get her to sign his detention slip. There was no point getting embarrassed about it in front of Sammy, since she not only knew about the detention, but also had to do it with him. If he brought it up with her here, his mum might not question it as much as she normally would.

He gave his mum the detention slip to sign and although she said, 'That's not like you, Theo,' when he explained that he had forgotten to do his homework, she let the subject drop. He felt like he had got off lightly.

After dinner, Theo told his mum he was going to take Sammy on a short tour. She nodded absent-mindedly before she took Milly off for a nappy change.

They left the flat with Larry, who slipped out after them. He watched Theo expectantly, as if he thought he was going on a trip with them.

Sammy started rattling off their plan. 'When we get there, you're going to lure him out of his office.'

'You make it sound like I'm the Pied Piper.'

'I hope you brought your pipe. Then I'm going to sneak in—'

In the Corridors of Power

'Shh,' Theo said, as someone passed them in the corridor.

As soon as they were gone, Sammy went on as if nothing had happened. 'And see what I can find, while you distract him.'

'I'm still not sure I can distract him,' Theo said. The whole plan was outrageous. He could only imagine the trouble he would be in if they were found out. There would definitely be no ring after something like that.

'Sure you can. You just ask him about the House of Lords Reform Bill, like we agreed.'

'I don't know.' Theo stopped at the top of an old set of stairs. His dad had told him it was originally the servants' staircase. It was steep and narrow, the wooden steps worn with deep grooves. He had chosen this route because he knew most people didn't use it. 'Is this really a good idea? I don't think you're going to find anything. Everything is bound to be on his computer or his phone and you'll never get into them. They'll be password protected.'

'I know you're worried,' Sammy said, 'but we have to check. I don't think anyone would suspect him. He might not have been interviewed by the police. Someone has to investigate him.'

Theo nodded; she was right. The thought didn't stop him from feeling nervous, but he knew he had to ignore it.

They took the stairs down, Larry out in front as if he was leading them. Theo shooed him away, but the cat was undeterred. The trio arrived in a corridor with a high arched window that looked out over the Rose Garden behind the house. Felix's office was the only one here. There was a broom cupboard at the other end – Theo had found it while playing hide-and-seek with Harry when they first moved in. He knew it wouldn't be locked. Pressing his finger to his lips, he waved for Sammy to go to the door.

Larry sat at the entrance to the corridor, watching them as if he was wondering what on earth they were doing.

Fortunately Felix's door was closed and Theo could wait outside it while Sammy passed. He found himself holding his breath.

He had his hand raised to knock when they heard footsteps.

He panicked. And launched himself down the corridor towards Sammy.

She wrenched open the cupboard door and shut it behind them as quickly as she could.

Theo knocked a broom propped against the back wall. He grabbed it before it clattered to the floor. It wouldn't stay up unsupported, so he had to shuffle round and let it rest against his back. There was very little space and almost no light – just that coming through the crack under the door.

He pushed himself as far back from the door as he could get, breathing fast.

Sammy opened the cupboard door the tiniest crack. Larry was waiting for them on the other side. He meowed loudly, looking straight up at them.

Theo jabbed Sammy in the arm to tell her to close it, too afraid to speak.

'He's leaving,' Sammy whispered.

Keeping well back, Theo looked out through the crack. Larry was still staring at them, his tail flicking this way and that.

Felix closed his office door. He looked directly at them. 'You stupid article. Go on, get away.'

In the Corridors of Power

He made as if to come towards them and Theo's heart stopped. He couldn't breathe.

'What have you found there?' Felix came towards them, his eyes on the cat.

Theo wanted to shut the door, but he didn't dare move. Sammy's hair tickled his cheek.

Felix was getting closer. At any moment he would open the cupboard door and find them.

Larry meowed one last time and dashed out of the corridor.

'Mad cat,' Felix said and disappeared after him.

Theo's hammering heart slowed to a more normal pace.

'You were supposed to speak to him.'

'I panicked.'

'It doesn't matter,' Sammy said. 'He's gone now anyway. Let's go.' She opened the door.

'Wait! He might come straight back.'

'We better be quick then.' She shot out into the hallway.

Before Theo had moved a muscle, she had slipped into Felix's office.

Theo restacked the cupboard so that the broom could stand upright once more. He didn't want someone to find their mess.

He hovered outside Felix's door.

'Be quick, all right.'

'Just keep watch.' Sammy was rifling through the papers on Felix's desk, leaving them at odd angles.

'Keep it tidy! We don't want him to know someone has been through his stuff.'

Footsteps echoed along the corridor and Theo's heart leapt into his mouth.

'Hide! Someone's coming.' He heard Sammy scuffling about, but when he looked into the office, he couldn't see her.

A young woman with unnaturally straight hair, wearing a pencil skirt and heels, rounded the corner onto the corridor. She looked surprised to see him.

Theo could tell she was about to ask him something and with a burst of inspiration he decided to get there first. 'Can I help you?' he said.

The woman's forehead furrowed. 'I'm looking for Felix, is he in?'

'I'm sorry, you've just missed him.' The woman looked as though she didn't believe him. His palms sweating, Theo went on, 'See, his office is empty,' gesturing to the open office door.

The woman peered around it and they both looked at the apparently empty room.

'I'll come back later then,' she said, still looking sceptical and turned back down the hallway.

Theo didn't relax. As soon as the woman was gone, he called to Sammy, 'Will you hurry up in there?'

'That was brilliant,' she said, climbing out from behind the desk.

Theo felt himself go slightly pink. 'Never mind that, just hurry.'

Sammy worked her way through each of the drawers in the desk, shoving things aside without bothering to put them back. Theo didn't tell her off this time. If it got them out of there quicker, he no longer cared.

The distinctive sound of shuffling footsteps approached the hallway. Theo's heart juddered to a stop.

'Get out, now,' he hissed.

'Just a second, I have one more drawer,' Sammy replied. 'But it's locked.'

'Leave it then!'

'The key must be here somewhere.'

Just in time, Theo walked up the hallway and met Felix at the end of it. His legs were turning to lead, his palms sweating.

'Felix,' he said, 'I was looking for you.'

Felix looked rather surprised. 'Why was that?'

Theo could barely remember what he was meant to say. 'I wanted to ask you about... about... the House of Lords Reform Bill and whether you think it should go through.'

'I can't talk to you about that, Theo.' Felix continued walking towards his office.

Theo resolutely stood his ground. 'Why not?' he burst out.

It did the trick, Felix turned back to look at him, now with an expression of concern. 'Because I'm in the civil service. We're apolitical. You must know that.'

Theo had that shrinking feeling he always got when he got something wrong. It was like something inside him was being squashed really small. It felt like his voice was being squeezed in with it.

Sammy peered around the door to Felix's office.

Theo wondered if Felix could hear his heart hammering in his chest.

'Sorry. I... I... forgot,' he stammered, his voice tiny.

Felix made as if to turn back to his office.

'Wait!' Theo said, a little too loudly. Felix's eyebrows rose halfway up his forehead. 'I've forgotten... how to... to get back to the flat. Could you show me? Please.'

Looking more than a little exasperated, Felix walked

with him back down the corridor. Theo checked back over his shoulder, to see Sammy tiptoeing some way behind.

Theo asked Felix to keep showing him around a few more corners, until he caught sight of Sammy sneaking into what he hoped was an empty room. Felix was shaking his head in dismay when Theo finally allowed him to go back to his office. He waited to see Felix go, pretending he was waiting to wave to him. As soon as he was gone, he retrieved Sammy from the room she had hidden in.

She threw her arms around him. 'Thank goodness. I thought I would never get out of there.'

Theo could tell he was bright red. 'We're never doing that, ever again.'

'It was worth it.' She reached into her trouser pocket and pulled out an external hard drive. 'Found it in that last drawer.'

'I thought it was locked?'

'Found the key under a model of a cruise liner on his desk. It was very cute actually, it had an inscription on the bottom from someone called Moira.'

Theo stopped abruptly. 'Next time, why don't you take your slippers and a cup of tea in with you so you can really relax, while I have the most awkward conversation since someone had to tell the architect of the Titanic that the world's first unsinkable ship had sunk.'

'Thought you said there wasn't going to be a next time.'

'There won't be. So let's hope there's something helpful on that hard drive. Let's get back upstairs before anyone else sees us.'

CHAPTER SEVENTEEN

Contraband

Back in Theo's room, he plugged the hard drive into his computer. Larry, who had followed them in the front door when they came back, jumped up on Theo's lap. 'Traitor,' Theo said. But the cat curled up contentedly and Theo didn't have the heart to tip him off. He purred as Theo absent-mindedly stroked him with one hand.

Sammy hovered over his shoulder. 'There's loads of files. How are we going to find out what's here?'

'We'll have to open each one and work our way through it.'

'Ugh!' Sammy said, throwing herself on to the bed. 'That's going to take ages.'

'We just need to be methodical. We'll write a list of the files and cross off each one as we open it.'

'You do that,' Sammy said. 'What's this?' She was holding his grandpa's research papers. Theo hadn't had the heart to look at them again since he first put them by his bed. They had sat there untouched ever since. For some reason, he hadn't wanted to move them.

'My grandpa was researching our house's architect before… That's all his work.'

'Your house had an architect?'

Theo shrugged apologetically. 'Charles Barry.'

'Woah. There's some incredible drawings in here. Is this a plan of your house?' She was flicking roughly through the pages in a way that made Theo wince.

'Guess so.'

'More like a castle.'

'Could you put them back? I don't want the pages to get muddled up.'

He said it more sharply than he intended and Sammy stopped abruptly. She shuffled the pages together gently and put the pile back where she found it.

'Did your grandpa finish his research?'

Theo shook his head. 'He… died. Six months ago.'

'I'm sorry, Theo.'

He couldn't find anything to say.

Sammy picked up a copy of *Bullseye* from the top of the pile that was still on Theo's bedside table.

Theo turned back to the computer. He didn't mind going through the files, he was quite interested to see what a civil servant actually did.

Half an hour later, Theo's enthusiasm had trickled away to nothing. Larry had gone to sleep on his lap. Sammy hadn't looked up from *Bullseye*. There was report after report after report. Felix didn't have a good filing system either. He was losing hope. He dreaded to think that they might have stolen the hard drive for nothing.

He clicked on a folder titled 'Enquiries' and found another called 'Leads' and then another called 'Follow ups'.

This immediately struck him as odd because none of the folders had anything in them except another folder. Until the last one, 'Follow ups', which contained several photos. Theo opened the first one. It was a photo of two men sitting together in a busy bar that looked like it was in the Palace of Westminster. One had his back to the camera, the other was facing it. Theo didn't recognise him.

He opened the next photo. It was similar, but this time there was a different man in the picture and it had been taken in one of the palace's restaurants.

'Sammy,' Theo said, 'come and look at this. I don't understand...'

He opened the next photo. This time he recognised one of the people in it – it was Rupert Spencer. He was in a pub, talking to a woman.

'What?' Sammy said, coming to look over his shoulder.

'Hold on.' Theo clicked through more of the photos and back to the earlier ones. His suspicions were confirmed. 'They're all of Rupert. He's got loads of photos of Rupert.'

'But he's just talking to people. Why would Felix want photos of Rupert talking to people?' Sammy said, scanning the pictures.

'Rupert is the Chief Whip. Sammy, what if...' Theo trailed off. He wasn't sure, maybe he was being ridiculous.

'Go on,' Sammy said gently.

'It's Rupert's job to persuade all the MPs to vote with the government. What if these are the people Rupert had to persuade? Felix has been trying to get a list of people who could swing either way on the vote from the very beginning. That day we met at the Palace of Westminster – Felix asked Rupert for a list then, but Rupert wouldn't give it to him.

Then he was asking that person on the phone for names. That must not have worked either. So now he's been spying on Rupert to find out who was voting which way. Maybe… maybe he wants to know who to persuade to vote *his* way.'

'That's genius. I think you're right. That must be it.' Sammy leant over the desk, propping herself up on her elbows. 'Do you recognise anyone else in the pictures?'

'Hang on.' Theo scrolled through them again. He stopped on one of a woman he recognised. He typed her name into a search bar and waited.

'That's her!' Sammy said, slapping him on the arm.

'I know.' Theo rubbed the sore spot. He typed in her name, along with 'House of Lords Reform' and waited for the results to load.

Sammy gasped. 'She was a known sceptic of House of Lords reform. Check some of the others.'

Theo looked up any others whose faces he could put a name to. For a couple he could find no information about their views on the Reform Bill, but there were more who had voiced their concerns about it.

'This is it, Theo! Felix has been keeping a file on all those who might rebel against the government. He's been finding out who to persuade to vote against the Bill. It could be him, he might really be the thief.'

'I can't believe it,' Theo said. He was astonished that they had actually found something.

'Wait though,' Sammy said. 'Hold on. We don't actually know he took the mace. This shows he's trying to alter the vote. But it doesn't mean he definitely took the mace.'

Theo's heart sank. 'You're right. And he was talking to someone else about it on the phone. That could have been the person who took the mace.'

His mum called him from down the corridor. Theo shut all the files, pulled out the hard drive and shoved it quickly into a drawer before his mum came in.

'It's getting a bit late,' she said from the doorway. 'I think Sammy should be getting home.'

'OK,' Theo said, not meaning it. 'Just another half an hour.'

'It's past seven o'clock, it's already late for her to be on public transport on her own. Sorry, Sammy, I would say you can stay, but I don't know if your mum would mind.'

'No problem. You're right, I should get going.'

Theo reluctantly walked Sammy to the tube stop. He had wanted more time to talk about their discovery. They would have to make do with lunchtime at school. On the way she reminded him that it was Ruth Morris's event the next day. Theo felt a flutter of nerves. This wasn't like sneaking around the Downing Street corridors. This was out, in public, where the press could find out. But Sammy argued there was no other way to find out more on Ruth.

'You could just go without me,' he said.

'I could, but then you would miss all the fun.'

Theo snorted. 'What like this evening, when we had to sneak you out of Felix's office with stolen government property?'

'It's not stolen, it's still in the building.' Something about her words rang a bell, but he didn't get a chance to dwell on them. 'I need you to come. I couldn't have done tonight without you. I only got out of there because you helped me. And I messed it up with Thompson. I need your help.'

Although he continued to resist, Theo knew that he would

give in. He wouldn't have found out Erin's secret without Sammy's insistence. He never would have followed her on his own. Sammy wouldn't have found the hard drive without his help. They needed each other. Everything seemed to work better when the two of them worked together.

When he got home, his dad met him in the hallway. To his surprise, his dad asked to have a chat with him and they went into his bedroom together.

Theo perched on the edge of his bed nervously. Had his dad found out about the hard drive? If Felix knew it was missing, he was bound to put it together with Theo's weird behaviour.

His dad leant against the desk with his arms folded. 'Your mother tells me you have been given a detention.'

Perversely, Theo relaxed. This wasn't nearly as bad as being found out as a thief. 'Yeah, I forgot to do my homework,' Theo said, a little too offhand.

'I don't like your tone, Theo. This is a serious matter – getting into trouble at school. You know how important it is to work hard.'

'I know.' He thought with growing unease about what his dad might say if he found out that this was the least of his recent misdemeanours.

'There's no such thing as a free lunch, you know. Just because you're my son doesn't mean you'll have everything handed to you on a plate. You have to work for it, just like everyone else.'

Theo never thought he would get everything handed to him on a plate. Didn't his dad know that? It wasn't easier for him because of who his dad was, it was harder. He wasn't allowed to make mistakes. 'It was just one homework.'

Contraband

'Every action counts and every action has consequences.'

Theo knew arguing was pointless. He kept back all the angry things he wanted to say. It felt like trying to swallow a block of salt, its jagged edges scratching on the way down.

'You're usually very good with your homework. What's changed recently? Is it this new friend of yours – Samira?'

'No. No, it's not that.'

'What is it then?'

'I just got distracted by everything happening with the mace and I want to help you. I want to help you find it.'

His dad uncrossed his arms and sat next to him on the bed. 'You don't need to worry about that. We're going to find the mace, all right?' He squeezed Theo's knee, his ring digging into Theo's leg.

'Do you have any suspects?'

'We know what we're doing, Theo. You just concentrate on your school work.'

His dad didn't trust him to help. He thought he couldn't do it. He treated him like a child while expecting Theo to behave like an adult. He was a child when it suited his dad – telling him to get on with his homework quietly – but when the time came for political manoeuvring, he expected Theo to be as mature as any adult – not to put a toe out of line, never to say something indiscreet. He had to meet the same high standards of behaviour as any MP or he risked jeopardising his dad's career.

His dad stood up to leave. 'No more detentions. And tell your mother next time you're bringing a girl home for dinner.' His dad winked as he made to close the bedroom door behind him.

'Dad!' Theo stood up, his nerves tingling. 'Actually, can

I go to Sammy's for dinner tomorrow night? We're working on a project for Citizenship together.'

His dad paused for a moment. 'Sure, no problem.'

As he shut the door, Theo felt a lead weight of guilt settle in his stomach. He knew he shouldn't go to the meeting. But he was determined to prove that he could do this. He could solve the crime. And he wanted his dad to know it.

CHAPTER EIGHTEEN

The Leader of the Opposition

The chilly evening air whistled through the cracks in the drafty car door and got under Theo's scarf, making him shiver. He was quivering with a combination of cold and nerves. He had to clench his teeth to stop Sammy from noticing them chattering.

Karminder had driven them to a community centre. It was a rectangular block with other inexplicable blocks of varying sizes looming off it, some square, others oblong. It reminded Theo of those pencil cases with all the hidden compartments; it looked like they had popped suddenly out of nowhere, with no obvious function.

Although Sammy had talked most of the way, Theo was aware of an awkward atmosphere in the car. When Karminder stopped, she didn't immediately get out. She turned around in her seat to face Theo.

'Are you sure this is a good idea?' she said, for the second time. She had asked him before they had left Sammy's house too.

'It will be fine, Mum.'

The Leader of the Opposition

'You mustn't make light of this, Samira. This is a very important decision for Theo.'

'We're here now,' Sammy went on. 'What are you planning to do, go all the way home again?'

'If Theo wants to.'

Theo's throat felt tight and he wasn't sure what to say.

'If you don't want to go in, you don't have to,' Karminder said. When Theo didn't answer, she went on, 'I think you have the right to make up your own mind about your political beliefs.'

Theo looked at the bleak concrete building. It was ugly and uninviting. He didn't want to get into trouble with his dad. But if he was honest with himself, he was curious about the meeting. He was under no illusion that it would influence his political beliefs. His dad had told him all about the Opposition's incompetence. He was still interested to see something of them for himself. And it was all to help his dad. He surely couldn't be annoyed about that. He reasoned that it was unlikely anyone would recognise him anyway.

'Let's go,' he said and got out of the car.

He wrapped his scarf around the bottom of his face as they went through the main door. Inside, the community centre was crammed with people. Chairs had been laid out in rows facing the front, but most of them were full. Karminder took a seat, while Theo and Sammy joined the crowds standing around the edges.

The hubbub in the crowd died down as the door at the back of the room opened. Applause and whistles went up and Ruth Morris made her way to the front of the room. It was slow progress. She shook hands with people at the

The Leader of the Opposition

end of every row she passed. She even exchanged a few words with some. Theo wondered whether she knew them. She was accompanied by a tall man wearing loose trousers and sandals, and a young, very professional looking woman, who had a chic, close-cropped afro. The man, who said he was a local councillor, introduced Ruth to the stage and then she began her speech. She talked about funding for schools and universities, about striving for a more equal society and about helping prisoners rehabilitate after they left prison.

Theo listened to it all with interest, but it was her comments on the House of Lords Reform Bill that really caught his attention.

'The government's Reform Bill is a plaster on a gaping wound. They're proposing that only thirty per cent of the House of Lords will be made up of elected members. Only three out of ten places will be available for people from ordinary backgrounds. They want to keep it as a jobs-for-cronies establishment. Duncan wants to make sure he can promote all his loyal lapdogs when his term comes to an end.'

Theo pulled his scarf up a little higher over his red face as the crowd jeered in agreement.

'The government want to keep the bishops but they have made no provision for other faiths. What about our Muslim friends?'

Several people muttered, 'Hear, hear.'

'What about the Jewish community?'

The noises of agreement were gathering.

'What about Hindus and Buddhists?'

People stamped the floor and clapped enthusiastically.

The Leader of the Opposition

'We say the House of Lords should be more representative of Britain today. We are a multicultural nation and we are proud to count people of all faiths amongst our citizens. The government's Bill doesn't go far enough. We want to see all faiths represented in our House of Lords.'

Ruth was drowned out by whoops of agreement. Next to him, Sammy was clapping. Theo raised an eyebrow at her.

'She's got a point.'

He couldn't deny that. Why should the House of Lords only have representatives from one religion? Why hadn't his dad worked this out? He wondered if and how he could bring it up with him.

After Ruth had finished her speech, she took questions from the audience. Lots of people wanted to speak to her and she gave each person a full answer. Theo looked at his phone; it was getting late. He didn't know how much longer it was going to go on for and they hadn't really found out anything useful. He thought about asking Sammy to leave, but he didn't know how they could signal to her mum without drawing too much attention to themselves.

Ruth finished answering a question and looked around for more. Sammy's hand shot in the air.

Theo nuzzled down inside his scarf as someone brought her a microphone to speak into.

'I just want to know who you think stole the parliamentary mace and when you'll get it back?'

Everyone was looking their way, but they were looking at Sammy. Theo felt like he couldn't move.

'That's a very good question,' Ruth said and the room turned back to her. 'I'm glad to see some young people here, engaging in our debates. But I'm afraid it's not for me to answer. The police are conducting an investigation and I'm sure they'll make us aware as soon as they have a suspect in custody. I do think the government's response to the crisis has been a shambles. This should never have been allowed to happen and it's an outrage that our democratic process has been disrupted in this way. I have told the Prime Minister how vital it is to solve this problem swiftly and we will continue to put pressure on him.'

Theo shifted uncomfortably from foot to foot.

Ruth took a question from another audience member. It was a man in the front row. His chin was speckled with stubble and there was a stain that looked like ketchup on his jumper.

'What are you going to do about the government's plans to scrap school meal vouchers? None of us wants to rely on help, but I was made redundant last year after my wife passed away from cancer. The meal vouchers have been a lifeline for us. I don't know what I'll do without them.'

Theo felt distinctly uncomfortable. He hadn't heard about this plan and didn't know what the vouchers were.

Ruth nodded sympathetically while she listened. 'I'm so sorry to hear about your wife passing. As you know, my husband died of cancer a few years ago, so I know how difficult it can be. I want you to know that we will hold the government to account over this. We won't let them get away with taking away the vital help that our community so desperately needs.'

Many people in the room clapped. Theo squirmed. He couldn't look at Sammy. He wondered what this was all about. Was his dad planning to get rid of a scheme that helped vulnerable people? It didn't make sense. He always said he wanted to help the vulnerable out of poverty.

Someone else was asking a question now, but Theo wasn't listening.

'Let's go,' he whispered to Sammy. 'We're not going to find out anything here.'

'Wait. It'll be worth it, I promise.'

Theo waited through more questions with only half an ear open. Every question brought fresh criticism of his dad and his policies.

They hated his dad. Hated him. Some of them with a vengeance. People accused him of being heartless, cowardly, one person called him an elitist snob. Theo was prepared to be bet that none of them had ever met him. His dad wasn't heartless. How could anyone think that? Theo thought of the time his pet hamster George had died and his dad had given him a proper funeral in the back garden. He dug George's grave himself. And no one who had ever met him could call him a coward! His dad was the bravest man he knew. He had seen older, much more experienced men come out of meetings with his dad shaking from head to toe.

By the time the discussion was brought to a close by the councillor, Theo was sorely glad to hear the end of it.

'Let's get out of here,' he said as people started to drift out of the room.

Sammy clung on to the elbow of his jumper. 'No, wait.'

He couldn't go without her – Andy was picking him up from her house. He looked at his phone again. It really was getting late now.

People slowly drifted out of the hall. Some spoke to

The Leader of the Opposition

Ruth on their way out, asking her questions or thanking her for coming. Sammy waited through it all. Karminder didn't seem to be in a hurry to go anywhere either.

As people left, Theo felt more and more conspicuous. Ruth looked their way and her eyebrows rose when she spotted him. She recognised him. Theo was tempted to wait out in the hall, but he didn't want Sammy to know he was too chicken to speak to Ruth.

Finally, they were the last ones left.

'Still here, Karminder?' Ruth said, as they made their way towards the door. 'And with Theo, too.' She said it gently, but Theo could feel her interest in the implied question.

'He's at school with my daughter, who, I think, wants to have a word with you.'

They turned to look at Sammy, who bit her lip.

When Sammy said nothing, Karminder went on, 'I think she wants to ask you if *you* stole the mace. Is that right, Samira?'

Sammy had gone bright pink.

Theo had never seen her embarrassed before. It felt unnatural, like seeing an adult cry. 'It's a legitimate question,' he said. 'Someone took it. You must admit you have a motive.' His heart hammered in his chest, but he fought back the warmth he could feel threatening to creep across his cheeks.

Ruth considered him for a moment. 'I'm sorry to disappoint you, Theo, but I didn't take that mace. Just before the theft, I was with my doctor. He has already vouched for me with the police.'

The young woman who had come in with her appeared at her elbow carrying a walking stick.

The Leader of the Opposition

'Thank you, Wunmi.' Ruth took the walking stick from her. 'My knees aren't what they used to be. Early-onset arthritis. Not something I choose to share with all of our supporters, which I hope you will respect.'

Theo's stomach squirmed.

'Always a pleasure to see you, Karminder.'

'It was a fantastic speech, well worth the journey,' she replied.

'Give my regards to your father, Theo.' Leaning heavily on her stick on one side and Wunmi on the other, Ruth ambled away.

The hall was eerily empty with just the three of them in it. Karminder looked from Theo to Sammy slowly. Sammy was still red in the face and didn't meet her mother's eye. Theo was experiencing something like how he imagined shell shock must feel. He couldn't quite believe what had just happened. Except that there was no other explanation for how deeply ashamed of himself he was. He had accused a fragile old woman of being a thief, with no evidence to back himself up. What had he been thinking?

He thought Karminder was going to shout at them, like his dad would have. Instead she quietly said, 'Let's get you both home.'

CHAPTER NINETEEN

Detained

The next day after school, Sammy and Theo trudged up to Mr Gatimu's room for their detention. Although Theo wasn't looking forward to it, the shame of the previous evening had put the detention into perspective.

Karminder had driven him back to her house in silence. Theo wasn't sure how angry she was with them until she stopped the car. Somehow he felt even worse when she asked them whether they were all right, rather than shouting at them. He had felt enormous relief when he got out of the car to find Andy and a government car waiting for him. It hadn't lasted long. Left with his own thoughts on the car ride home, he had slipped into a miserable slump.

He couldn't believe he had let Sammy convince him to investigate Ruth. He had known from the start that the walking stick had nothing to do with the theft. She hadn't injured herself getting the mace away. She had a medical condition. Theo had looked up early-onset arthritis on his phone. She probably couldn't lift the mace, let alone make an escape with it. Why had he listened to Sammy? He had risked so much going to that meeting, all on her insistence. And it had been for nothing. With no trace of satisfaction, he had crossed Ruth's name off his list of suspects.

His mum had worried about him when he arrived home. She kept asking whether he had had a good time at Sammy's. Eventually he realised that she thought they had fallen out. He felt an uneasy uncertainty about whether she was right.

'Did your mum shout at you yesterday?' Theo asked.

Sammy shook her head.

She wasn't saying much and Theo tried to fill the silence. 'At least we've crossed someone off our suspect list.'

Sammy picked at her nail polish. She wasn't usually this quiet. Theo felt nervous. He was annoyed at her from the night before, but somehow it still worried him that she might be annoyed with him too. He could pretend everything was all right. It didn't seem like she could. Were they going to have an argument?

'We shouldn't have gone,' Sammy said. 'I never should have got into this.'

Theo felt really cold inside. How could she say that? It had been *her* idea to go to the meeting! She had made *him* do it. But still a little part of him was worried that she wanted to quit their investigation. She might not even want speak to him any more. She definitely didn't want to right now.

They fell into silence as they walked the last corridor to Mr Gatimu's room.

Theo could manage without her on the investigation; it might even go better. It would probably take longer, but he could take fewer risks, do everything under the radar. No one would ever find out what he was up to. But he dreaded to think of everything going back to the way it was before, before they had become friends. If that was what they were. He suspected she might only be spending time with him because she wanted to solve the case. After all, they didn't exactly have a lot in common. Why would she want to be friends with him? If she didn't want to help him on the case any more, would they still sit together at lunch? During Citizenship classes?

There were two others in detention when they arrived – two boys from the year above, sitting in the front row. Mr Gatimu sent Theo and Sammy to seats at opposite ends of the back of the class and told them they would be writing an essay. He had written the question on the whiteboard: 'With reference to the British political system, explain what an uncodified constitution is and two ways in which it is changing in Great Britain.'

This would be easy, Theo thought. He knew enough about the British constitution and he could write about the House of Lords Reform.

Theo set to writing his essay. He thought that if he finished early, Mr Gatimu might let him leave. After half an hour of furious scribbling, he put down his pen.

As he read through what he had written, he noticed Sammy on the other side of the classroom, doodling idly on her page. His heart sank. There was no way she would be leaving early with him. Why couldn't she just follow the rules? Didn't she understand that that made everything so much easier? Sometimes he suspected she liked being in trouble, although he couldn't see why.

He presented his finished essay to Mr Gatimu at the front of the class, who sent him back to his seat. Theo waited and watched while Mr Gatimu read his essay. His red pen sliced through Theo's words like a scalpel cutting out a tumour.

He felt uncomfortable. He couldn't watch Mr Gatimu judging his work, correcting his mistakes. He took out the latest issue of *Bullseye*. He particularly liked the column called 'Whispers from Westminster'. In it, journalists reported on the gossip that was going around Westminster's bars and pubs. It wasn't usually about politics; it was more to do with the politicians themselves and the questionable or embarrassing things they did.

> *Bullseye* recently uncovered the Health Secretary's aversion to the sight of blood (previous issue). We can now reveal that the Rt Hon Martin Fields MP also has an abhorrence of incisive points. We refer not to his style of rhetoric (as one may be forgiven for assuming), but to his phobia of needles. This problem became apparent to his team after he posed for last week's flu vaccination photo shoot at St Thomas' Hospital, during which a nurse presented the wan-looking Minister with a three-inch needle. The Minister suffered a fainting fit immediately afterwards and was only brought around after a lie down and a strong coffee. His staff would be well advised to carry smelling salts and a fan for milady, in case another swoon should come on again in future.

Theo snorted. He looked up to find Mr Gatimu watching him and ducked his head.

The article had given him an idea. Some of the anecdotes referenced places where discussions had happened. One mentioned a pub in Westminster called The Queen's Head. He had often seen it mentioned and he started to think that perhaps several people who worked in politics frequented it. If he went, he might overhear something interesting.

There was one problem. He wasn't eighteen. If someone asked him for ID, he would be chucked out, or worse, reported to his dad, leaked to the press, punished by the school. This wasn't the less risky investigation he had just been contemplating. What if he was recognised? He thought of all the times he walked down the street without anyone noticing him. He could go almost anywhere without being recognised, thanks to his dad's policy of not allowing pictures of him and his siblings to get into the papers. The only one they had was from the day his dad was elected. Most people wouldn't recognise him from it, it was so old. And being tall had its benefits. He might not get questioned. *Might*.

'Theo,' Mr Gatimu said. Sammy and the two other boys all looked up too. 'Your essay was rushed. You spent most of your time discussing the possible changes to the House of Lords and very little on your other example – devolution of powers to the Scottish Parliament.' Theo's cheeks began to warm. 'You must remember to give equal weight to your points or you risk losing out on valuable marks.'

The shame of the previous evening came rushing back to him. He had messed up. Again. He couldn't believe Mr Gatimu had said it all in front of the others. Wasn't there a privacy law preventing that? Grades should be counted as private information.

Sammy had heard all of it. She would never say he was clever again.

Mr Gatimu held out his essay to him. Theo would have

to get up and retrieve it. His face beaming with heat as though he had just been sitting by the open fire in his grandpa's living room, Theo trudged back to Mr Gatimu's desk.

Mr Gatimu had put the essay back down, his hand clamped over it like it was a spider he had caught and didn't want to release. In a quiet voice for only Theo to hear Mr Gatimu said, 'This is very unlike you, Theo. I've seen how well you can structure your essays. What's going on?'

Theo looked at his feet. 'I don't know.'

'I think you do know.' Mr Gatimu waited. Theo had the feeling Mr Gatimu knew he wouldn't reply. He was keeping him dangling there deliberately, like a fish on a hook. After an excruciating pause, he said, 'You seem very distracted by the House of Lords Reform Bill. Is everything all right at home?'

Theo's head snapped up. 'Everything's fine.'

Mr Gatimu nodded slowly, knowingly. 'Are you worried about the mace?'

Theo nearly recoiled. How did he know? 'I don't know… I mean, isn't everyone?'

Mr Gatimu looked at the other students in the classroom. Theo wondered if that really was the shadow of a smile he saw playing at Mr Gatimu's eyes. A moment later, it was gone. 'It's not in our power to help. It's not a good idea to invest your energy in things you can't control. Better to focus on things you can, like your school work.'

His hand lifted off the essay. Theo picked it up and Mr Gatimu nodded to the back of the class. 'You can spend the rest of the hour editing what you have written.'

When the hour was up, Theo waited outside the door for Sammy. He watched as Mr Gatimu preceded them down the corridor and out of earshot. He had been unsure whether to tell Sammy about his plan, but in the end decided he would feel too guilty if he didn't involve her.

'I've had an idea. We should go to The Queen's Head pub.' He showed her the page of *Bullseye* with the 'Whispers from Westminster' section. 'In here they talk about it all the time. Loads of politicians go there and I think we could get some really good clues.'

'I can't,' Sammy said.

'But, we'll go now. Our parents think we're in detention. We'll be there half an hour. Tops. No one will ever know.'

Sammy stopped and turned to face him. 'Do you know how much trouble I could get in if I was caught drinking underage?'

'We won't drink, we'll just—'

'It's all right for you. You're protected. Your dad would cover it all up. It wouldn't go on your record. It would all be forgotten. I'm an Indian girl, with normal parents. *I* would get into trouble. It would go on *my* permanent record. This isn't the same for me as it is for you.'

Theo was gobsmacked. He had gone along with every idea she had suggested, not matter how reckless. The only one he had come up with, she had turned down flat.

When he didn't respond, Sammy said, 'Sorry, I just can't.'

She looked really sad as she walked away, but Theo felt suddenly angry.

What she had said wasn't fair. Didn't she know that everything would go on his permanent record? Not his private school record, not a police record, but a public record made up of newspapers and blogs and TV panel shows. If he was caught, they would never let him live it down.

Detained

As he marched out of the school, he got increasingly wound up. Sure his dad had made some problems go away – that video of his rugby match, his first detention. But not a police record. And he couldn't, because if that was found out it would be political suicide. That was why it was so important that Theo didn't mess things up. It could be the end of his dad's career, at any moment.

He didn't like to think about what she had said about being an ordinary, Indian girl. Part of him knew he didn't know what it was like for her. He knew he came from privilege.

But in this one area of his life, he wasn't privileged, he was disadvantaged. Sammy had said she was a nobody like it was a tragedy. She had no idea how much he envied her. He dreamed about anonymity. About another life in which he didn't have to think about newspapers, journalists, social media trolls, the twenty-four-hour news coverage – public scrutiny.

He stopped. The Queen's Head was on the opposite side of the road. He didn't know whether to go in. He could get into trouble. So much trouble that not even Sammy wanted to risk it. She had stolen government property, stalked a journalist, confronted the Leader of the Opposition. She drew the line at this.

Theo pulled back his shoulders. This was nothing in comparison to any of those things.

A shiver of fear ran through Theo as he crossed the road. He stopped outside the pub door. He pulled off his blazer, tie and school jumper, and stuffed them in his rucksack.

As he opened the pub door, he had a sudden memory of Sammy searching Felix's office, how fearless she had been. He tried to be fearless as he went in.

CHAPTER TWENTY

The Aides' Revenge

The pub was dead. An old man was hunched over a pint glass, watching horse racing on a TV screen over the bar. A young Asian couple consulted a tourist map in whispers in the corner. There was a yawning gulf between them that simmered with the low sounds of the commentator on the TV. The bartender was nowhere to be seen.

Feeling grateful that he was unlikely to be recognised, Theo chose a tiny round table with a couple of missmatched stools next to the window. He couldn't see out. Panelling obscured the bottom half and the glass above was leaded and mottled. That was good; it meant no one could see in at him either.

He didn't want to order a drink, he would rather not speak to anyone at all. But he had to do something. He couldn't just sit there twiddling his thumbs. Reflexively, he reached for a book from his bag. He froze. He couldn't take out a school book! He had almost given himself away within moments of sitting down. He could feel warmth creeping up his cheeks. *No, stop it*, he thought. He gritted

The Aides' Revenge

his teeth and breathed deeply through his nose. His face returned to normal temperature. He took his *Bullseye* magazine out of his bag and flipped it open to a random page.

A few dull minutes passed in which Theo wondered whether he should have bothered. He had read the whole of this edition and his eyes glazed over the words. There was no one in here that he could get any gossip from. He might as well go.

'Can I get you anything?'

Theo jumped. He hadn't heard the bartender return to the bar. He was looking straight at Theo. He had long hair, a thick beard and a nose ring.

'I'm waiting for someone.' Theo tried not to mumble, but to sound like he had every right to be there.

'Suit yourself,' the bartender replied. He opened a dishwasher and stacked away the clean glasses onto their shelves.

Theo let out a sigh of relief. The man didn't seem to care about him sitting there.

The pub door swung open, letting in a young man and woman. The man was wearing a tweed jacket and tortoiseshell glasses. His brown hair was artfully swept to one side in what looked like a deliberately dishevelled way. The woman was Asian and had short, bouncy shiny hair. She walked with a spring in her step, giving off a powerful aura of happiness.

'I told the Minister not to pose for the photo, but he wouldn't listen to me,' the man said.

'They never do,' the woman replied.

The rest of their conversation drifted away as they walked to the bar.

Theo tucked away his magazine as surreptitiously as he

The Aides' Revenge

could. He didn't want them to spy him reading it.

The young man laughed loudly, but otherwise, Theo couldn't make out what they were saying. He would have to get closer. He fished his wallet out of his bag, taking care to keep his blazer out of sight.

He went over to the bar and watched the bartender pouring out two glasses of wine for the pair.

'Still, it gave me a giggle, anyway. We've got to be able to laugh about it,' the young man said.

'What can I get you?' the bartender asked Theo.

He wasn't expecting to be asked yet. The bartender was still serving the drinks for the other pair.

'Could I get a coke please?' he said.

'Half or a pint?' the bartender asked, as he typed something into a card machine for the couple.

Half of what? Theo wondered. 'Pint, please.' He would never manage a whole pint, but it was the measurement he understood best.

The bartender ripped off the receipt for the woman – who, after some wrangling with the man, had just paid – and selected a pint glass from the shelf. Too late, Theo realised he had meant a half pint. He needed to be more on the ball than this. Besides, his drink was nearly poured and he hadn't managed to catch any of the couple's conversation.

'I *told* him not to try to push that reform through,' the man said.

'You were right.' The woman's eyes were sympathetic behind black-framed glasses. 'Chris is going to tell him to drop it on Monday.'

'Two fifty,' the bartender said. Theo handed over a note and turned his attention back to the couple.

The Aides' Revenge

'It was a crazy idea, so overcomplicated. I don't know where he comes up with this stuff. I was saying to Marco the other day, sometimes I think he reads this stuff on social media.'

'No!' the woman said, sounding scandalised.

'Yes.' The man angled himself out, as though he was looking for more of an audience. He did a double take as he noticed Theo for the first time. 'You're not. Oh my god. Are you?'

He looked from the woman to Theo with an expression of growing excitement.

'Ermm.' Theo picked up his glass. Luckily the bartender had already given Theo his change and gone out to the back. But he might return any moment, just in time to hear him outed as a minor.

'You're Duncan's son aren't you?' the man said, in a stage whisper.

The woman's eyes became round then too. 'Oh my god!'

'I, errr...' Theo had no idea what to say.

'Oh, of course, mum's the word,' the man said, nodding sagely. 'You're here incognito. We won't breathe a word, will we, Rachel?'

'Oh no,' Rachel said, breathlessly.

'Thanks.'

Touching his collarbone, the man said, 'How silly of me not to introduce myself.' He held out his hand to shake. Theo had to put down his over-full pint glass before he could meet his hand. 'I'm Tom Davies, aide to Martin Fields, the Health Secretary. I'm sure I don't need to tell you that.' His laugh was like a tinkle on glass.

Theo reached out his hand to the woman. 'Rachel Wong.

The Aides' Revenge

I'm a spad, sorry special advisor, for Chris Elliot,' she said.

'Oh riiight.' He didn't mean to be talking to them. He should find a way to get out of the conversation. But Rachel might know something helpful about Chris.

'We were just discussing the NHS reform programme the Minister has been working on. What do you make of it, Theo?' Tom's eyes were alert in a slightly frightening way.

Theo had no idea what the reform programme was. He wished he had stayed in his corner. They might have come to sit at the table next to him and he could have overheard their conversation without being noticed.

'You can't ask him about that,' Rachel said, after a silence just long enough to turn awkward. 'He can't tell us what his dad thinks.'

'Well...'

'But we won't tell anyone,' Tom cut in. 'We will be the souls of discretion.'

'It doesn't really matter what anyone thinks of the reform. Until they get the mace back, the government can't pass any laws anyway,' Rachel said.

'Do you think they'll find it?' Theo said, seizing on the topic he really wanted to discuss.

'It will be disastrous if they don't. They can't use the Lords' mace for ever.'

As Rachel talked about the possible calamities that might befall democracy if the mace wasn't found, Theo was distracted by Tom furiously typing on his phone.

Seeing his line of sight, Rachel's gaze also fell on Tom.

'Who are you texting?'

'No one,' Tom said, flipping his phone case shut. 'I don't think they'll find the mace. Whoever masterminded this knows exactly what they're doing. Think about it. They got the mace past all of that heavy security. The police haven't found a shred of evidence. The culprit is a genius.'

Theo took a sip of his coke and then tried to say as casually as he could, 'Who do you think has the brains to pull that off?'

'None of the ministers I've met!' Tom roared with laughter.

Rachel was more thoughtful. 'I don't know. They're a lot more devious than we sometimes give them credit for. And ruthless.'

'Ruthless?' Theo pressed.

'I've heard Chris say he would rather give up the House of Lords Reform Bill and stay in power, than fight for it and lose in the next election.'

Theo was stunned. 'But it was his manifesto promise.' He felt like he might have given his interest away. 'Wasn't it?'

Tom nodded with a look that said he had heard it all a thousand times. 'They would all give up their passion projects for one more term in office.'

'Not *all* of them,' Rachel said.

Worried that the conversation was veering off course, Theo cut them off. 'It's lucky Chris was in Clapham the morning of the theft or the police might get suspicious.'

'Clapham?' Rachel said. 'No, he was at home. He called in sick that morning, his wife vouched for him with the police.'

Theo tried not to gape. 'Are you sure?'

'Of course. I have access to his diary.'

Rachel and Tom were looking at him funny.

The Aides' Revenge

'I must be thinking of someone else,' Theo said.

Tom picked up the topic of ministers who had sold out their policies in order to get another term in office. Rachel began listing those who had resigned rather than force through policies they disagreed with.

Theo felt the time had come to make his excuses and go. He had the best clue he was likely to get. It turned out Chris had a motive to steal the mace and he had lied about his alibi. He had to be the main suspect now.

The pub door swung open and three other people walked in. There was a short young woman leading the way – straight towards them. She had unkempt hair and an ill-fitting blazer. Her eyes bored into Theo. She was followed by a man who looked younger than Theo, but his suit suggested he was as old as the others. At the back there was a young woman who had dyed blonde hair and those nails with the white tips, which Theo hated. Although he had to admit they had been done well and they didn't seem to be the fake, plastic kind of nails, which were worse. She was wearing a large diamond ring on her wedding finger.

'We were going to the Masons Arms, but I thought we would just check to see if anyone was here first,' the short woman said, in a voice that was just a bit too loud. Theo didn't believe her. He had a feeling this was who Tom had been texting.

Theo was introduced to the group – more aides of MPs. The blonde, Hannah Ingram, worked for Rupert Spencer. He was pressganged into joining them at their table.

Insisting that he couldn't stay very long, Theo brought his bag over. He gulped down his coke, saying as little as possible, while the others complained about their bosses. He kept

The Aides' Revenge

one eye on the door, fearful that more people would come to join them. What if one of them told their boss he had been here? The more people that came, the greater the risk that his dad would find out. He could barely sit still on his stool, ready to jump out of his seat at the earliest opportunity.

They were all laughing at a story Tom was telling about the Health Secretary asking him to return his wife's online shopping because he didn't know how to do it himself. 'Imagine not knowing how to use the post,' Tom cried.

The door opened and Mr Gatimu walked in with a man Theo didn't know.

Theo froze. His eyes followed Mr Gatimu to the bar. He was afraid to move in case he drew any attention to himself.

As Mr Gatimu ordered from the bartender, Theo rested his head in his hand, facing the opposite direction.

Luckily, Hannah was speaking at that end of the table, so he pretended to focus on her.

'The other day I found out Rupert has never even painted a room himself. My fiancé and I are doing up our new flat and I was telling him about it. He couldn't believe we were doing it ourselves. I suppose if you have as much money as his family, you don't need to.'

Theo turned his head a fraction to see what Mr Gatimu was doing. He wasn't paying their table any attention, but if he just looked Theo's way once…

'Chris doesn't know how to put bullet points in a document. He asked me to do it for him,' Rachel said.

The short woman said, 'I do all of Marian's printing. She's never worked out how to connect her computer to the right printer. Whenever she does it, it comes out on a printer on the other side of the building. Once she printed off plans for tax breaks on the car industry in the Green Party's office by mistake.'

'Was that her?' Rachel exclaimed.

Mr Gatimu disappeared out of the back of the pub, leaving his friend at the bar. Now might be Theo's only chance.

'I'm really sorry,' he said, grabbing his bag. 'I've got to go.'

Everyone pressed him to stay and promised to buy him a drink. Shaking his head, Theo rushed out of the door, leaving perplexed stares behind him.

Back out on the street, he breathed an enormous sigh of relief. He didn't waste any time turning his feet towards home.

CHAPTER TWENTY-ONE

Truce

That night, Theo sat at the desk in his room typing out and deleting text messages to Sammy. He didn't know what to say or whether they were even on speaking terms. His anger from earlier in the day had burnt off with his success at the pub. Now that he had such a vital clue, all he wanted to do was tell Sammy about it. He needed – and wanted – her help. He couldn't solve the mystery without her. She was the one who always had the ideas. It was her idea to go to the meeting, her idea to follow Erin. She had stolen the hard drive from Felix's office. He would have nothing without her. If it wasn't for her, the investigation would have ended before it even began.

He just wasn't sure she wanted to hear from him. He remembered what she had said about how it was different for her, because she didn't have a parent who could make her mistakes disappear. He had got so frustrated with her earlier, he hadn't stopped to consider how true that was. She was right. He had no idea what it was like for her. But he wanted to understand.

Truce

He decided that he would text her and settled on something simple, explaining what he had found out in the pub.

The next day, as soon as the lunch bell rang, Theo jumped out of his seat. He rushed down the hall into the old part of the school. He knew Sammy had English in one of those rooms and he didn't want to miss her coming out.

He stood in the hallway opposite the classroom door as students flooded out. Sammy was one of the last to leave.

'Hey, you didn't reply to my text last night,' Theo said, falling into step with her.

'I'm sorry, I didn't know what to say.' Her hand went to her fingernails but there was no polish there to pick off. Her hands looked a lot younger without their trademark dark polish.

That was it, Theo thought. She had nothing left to say to him. He should walk away now. He didn't want to pressure her into speaking to him when she obviously didn't want to. Somehow his feet kept following on beside hers, putting off the moment when he would have to say goodbye.

'It was great that you managed to get such an important clue. See,' she said, elbowing him gently in the side, 'you didn't need my help.'

She was trying to get rid of him, subtract herself from the equation.

Theo forced himself to say, 'Obviously if you don't want to be involved in the investigation any more, then I'll leave you alone.' He could hear the resigned sadness in his own voice. But it was too late to retract it now.

They had walked out into the playground, which was mostly empty because all the other students were flooding into the cafeteria. Through the cafeteria windows, Theo could see them shoving each other in the queue for the counter.

'I want to be involved, but I *can't*,' Sammy said and she plonked down on a bench and put her head in her hands.

'Why? I don't understand what's happened.' When she didn't answer, Theo went on, 'Is this about what happened with Ruth Morris?'

Sammy nodded into her hands. 'Afterwards, when we got home, my mum told my dad about it.' She rested her head on her chin. 'He said my mum let me have too much freedom and then they had a big argument. Mum sent me up to my room, but I could hear her shouting down the phone from upstairs. I just know when I go there next he's going to make me spend the whole time with my grandmother.'

'Don't you like her?'

Her head shot up. '"Don't say this, Samira, don't wear that. Respect your elders. *Let me show you how to make chapatis, Samira.*"' She did a very good Indian accent. '"*Why has your mother let you dye your beautiful hair? She shouldn't let you walk around in these skimpy clothes.*"' She blew out her cheeks. 'My dad's always dumping me with her on his weekends, so he can go off with his girlfriend.'

Theo's eyebrows rose. 'What does your grandmother think of that?'

'She pretends not to hear whenever I mention her. To her, my mum is the baddie. She left my dad, so she's decided it's her fault their marriage ended.'

Theo felt awful. 'I'm sorry, Sammy. I had no idea.'

'It's OK, it's not your fault.'

'I don't think it is OK.'

Truce

They were silent for a bit.

Theo felt a bit better that she wasn't avoiding him, but he hated that she was so sad about her family. He didn't know her dad had a new girlfriend. He didn't know that most weekends she was meant to be with her dad she spent with her grandmother, who she didn't like. There was a lot he didn't know about her.

'What about your mum's parents? Do you get on with them?'

'Naniji and Nanaji are great. Especially Nanaji.' She turned towards him with a smile. 'The other day, we were all round at their house and my cousins ate all of the gulab juman – this yummy dessert,' she said when she saw Theo's puzzled expression, 'because my aunty Tanny lets them get away with everything. But then it turned out my nanaji had secretly saved me one and he slipped it to me in the kitchen when the others weren't looking.' Theo could tell she was feeling satisfied, knowing she had got one over on her cousins. 'Have you really never tried gulab juman?'

'Nope.'

'I'll ask my mum to make it next time you come round.'

Buoyed by the idea that she still wanted him to go round to her house, he found the nerve to ask the question he was dreading. 'Do you want to stop helping out with the investigation? I understand if that's how you feel,' Theo added quickly; he didn't want to push her. She chewed on a corner of her lip. 'If your dad already dumps you with your grandma at the weekends, it sounds like he can't do any worse.'

'If I give in now, he's won. He'll try to grind me down, like he did to my mum.'

She was speaking more to herself and Theo sensed it

was too soon to ask what she meant.

'You're right,' she said, standing up. 'What's the worst that can happen?'

'So you're still in?'

'As long as you are.'

'I'm in.' Theo stood up. 'Let's get some lunch before it's all gone.'

Theo and Sammy met at the school gates after school. Before lunch ended, Theo had suggested that they follow Erin again. His sister was going over to a friend's for dinner, so he only had to text his mum to say he would be in the library to create a solid alibi.

He didn't think Erin was responsible for the theft. His gut was telling him that Felix was involved – the phone conversation, the photos on the hard drive were just too much evidence to ignore. He couldn't see how Erin might be tangled up with him. Unless she had collected the photos for him, using one of the photographers who worked for her paper. The paper must know a lot of investigators too. She was a loose end and they needed to tie her up.

This time they were waiting outside her office for an hour before she emerged. Just like last time, she crossed the road and went into the corner shop.

Theo's phone rang – it was his mum. He pressed the button to ignore the call.

Theo and Sammy hung back on their side of the road, waiting for Erin to leave the shop. As she did, her eyes flicked their way, but didn't settle.

She set off walking in the same direction as last time and they hurried to follow. She took them down a narrow, winding street. Then turned onto another. Instantly, she turned again. Theo no longer recognised whether they were going the same way as the last time.

She slowed down and got out her phone, as if she might be checking for directions. They hung back, trying to keep enough distance between them to make sure she didn't spot them. Theo's stomach was squirming. Adrenaline pulsed through him. He wanted to move. The sun beat down on him, making him uncomfortably hot. He could feel sweat forming under his collar.

Erin set off at speed again and they trotted to catch up. She turned down an alleyway. Theo and Sammy waited just short of its entrance. If she looked back down the alley, there was no way she could miss them.

Sammy peered around the corner. 'She's gone.'

They half ran the length of the alley, their footsteps echoing eerily in the enclosed space.

Erin stepped into their path, blocking the exit. 'What do you think you're doing?'

Sammy yelped, Theo's heart leapt into his mouth.

'You've been following me,' Erin said. She had the hint of an Irish accent, like it was part of an alter ego costume that she could put on or take off whenever the mood struck her.

Theo and Sammy exchanged alarmed looks.

Erin's eyes sparkled with anger. 'I want to know why.'

'Did you cut the feed to the security cameras or did you get your boyfriend to do it for you?' Sammy said. She was standing tall, staring Erin down.

'What security—?'

'There's no point denying it,' Sammy continued. 'We

know all about your affair.'

She narrowed her eyes. 'It's not an affair if neither of you are married. What's this about?'

Sammy said nothing and Theo could tell she didn't have an answer. Wanting to back her up, he said, 'Where were you on the morning of the theft of the mace? We know you had the means to tamper with the security and the motive.'

Erin's eye's widened. 'You think... you think I did it?' She began to laugh.

She didn't seem to be angry any more, she actually seemed genuinely amused. Theo hadn't expected that. It took the wind out of his sails.

'I didn't steal the mace, ye eegits.' Her light accent thickened for a moment. 'Why on earth would you think that?'

'You've been campaigning to abolish the House of Lords for years.' Sammy seemed to be holding her conviction more than Theo. 'You didn't want the Reform Bill to go through because it didn't go far enough for you, did it?'

Erin's smile faded. 'I do want to abolish the House of Lords, but it's not going to happen. Not in my lifetime. The Reform Bill was the next best thing. I wanted it to go through. Still do.'

'But in all your articles you were so sure you could get rid of it,' Theo said.

'I was young.' She considered them both, then nodded to herself. 'My fiancé died in a car accident, did you find that out in all your research?'

Neither of them answered.

'First rule of investigating – do the background research. When my fiancé died, I got involved in the lobby for a Road Safety Bill.' This rang a bell and Theo realised they had read about it, but dismissed it as unimportant. 'It looked like we were going to get it through, but it was defeated in the Lords. I was grieving and I became... fixated on it.

'I'm past all that now. I'm with someone new and I'm happy. I had nothing to do with the mace theft. I was with Gary, my boyfriend, when the theft happened. Did you not think the police might have already checked?'

Theo's phone rang again. It was his mum.

'Do you need to answer that?' Erin said with a knowing look.

'No.' Theo sent the call to voicemail, turned his phone to silent and stuffed it in his pocket. 'You've been really critical of the Bill. Why did you say all that stuff if you want it to go through?'

She shrugged. 'That's how it works. Sometimes you can pressure the government into amending a Bill if it's really unpopular.'

Theo and Sammy exchanged awkward glances. He felt a little bit like how they had felt after they spoke to Ruth. He wasn't as embarrassed this time. At least no one else was there to see what had happened.

'So are you trying to find out who took the mace then, Theo?'

Theo said nothing.

'Does your dad know what you're up to?'

'Come on, Sammy. Let's go,' he said.

They turned to walk back down the alley.

'Sammy, if there's ever anything you want to tell me about your friend, you know where to find me!' Erin called after them.

'Leech,' Theo said.

'She's just doing her job. I think she was telling the truth.'

'Maybe. If Gary's her alibi then they could just be vouching for each other.'

They came out at the other end of the alley. Theo followed their footsteps back the way they had come.

'Hold on, let's work out where the nearest tube station is.' Sammy took out her phone and opened up her map app. 'That way.' They set off in the direction she had pointed.

'So we're no closer to crossing her off our list then. Who else is there? Chris and Felix?'

'And Trevor, we still haven't ruled him out.'

'I don't know how we're ever going to rule him out,' Sammy said.

'We don't need to, we just need to prove that it was one of the others. Or someone else.'

They walked silently for a moment. Theo considered how likely it was that they would ever find the culprit.

'How are we supposed to work out what anyone believes?' he said, throwing up his hands. 'Ruth and Erin both campaigned to get rid of the Bill, when actually they want it to go through. Chris created the Bill, but if push comes to shove, would rather drop it. Rupert was right. Nobody actually argues for what they really believe in.' Theo felt even angrier than the first time Rupert had said it to him. A part of him had wanted to believe that MPs only argued for causes they really agreed with. That was their whole job. But Rupert was spot on. They all had an agenda.

They came onto a main road. Sammy consulted her phone and then pointed them towards a zebra crossing.

'But that's just it – we've worked out what Erin and Ruth and Chris really believe. None of them told the truth straight off, but we know what the truth is now. We did that.' Sammy's hair flew into her face and she flicked it off like she shrugged off detentions. 'We're going to solve it, Theo. I know it.'

They took the steps down into the tube station. Theo was going west and Sammy was going east, so they said goodbye at the top of the escalators.

Theo reflected on Sammy's confidence. He couldn't deny that they had done better than he had thought possible. And they still had leads to follow. They needed to find out where Chris really was on the morning of the theft. And they needed to find out what Felix was up to.

He walked the last few stairs of the escalator, standing taller.

CHAPTER TWENTY-TWO

Reckoning

Theo was still feeling buoyant as he walked through the front door. He was confused by the sound of rushing footsteps. His mum came into the hallway. Her face was ominously unreadable.

'I need to speak to you,' she said.

She pointed to the living room and Theo followed, his palms sweating.

Milly was on the floor, banging a hammer meant for a child's xylophone against a pile of her books. She smiled when she saw him. Her smile quickly dropped. She could sense the tension.

'Why is your phone off?' his mum said as soon as he was sitting on the sofa. She perched on the coffee table, directly in front of him.

'I... was in the library. Sorry, I must have forgotten to turn the sound back on.'

'You haven't seen the news?'

Theo's stomach shrivelled. They had found the hard drive. They knew he had stolen government property.

Reckoning

Somehow the news had got hold of it. He was done for.

His mum switched the television on. She said nothing as the reporter finished her story and Theo didn't dare ask what was coming. He didn't think he could bear it.

'More than one witness has reported seeing the Prime Minister's fourteen-year-old son, Theodore Duncan, this week at a speech given by the Leader of the Opposition, Ruth Morris. He was seen at the meeting with a young Asian woman, thought to be one of his school friends. There are also suggestions that he approached Ruth Morris at the end of the session and spoke with her privately. Commentators have questioned whether this shows that the Prime Minister's son might have doubts about his father's policies.

'With rumours circulating that the Prime Minister intends to reopen the Commons next week using the Lords' mace, some MPs have formed an alliance with the Lords and are now threatening to take legal action against the government to prevent them. The pressure on the Prime Minister to change course is mounting daily.'

His mum pressed the mute button.

She stared at him for a long while. Theo couldn't meet her gaze.

'Your father will be up in a minute.'

She went into the kitchen, leaving Theo alone with Milly.

Theo sat motionless, in a daze. He had been so worried about the hard drive, he had completely forgotten about the meeting. This was exactly the type of thing he wasn't supposed to do and he knew it. If his mum was this angry – when she was normally level-headed about political dramas – he could only imagine how his dad would be.

Chris Elliot's face appeared on the television screen.

Theo didn't dare turn the sound on, so he turned on the subtitles instead. They were slightly behind the picture, because now Chris was speaking but it was obviously the newsreader's words below him.

'The Prime Minister's Deputy, Chris Elliot, has today condemned the government's decision to use the Lords' mace and Chris joins us now. Chris, do you think the use of the mace is a mistake?'

'Good evening,' the subtitles read, now in a different colour, although it was still Chris's face speaking from the screen. 'Yes, I'm sorry to say that I do believe this is a mistake. There is no constitutional precedent for the Prime Minister's decision. This decision would prevent the Lords from sitting at the same time as the Commons – a measure that has not been seen in all of Parliament's long history. Even during the Second World War, when the Commons were bombed and the Lords graciously gave up their chamber for MPs' use, they still continued to sit in another venue. We cannot repay their generosity by resorting to methods that benefit solely the Commons and not the good of all Parliament...'

Theo couldn't believe what he was reading. He had heard Chris agreeing the plan to use the Lords' mace with his dad. He couldn't believe he would publicly criticise him. His dad must be furious. And on the same day they had reported that he had gone to the Opposition meeting.

Theo was startled from his thoughts by Milly resuming her banging.

He went over and absent-mindedly wiped her dribbling nose on his sleeve. 'You don't want that in your mouth.'

She scrunched up her face as he wiped it, her feathery

auburn ringlets bouncing. She went back to her books, tossing one out of reach in her eagerness to turn the pages.

The front door slammed. Theo couldn't turn around.

'In my office,' his dad said from over his shoulder.

Theo returned his sister's book to her and followed his father down the hallway, to his office.

It was a tiny room – just a desk with a computer, sitting under a dormer window. A small sofa filled the opposite wall.

His dad swung the swivel chair around to face the sofa, as if he was an interrogator about to address a prisoner. Theo sat on the sofa.

He faced his dad for the first time and flinched. He was almost twitching with rage.

'What were you doing at that meeting, Theo?'

Theo stared at his hands. Out of the corner of his eye, he could see his dad's ring on his clenched hands. He had no lie prepared. All he had was the truth.

'I wanted to question Ruth about the mace.'

His dad sat back in surprise.

'I wanted to help you find it and I thought she might have taken it, so I went to her meeting to find out.'

His dad gripped the armrests on his chair, his ring digging in. 'That's ridiculous, Theo. She's the Leader of the Opposition, of course she didn't take it. Don't you think the police have already questioned her?' His dad's eyes fell where Theo was looking. His forehead creased and he began twisting the ring around his finger.

'I just wanted to help you.' Theo hated how small his voice sounded, but he felt as though a great weight was pressing down on him, squeezing him small. The colour was rising in his face and he couldn't fight it. He couldn't bear for his dad to know that he had done it all for the ring.

'You shouldn't have got involved. Don't you understand how bad this looks? I can't tell the press you went there to question her about a theft. They're saying you agree with her politics – my own son! And I can't say anything to contradict them. I really didn't need this today, Theo.'

Theo remembered the discussion about school meal vouchers and wondered whether he might agree with some of Ruth's policies. He felt like saying it, just to spite his dad. A premonition of the resulting fallout held him back.

'It was very noble of you to want to help, but you must understand the proper authorities have it in hand. You're just a boy, Theo, you have to leave it to the professionals.'

Theo looked up. His dad was staring at him with wide eyes, as though he hardly knew him. Maybe he didn't. Theo didn't feel like a boy much any more. Boys could cry and scream when something was unfair. They could break things and run around causing trouble. Theo couldn't remember the last time he could get away with doing any of those things.

'Have the professionals found out who did it then? Have they found the mace?' Theo said.

His dad's face hardened. 'They will.'

Theo's anger was mounting. 'Have they got any leads at all? Are they any closer to finding the mace than they were a week ago?'

'I get this from the press every day,' his dad suddenly thundered, 'I won't take it from my own son!' He was breathing heavily, his chest visibly rising and falling.

'They've got nothing, have they?' Theo exploded. 'They

haven't got any leads, but I have. You just don't want to listen to me.'

His dad rolled his eyes. 'What leads could you possibly have?'

Theo was on his feet. 'Where was Chris on the morning of the theft? He's lied about his alibi. And now he's telling everyone who will listen that you're getting everything wrong. How do you know he didn't take the mace?'

His dad put his head back and laughed. 'Chris? Chris was with his sister in Clapham during the theft. She's...' He hesitated, his smile gone. 'She has a drug addiction,' he said quietly.

Theo's cheeks were warming. 'What do you mean?'

'You're not to tell anyone, you understand.' Theo stared. 'He told me as soon as we agreed to go into government together. She often has... crises. He was with her that morning. That's why he lied about where he was. But he told *me* where he was. At least he was honest with me about that.'

Theo felt foolish and he could feel his cheeks burning with shame. He had been so sure. His dad gave him a pitying look and suddenly that was worse than any of it.

'What about Felix Humphries? He's been lobbying people to change their vote on the Bill. He—'

'How would you know that?'

Theo looked away. He couldn't tell his dad about the hard drive.

'Felix is apolitical, you *know* that.' At the look of defiance on Theo's face his dad went on, 'Besides, Felix was with me the morning of the theft. The police have ruled him out of their enquiries and –' he raised his voice to prevent Theo from interrupting – 'that's all there is to it.'

Reckoning

Despite the fact that his father was seated and looking up at him on his feet, Theo felt very small again. His dad was never going to believe him. He could tell by the look on his face. He was treating Theo like he was stupid. No matter what he said, he wasn't going to be taken seriously.

He sat down, resigned.

'So you've been investigating this for a while then,' his dad said. 'Where else have you been and who else have you questioned?'

Theo had no intention of telling him.

After a silence thick with the force of both their wills, his dad held out his hand. 'Phone,' he said.

Theo took his phone out of his pocket and slapped it down on his dad's hand. He got up to storm out.

'And you're grounded. There's no going to friends' after school, no library, no friends here. You're to come home as soon as the school bell rings. Do you understand?'

'What about the trip to Montgomery tomorrow?' The thought of missing out on his one opportunity to speak to Lord Thompson filled Theo with the hollow feeling of failure.

His dad swore. 'The team have already briefed the press that we're going.' He considered silently for a moment and Theo barely dared breathe. 'Fine, we'll go to the fundraiser, but that's it.'

'Fine.' Theo felt no sense of victory. His dad was only keeping the plans for appearance's sake. Typical of him.

He stormed out of the room.

CHAPTER TWENTY-THREE

Gommers

The next morning, in his parents' efforts to punish him, Theo was kept home from rugby. In this at least, he felt he had the last laugh. He couldn't have been happier to have an excuse not to go.

He felt rather differently after a couple of hours cooped up in the flat. His dad had changed the password on his computer; he was only allowed to use it to do homework. He wasn't allowed his phone, so he couldn't text Sammy. He was worried he might have missed some texts from her. Not for the first time, he was glad his notifications were turned off, so any texts wouldn't appear on the home screen. At least his parents couldn't get into his phone without his fingerprint.

He would usually have caught up on social media in the morning. Instead he picked up his dad's discarded newspapers. They had every one – they were brought up by a civil servant each day and taken away again at the end of it. He sifted through them until he found one with a headline that wasn't about the mace.

Gommers

A few pages in, there was a feature about the plan to scrap school meal vouchers. It was part of several planned cuts, which the Chancellor of the Exchequer said would create 'a fairer society and a leaner economy'. More like leaner children, Theo thought. The paper had done an analysis of the possible impact on children living in poverty. It was damning. His dad couldn't possibly have missed it. Did he care? He had never had to rely on vouchers when he was growing up. Whereas since he had heard Ruth talk about them, Theo had noticed several of the kids at school using them. They walked around in trousers too short or shirts with fraying cuffs. There weren't many of them, but that only made them stand out all the more. He wondered what life was like for them at home.

Today it was easier to imagine his dad flicking away the concerns about the policy; single-minded, unwilling to listen to other points of view. Theo stuffed the newspaper angrily in the bin.

He sat with Harry while she watched the cookery programme she liked, trying not to dwell on everything his dad had said the day before. When the news came on, his mum came in and switched off the TV. But not before they announced that the legal challenge to prevent the government from using the Lords' mace in the Commons had been quashed. The House of Commons was due to reopen the next day and the vote on the House of Lords Reform Bill would go ahead.

'That's enough lazing around, Theo,' his mum said. 'Into the shower, now.'

He thought about the new vote as he brushed his teeth. The thief's time was up. The vote was going ahead, whether they had persuaded anyone to change their vote or not.

Before lunch, one of his dad's assistants came up to collect him for their trip to Montgomery. Rather than taking Theo out of the front door on to Downing Street, he took him out the back.

'Why are we going this way?' Theo asked.

'Too much press around the front.' Seeing Theo's grimace, he went on, 'Your dad didn't want them questioning you.'

Theo had an uncomfortable swell of gratitude towards his dad, which he shoved away with the thought that his dad was probably only doing it to protect his own reputation.

When he reached the car, Theo found his dad already inside, speaking into his phone. He acknowledged Theo with one tight nod and then they set off, one police outrider following on a motorbike behind.

His dad spent the hour-long journey out of London talking on his phone. He finally hung up when they reached the school entrance. At the side of the otherwise quiet country lane, photographers clustered in the dirt next to the school's wrought-iron gates. They snapped into action as the car approached, darting forward, their cameras flashing.

'Andy, could you make sure none of them get inside the grounds please?' his dad said.

'Of course, sir.'

The driver stopped at the gates and Andy got out of the front passenger seat to keep the press back, while the school security officer let them through.

'Theo, Theo!' they shouted. Theo shrunk into his seat.

Gommers

On the other side of the gates, Andy got back in. Then they set off up the sweeping driveway towards the school building.

They drove through dense woodland. There was a flash of red and yellow between the trees. Theo's stomach clenched. Photographers had broken into the grounds. He searched for them among the brown of the mud and trees. He relaxed. It was only three boys, about his age, dressed in the school PE kit. They whooped as they ran along a dirt track that followed the road. The leader turned back to egg on the two behind him. Theo had a flash of yearning envy. If his dad hadn't become Prime Minister, he would be at this school. He might be racing his friends through the grounds, with nothing more to worry about than his next homework deadline. The boy caught sight of the car and met Theo's eyes. Theo looked away.

They emerged onto a neatly clipped lawn that stretched like a red carpet leading up to the school building. It was magnificent red and white brick, with red-brick chimneys and three distinct wings. Perfectly sculpted box hedges lined the foot of the building and scarlet flowers tumbled from barrels that edged the road.

Theo couldn't imagine any of the students here receiving school meal vouchers. If they couldn't afford the meals, they definitely couldn't afford the school fees. He wondered whether his dad had ever known anyone who needed meal vouchers.

They were dropped off on the circular driveway just as another car was pulling up. They went through the main doors into a vast entrance hall. The floors were marble. Ornately carved wooden pillars stretched to the distant ceiling, holding aloft a gallery that ran above. A student in a tailcoat met them and led them down a hallway lined with oversized photographs of illustrious alumni – famous actors, past politicians, a man who filmed wildlife programmes. The last was a photograph of Theo's dad. The student pointed it out to them and Theo's dad responded with a strained smile. Sometimes, he suspected, even his dad didn't like being Prime Minister.

They went through a door out of the side of the building into the gardens. A pathway took them to a terrace that overlooked a lawn embroidered with crisp golden gravel walks and sparkling fountains. The terrace was packed with people milling around a buffet table, waiters wandering between them with trays of drinks. They were all dressed as if they were going to a garden party, which, Theo supposed, they were. You wouldn't have guessed it was a fundraiser for charity. Theo thought of the times his school raised money for charity, when aggressive students cornered you in the corridor and forced you to sponsor them for a run. He gave them a quid just to get rid of them.

His dad's arrival had a palpable effect on the crowd. Conversations around them juddered to a halt, then restarted with an odd stiffness. Laughs became fuller, more forced. Some openly gawped at them. Most kept anxiously checking that they were still there, as if his dad were a friend's toddler they had been asked to keep an eye on.

His dad found a few of his old teachers to greet and Theo loped off to the buffet table, hoping to catch sight of Trevor Thompson. While he was loading his plate – real china, not plastic – with sticks of chorizo and manchego, he spotted Thompson speaking to a very tall, square woman who was clutching nervously at her pearls.

A woman who had that unmistakeable teacherly quality, Theo could smell it a mile off, called their attention with a microphone.

'Ladies and gentlemen, thank you all for coming today. Our keynote speaker for the day will be Lord Trevor Thompson. Lord Thompson was once a pupil at this school, then went on to become MP for Blatchington South for thirty years. He spent time in the Cabinet Office, first as Secretary of State for Housing and later as Secretary of State for Work and Pensions. He has remained in Parliament, serving his country, ever since and is now the Speaker of the House of Lords. Please give him a very warm welcome.'

Everyone applauded politely as Thompson came to the microphone.

'Imagine, if you will, a young boy of obscure background,' Thompson began. 'He lives in a two up, two down, courtesy of his father's job down the shipyard. The boy is unusually bright. This has gone unremarked during most of his school years, because his teachers are too busy worrying about the children who are still struggling to grasp the basics of reading at ten years old to pay him any attention. But this all changes when one teacher does notice.' The audience was totally silent. Thompson wasn't using his booming voice now, he didn't have to. He was an expert public speaker, able to hold the attention of the whole crowd. 'This teacher tells the parents that their son is gifted and that his gifts will be wasted in their small school. She suggests the parents try to get him in to the private school in the next county. It has just set up a new scholarship programme.'

Thompson paced up and down the small space that was

his stage, taking his time over his story.

'After several discussions, the parents decide to send their son for the entrance exam. To their surprise, the school offers their son a place. So they drop their son off at the school on the first day of term.' He paused dramatically. Theo imagined that boy arriving at a school like this after living in a tiny house. Imagined him tearfully saying goodbye to his parents as they left him in what might as well have been a foreign country, for all that he could go home. 'And that was the day that changed his life – my life – for ever.'

Theo felt a small jolt. They hadn't read that in their research about Trevor Thompson – he had been at Montgomery on a scholarship.

'I am certain that the list of achievements read out to you at the start of my speech would have been a lot shorter, had I never come to Montgomery School. In fact, I would never have given speeches. I would probably have got a handful of qualifications and, for want of any better ideas, followed my father down to the shipyard.'

Lord Thompson went on to describe some of his experiences at Montgomery, like learning to row on the river that ran through the school grounds and joining the Debate Society. He was painting a picture of an idyllic school life, one that he might never have had, had it not been for the scholarship programme.

'I was that boy in that tiny house, but there are other boys just like me, out there, waiting for their chance. Let's make sure they get it.'

Thompson encouraged them all to dig deep, to make pledges to the scholarship programme they were commencing in his name. Several students materialised out of nowhere and dispersed among the crowd, handing out pledge forms. Theo's dad took one and started filling out his details. Perhaps he did care.

Trevor thanked them and the crowd applauded again as he sidled off. The electric glow about him that had seemed to switch on when he took the stage switched abruptly off and he melted into the crowd and back into obscurity.

Theo was worried that he might be leaving straight away. Without any idea what he was going to do when he found him, Theo decided to follow.

'Just going to the toilet,' he said, as much to Andy as to his dad. They both nodded to release him.

Theo craned his head over the crowd and watched as Thompson headed back towards the house. He was unusually fast for an old man. He was like one of those tiny dogs that inexplicably hurtled everywhere. Theo jogged to catch up with him.

Thompson followed the path around the school building and turned into an alleyway that ran between what looked to be the gymnasium and the main building. He pushed through one of the doors into the main building and Theo saw that it was the men's bathroom. He hesitated. He couldn't follow Thompson in there – he could hardly stop him for a chat at the urinals.

As Theo dithered by the entrance to the alleyway, another door swung open so violently it banged against the wall with a crash. A very small boy hurled himself out of it. Instinctively, Theo shrunk back. He leant into a hedge at the corner of the building.

Before the boy had taken more than a few steps, two

boys much taller than the first – Theo guessed they were a few years older than him – had appeared through the door and pulled the boy back by his collar. The small boy fell backwards, neck first, with a cartoonish snap. One of the taller boys laughed as they both leered over him. When they straightened up, they had his backpack off him. One unzipped it and tipped it upside down over the small boy's head. A cascade of books and pens rained down on him.

Theo took a step forward. What were they playing at? Someone had to stop them.

The door to the school opened again and out came Rupert Spencer. He marched with authority on the boys.

Theo pressed himself back into the hedge, anxious not to be seen spying.

'We were just—' one of them began, as he bent to collect the boy's things from the ground.

Rupert yanked him roughly back up by the scruff of his neck. 'I know what you were doing. Do you want to jeopardise the reputation of the whole school?'

Theo had to hold back a whoop of victory. He felt a deep sense of satisfaction at the thought that Rupert would see justice served.

'Now,' Rupert continued, he still had the boy by the collar. He forced the boy round to face the smaller one, who seemed to be transfixed on the floor. 'Help him up and make yourself scarce.'

He released the boy, then scanned the area – perhaps himself wondering if there had been any witnesses. Theo retreated around the corner. He didn't want Rupert to know that he had seen everything and been too timid to intervene.

After a moment, he abandoned any hope of getting a

moment alone with Thompson. He could still hear Rupert speaking to the boys in the alley. When Thompson came out they would most likely still be there.

Theo turned back the way he had come. As he followed the path around the school, he wondered what Rupert was doing there. He strongly suspected that he had also attended the school. They seemed to churn out politicians here. He was surprised that Rupert had got in the middle of the action. Theo's teachers never touched students at his school. But didn't somebody have to? And, after all, Rupert wasn't a teacher. Thank goodness he had been there to protect the bullied boy.

Theo felt a stab of unease when he thought about that boy. He had been imagining the school as an idyll. Somewhere he could be free to be himself, without other students staring, jeering, mocking him. Somewhere he could find friends. Now he wondered if that was true.

It turned out there were gits everywhere.

CHAPTER TWENTY-FOUR

The Palace's Secrets

When Theo re-joined his dad, he was speaking to a teacher about his time at the school. He was telling the story of the time he was caught smoking on the roof by one of the masters, how his punishment had been to row the length of the lake every lunch break for two weeks. It was one of his favourite stories. Theo drifted away, to lean on the balustrade overlooking the gardens.

Andy kept one eye on him. 'Not too far, Theo.'

His dad had made his time at school sound perfect. Away from the critical eye of parents, he had had the freedom to get into trouble, to experiment and have fun. For the first time Theo wondered what else happened when adults left children to their own devices. He thought of *Lord of the Flies* – the boys alone on an island without adults and how they all turned on each other. If Rupert hadn't been there, what else would those boys have done to the younger one? What did they usually do?

'Are you all right?' his dad asked.

Theo turned to see that the teacher had left.

'Dad, was there ever any bullying when you were here?'

'Why do you ask?' His brow furrowed with concern. 'What has someone said to you?'

'No, I just—'

Someone else approached his dad then and he turned away.

Theo felt like he had his answer.

As they were leaving, they found Thompson in the entrance hall. Theo dreaded being approached by him with his dad there. What if Thompson mentioned their conversation in the Houses of Parliament? He sped up a little, hoping to get out without Thompson seeing him.

Thompson's gaze fell on them, unfaltering. He didn't look away. Theo's dad hesitated. Theo slowed down with him, looking between him and Thompson, his heart beating fast.

His dad stopped. 'Good speech today.'

'Thank you,' Thompson replied coldly. He watched Theo's dad calmly as if waiting for him to say something more. His dad seemed to feel this too.

'No hard feelings about the court case?' His dad twisted the ring on his little finger.

'What you're doing is wrong.'

His dad dropped his hand. 'Do you mean the mace or the Reform Bill?'

'You know exactly what I mean.'

'The court found in my favour, Trevor.'

Thompson nodded slowly, then he seemed to notice Theo. Theo fought against the colour rising in his cheeks. He wanted to tell his dad they should go, but he couldn't find his voice. Thompson nodded to him once and walked out.

The Palace's Secrets

As their car drove them back into London, Theo felt disappointed in himself for asking Thompson nothing. Although, he reasoned, he didn't know what he could have asked him. Whether he had stolen the mace? He certainly couldn't ask him what he thought of the House of Lords Reform Bill. That hadn't gone well the first time. He thought of Sammy striding straight up to Thompson at the Palace of Westminster. If only she could have come with him to Montgomery, she would have had a plan to get some information out of him. All Theo had found out was that it seemed as if Thompson had brought the legal challenge against using the Lords' mace in the Commons. And that he was a scholarship student. But he could have looked up both of those things online.

He thought back over everything Thompson had said and tried to imagine what it was like for him going to school at Montgomery. He must have felt like an outsider, like Theo did at Anderson. Perhaps they should have swapped places. Theo had always thought he wanted to go to Montgomery, as if that was where he was meant to be, before his life took a wrong turn. After today, he wasn't so sure.

His dad was typing on his phone, barely acknowledging that Theo was there. Theo wondered whether he had ever been pushed around by other kids. He couldn't imagine it. He had never seen anyone push his dad around. He thought of him signing the pledge form to donate to the scholarship fund and wondered again whether his dad cared about the kids on meal vouchers.

'Dad?' he said.

His dad looked up as if he was coming out of a dream. 'Yes?'

'Why are you cutting the budget for school meal vouchers?' His palms were prickling with nerves.

'We need to make cuts, there isn't enough money to pay for all the welfare commitments.'

'But why the vouchers? They're for children in poverty.'

'Sometimes difficult decisions have to be made.' His dad looked out of the window, as if that was the end of the conversation.

'I read this article in the newspaper this morning. They think the cuts are going to seriously impact the lives of young people.' When his dad said nothing, he ploughed on, 'There's this girl at my school, I've seen her using the meal vouchers—'

'Theo, drop it. I don't have time to explain the economy to you.'

Theo's stomach shrivelled.

'You'll understand when you're older,' his dad said, his voice softening.

That again, Theo thought. Everything seemed to come down to this now, with his dad. That he wasn't old enough, not clever enough. Yet when Theo tried to learn he felt squashed, shoved back into his place – like a child.

'I get it now,' Theo said. 'You'll donate money to a kid to go to a good school, to better themselves, but you won't help out the really poor ones because there's no help for them, is there?'

His dad's eyes boggled and he seemed on the verge of speech. He put his hand over his mouth and turned away. Theo looked out of his window and they sat in silence the rest of the way.

When they got home, he tried to do his homework.

The Palace's Secrets

After an hour wilting over the question of the nature of evil in *Macbeth*, he pushed his half-finished essay away. He glanced over the pile of *Bullseye* magazines next to his bed. It couldn't hurt to have a short break, just to clear his head.

He lay on the bed and shuffled through the pile until he found an old copy from a year ago that he didn't think he had read. He lay back to read.

Fifteen minutes later, Theo sat up suddenly. He held the magazine so tight, he crinkled its edges. He breathed heavily as he re-read the last article he had come across.

> This week it was reported that a lost passageway has been rediscovered in the Palace of Westminster. The passage, which historians knew of, but thought filled in during the building's Second World War renovations, had been hiding in plain sight for decades. It was uncovered as preparations began for next year's large-scale renovation project. Surveyors working on the project found a keyhole in wood panelling, which had always been assumed to open on to a broom cupboard. When the panel was opened, they found the passage, which dates back to the time of Charles II, when it was used for the monarch's coronation ceremony. The narrow corridor linked the House of Lords and Westminster Hall and was in use as recently as 1935. Plans are now underway to renovate the space and reconnect it with the main building.

Theo breathed heavily. This was it. There was a lost passageway in the Palace of Westminster. What if there were others that still remained undiscovered? What if the thief had found one and hidden the mace there? That would mean the mace had never left the palace. He realised the idea had been lurking somewhere in the back of his mind for a while. Why hadn't he realised before? He imagined a dark corridor and lying in the dust, the glittering mace.

He lunged for his phone on his bedside table, before remembering it wasn't there. His dad had taken it. He couldn't get in touch with Sammy. His parents had turned off the internet on his computer and he couldn't turn it back on without their permission.

Theo swore.

He jumped off his bed and began to pace. There had to be a way to find out if there were other passages. There must be maps of the palace somewhere. He had a sudden vivid memory of the architectural plans on Bob's desk in his office. Was Bob looking for passageways too? He must have access to every historical document about the palace. If he hadn't found anything, how could Theo? He was too energised by the possibilities to give up straight away.

He went into the living room and scanned the bookshelves against the wall. He had never paid much attention to his parents' books – they were old-fashioned volumes from the eighties with cover photos shot in such poor lighting that they looked like cartoons of themselves. They might have something on the Houses of Parliament. It was just the sort of boring book his dad would love.

'What are you doing?' Harry said, her voice dripping with scorn.

Theo had barely registered her when he came in. She had a pad and pen on her lap. She was taking down a recipe a celebrity chef was reciting on the television.

'You know they put all that information on the website for you.' He had no patience left for her today.

She turned cold and looked away.

The Palace's Secrets

Theo searched methodically through every book, starting in the top-left corner, working his way down.

Harry sighed. 'You're getting in the way of the TV.'

'If you help me, I'll be out of your way quicker.'

'What are you looking for?' A note of genuine curiosity crept into her voice.

'Something on the history of the Palace of Westminster – the building, I mean.'

'Everything political is in dad's study,' she said.

'It's not political, it's history,' Theo said, but Harry had already turned back to her programme.

He considered for a moment. She had a point. Although technically he wanted a history book, his dad might keep something like that with his politics books.

Theo went down the hall and peeked into his dad's study. He was still smarting from the memory of their argument in there the day before. His skin prickled with the shadow of his embarrassment.

He focused on the bookcase on the back wall. This time he was less methodical. He didn't think he would find what he was looking for in one of the smaller leather-bound volumes. He skipped over them and dropped to his knees to inspect the bottom shelf. Here were the large hardbacks. He ran his finger along their spines until his face broke into a smile. Bingo.

He pulled *The History of the Houses of Parliament* from the shelf. He laid it flat on the floor and flicked through every page. He paused at every illustration, hunting for a map.

Finally, he found one. But it was a map of the modern-day palace. He flicked on, until he had gone through the whole book. Nothing. He sat back on his heels, feeling dejected. A dead end. In desperation, he looked through the index to see if any other illustrations were listed that he might have missed. A name caught his eye. 'Barry, Charles.' The man his grandpa had been researching – the man who had designed parts of their house in Scotland.

Theo shuffled through the pages to find those on Charles Barry. He looked up from the page in astonishment. Charles Barry had rebuilt the Houses of Parliament in the 1800s after a fire destroyed most of the building.

He drew in his breath sharply.

The study door opened. His dad stopped on the threshold, surprised to see him. 'What have you got there?'

'A book,' Theo said, hastily getting to his feet. 'Can I borrow it for my homework?'

'Of course,' his dad said and he looked relieved.

Theo hurried out of the room, before his dad could question him any further. Back in his own room, he shut the door behind him and laid the book out carefully on the bed. His grandpa's notes were still in their pile next to his bed.

Carefully, he turned over each page. When Sammy had looked at them, she had said something about drawings. She thought they were of his house, but what if…? He didn't want to finish the thought. His heart was hammering against his ribcage.

Eventually he came to some drawings. He recognised the layout of the ground floor of the Glencoe house. Perhaps this was all there was. He kept turning the pages, there were still a few left.

He was down to the last handful of pages in the pile. Hope was slipping away like water through his fingers. He had to hold on. It had to be here.

He turned the page and there it was. Another drawing. He recognised this one too. But it wasn't the house in Glencoe.

Its lines were faint, soft pencil. It was so detailed he had to hold it up to his face to pick out the features. Central Lobby wasn't hard to find. He traced his finger up the corridor leading away from it, the corridor where the theft had happened.

He realised he wasn't breathing and let out a long breath. He read the cramped notes above the drawing.

> *Went to see Mortimer Barry today, descendent of CB and old school chum. Still has some of CB's original sketches. Let me copy them out. Fascinating to see how he worked. Not sure if they're accurate; to be checked against other sources.*

Theo followed his grandpa's advice.

Kneeling down next to the bed, he put the sketch next to the map of the modern-day palace in the book. In the sketch, there, leading away from the corridor where the mace had been stolen, was a tiny oblong with horizontal lines at the far end, indicating stairs.

Theo compared it to the map of the modern-day palace. The corridor wasn't on it.

Most of Sunday was agony for Theo. He was still grounded and he had no way of contacting Sammy. The knowledge of his discovery squirmed in his stomach, itching to get out. He wished he could tell someone. There was no point telling his dad. He could still remember his words two days before, *You shouldn't have got involved.* He had called Theo ridiculous. There was no way he would take him seriously now. Besides, Theo wasn't sure he wanted to share his discovery with his dad. If he was right, his dad would find the mace and get all the credit. The only way to prove him wrong now was for Theo to find the mace himself.

The family ate a tense lunch together. His mum tried to pretend everything was normal; Harry ignored him even more than usual and his dad was terse and preoccupied. He wolfed down his lunch before anyone else had finished.

'I've got to go back downstairs,' his dad said, getting up from the table. 'I've got Bob Piggott coming to see me. Will you be all right with clearing up?' he asked his wife.

Theo's mum pursed her lips but nodded. His dad kissed her on the forehead and swept out.

Theo helped clear up in silence. He kept watch out of the window, eager to see Bob when he arrived. He had started to have an idea. He saw a car pull up and Bob climbed out, a large artist's style case on one shoulder. He disappeared into the house.

Theo balanced as many plates as he could on his arm and took them into the kitchen.

'Is it all right if I go downstairs?' he asked his mum.

She was soothing a crying Milly on her hip and looked around, still distracted. 'What for?'

'Bit of fresh air. I'll just be in the garden.'

'Yes, all right.'

Theo dashed out of the room before she could change her mind. 'Don't be long!' she called after him.

Theo shut the front door quietly and rushed down the stairs. He didn't want to miss Bob before he left. He skidded down the tiled floors to his dad's office and came to a stop, panting outside his door. It was shut firm. Theo could just hear murmuring on the other side.

He looked through the door to the next room – the adjoining office where his dad's assistants worked. The room was unusually empty. Even at weekends, some staff worked here, but whoever was supposed to be there must have just stepped out.

Theo crept into the room and up to the door to his dad's office. It wasn't as thick as the one onto the main corridor.

'... need more time. We're still looking through the plans of the palace.' Theo recognised Bob's distinctive voice.

'Have you found any areas that we aren't already aware of?' his dad asked.

'Not yet, but if we could have another week—'

'Renovations must resume by Tuesday,' his dad interrupted. 'And I want the mace back by the end of the week.'

There was an ominous silence.

'If it isn't found by then, heads will roll. Security is your responsibility, Bob. Don't let me down.'

'Yes, Prime Minister.'

There was the sound of chairs scraping and Theo tiptoed quietly back out of the office, just in time to see his father's main office door open.

'Theo! What are you doing here?' his dad said.

'Just stretching my legs,' he said.

'Go on outside then.'

Theo walked towards the doors out onto the garden. He hung back as long as he could, listening as his dad said goodbye to Bob. When he heard the sound of the office door closing again, he whipped back around. Bob was

The Palace's Secrets

watching him with a gentle smile.

'Is there something you're wanting to say to me, Theo?' he said softly. He had the artist's folder that Theo had seen him arrive with still on his shoulder. Theo wondered whether he might have brought the palace plans to show his dad.

'How's your head?' Theo asked, coming back into the corridor.

Bob touched the spot. 'It were a nasty bump, but I'm fine.'

He waited patiently while Theo got up the courage to say what was on his mind.

'I've been thinking about what might have happened to the mace.' He hesitated.

'Go on.'

'There are parts of the palace that have been lost, aren't there? Like that passageway that was found last year.' He tried to keep the colour from rising to his face. There was no time now to be embarrassed. Either Bob believed him or he didn't.

Bob's eyebrows rose. 'There are some,' he said, very serious now.

His heart beating very fast, Theo said, 'There might be others that we still don't know about. But Charles Barry, the architect, might have known about—'

'Theo.'

Theo jumped.

'I didn't expect to see you here,' Rupert said. He had come around the corner into the corridor so silently, Theo hadn't heard him.

His beating heart slowed.

'I was just asking Bob if he felt better now.' Theo lied

instinctively. He felt foolish as soon as he had done it. Rupert had never laughed at his theories. But he couldn't take it back.

'I'm much obliged to you, Theo,' Bob said seriously. 'I hope I'll see you again soon.'

Theo opened his mouth to stop Bob from going. He hadn't told him everything he had meant to. But Bob was hurrying away. Maybe Theo had said enough and Bob was eager to consult his plans.

With a nod to Rupert, Bob left.

'That looked very serious,' Rupert said with a genial smile.

'I was worried he might still be unwell,' Theo said weakly. He considered Rupert for a moment. He wondered if he should warn him about the photos he had found on Felix's hard drive. Perhaps Rupert should know he was being watched. But how would he explain how he got the photos? He had a feeling Rupert wouldn't mind his unconventional methods. Rupert seemed to have those himself.

He had hesitated too long. The door to his dad's office opened.

'Rupert,' his dad said and stopped. 'I thought you were going outside,' he said to Theo.

'I did. I'm just going back upstairs.'

There was no time to linger. His dad waited in his doorway until Theo disappeared up the staircase.

CHAPTER TWENTY-FIVE

Sneaking Past Security

A car horn blared. Theo had tried to jog across the road in front of oncoming vehicles, but he hadn't been quick enough.

'Theo!' his sister yelled from behind him. She hadn't joined him in his mad dash.

He put up his hand to apologise to the driver, saying, 'Sorry!' even as he knew he couldn't hear him.

Harry had taken even longer than usual in the bathroom that morning. He had hurried her along for most of the way to school. The fact that she could tell he was desperate to get there had only made her walk slower. Theo wanted to get in early, to find Sammy in her form room and tell her everything before school began.

He jumped down the front steps and shoved through the ancient front door. He slowed down on the ground floor when Mr Shaw told him off for running. As soon as he was out of sight, he dashed up the stairs to the History corridor.

He found Sammy doodling in a notebook while the rest

of the class chatted loudly. He shot over to her table and swung his bag down with a thunk.

'I think I might know where the mace is,' he said.

At the same time, a girl called from across the room, 'Having a date with your girlfriend, Theo?' She and her friends shrieked with laughter.

'Sod off!' Sammy said and put her bag on the floor so Theo could sit next to her. 'What do you mean?' she whispered.

Theo quickly explained as much of the weekend as he could. It was eight twenty-five; the bell would ring for registration in five minutes.

'Are you sure the passageway is still there?' Sammy asked when Theo had finished. 'It could have been filled in or something.'

'I can't be sure. Not without actually checking it out.'

Sammy said, 'Hmm,' and picked at her navy-blue nail polish.

Theo was distracted by the girl and her friends whispering behind their hands on the other side of the room. Their eyes kept flitting his way.

'What do you think?' Theo said. It was only worth enduring the teasing if he found out what Sammy thought they should do. He had an idea, but he didn't think he could suggest it. It was too out there. Sammy might think he was mad. Maybe she would have a better idea, something clever that he couldn't think of.

'They're going to move it,' she said finally.

'What?' he said, surprised out of his thoughts.

'Felix, Lord Thompson, whoever it is. They're going to move the mace.' She pushed her newspaper towards him.

'The House of Commons is opening again today and the vote on the Reform Bill is going ahead. If we're right, and they were trying to stop the vote, then keeping the mace now is pointless. If they don't move it, it might be found and traced back to them. The vote is the perfect cover for moving the mace, everyone will be looking the other way. I think they're going to move it and we better get there first.'

'Really?' Theo's hopes rose. She was suggesting exactly what he had been thinking – that they had to get the mace, now.

'We'll go today after school. We'll have to queue up with the public and go in that way. We can't risk telling Rupert or Bob or anyone, in case they figure out what we're really doing.'

'No,' Theo said, his heart pounding.

'Do we have *any* idea who it is?'

'It can't have been Chris. We've ruled out Ruth and I believe Erin when she says it wasn't her. That leaves Felix and Lord Thompson. It must be one of them.'

'And they're not exactly spring chickens. I reckon we could take them if we had to.'

Theo was struck by the absurdity of the image of him or Sammy fighting Felix.

The bell rang and he got up to go to his form room.

'Wait.' Sammy put her hand on his arm.

Theo tried to ignore the sniggering that was growing behind him.

'You're grounded, Theo. You could get into a lot of trouble.' Her eyes creased in concern.

He patted her hand, still on his arm. 'So could you.' He swung his bag up onto his shoulder and walked out, the sound of jeering ringing in his ears.

Sneaking Past Security

*

Theo followed Sammy across Parliament Square towards the Palace of Westminster. He had never gone in this way, through the public entrance. The afternoon sun was low behind their backs, but bright. The palace's many windows reflected it back at them, twinkling like gemstones. Its sandstone bricks glowed rich gold; the freshly cleaned surface of Big Ben's clock face gleamed sapphire and gold.

They hurried along the road to the visitor's entrance, but they needn't have bothered. There was no queue. He supposed only tourists came in this way and they must have come and gone by now. It was nearly four o'clock; the visitor's entrance would be closing in an hour.

Sammy stopped at the tail end of the snake of queue barriers.

'What if someone recognises you?'

Theo's stomach crunched. 'Yeah, I know.'

'We should have brought you a hat or something.'

'And a fake moustache? I think we've just got to risk it.' Theo couldn't believe what he was saying. His stomach was doing somersaults like it was auditioning to join Cirque du Soleil. But every time he thought about turning around to go back, he remembered the mace and that this might be the last opportunity they would get to find it.

Sammy rocked on her heels. 'Have we gone mad? Is this totally mad?'

The woman manning the security station was watching them with curiosity.

'Yes,' Theo said.

Sammy seemed to be reassured by his honesty. 'OK.'

Sneaking Past Security

She turned to start down the empty queue.

'Wait, let's turn our phones off. My mum will start ringing soon, when Harry calls her to say I haven't come out of school.' He had run out of the gates as quickly as he could after school. He felt bad about leaving his sister waiting there for him, but he didn't suppose she would worry very much. His mum on the other hand…

Sammy nodded. As she took out her phone, Theo stared at his blank screen. His mum would be both furious and terrified when she couldn't get hold of him. Perhaps he should send her a message now, just to say that he was all right. He opened up his messages and hovered over the text box. He couldn't think what to say. If he lied about where he was and she found out later, he would be in even bigger trouble. Quickly, before he could change his mind, he switched the phone off and stowed it away in his backpack.

'Ready?' he said.

Sammy set off towards the woman on security and he followed.

The woman, who was young and frumpy, looked at them sharply as she said, 'What can I do for you today?'

'We want to go into the House of Commons gallery,' Sammy said, while Theo avoided eye contact with the security woman.

'You won't get in there today. There's a big vote on.'

'We don't mind waiting for someone to leave.'

The woman handed over two green laminated cards. 'You haven't got long. We're closing up soon.'

Theo mumbled his thanks and made for the security hut. It was also empty, apart from one guard who instructed them to put their bags through the airport-style x-ray machine. Theo swooped his bag off the tray on the other side and strode out into the open square of New Palace Yard. He scanned the lawn while he waited for Sammy to catch up. His eyes caught a familiar face. Rupert.

Theo turned away quickly, his heart hammering. After a few seconds, he checked carefully over his shoulder to see whether Rupert had spotted him. He was moving purposefully towards the entrance of Westminster Hall, his strides long and quick, a sports bag swinging from his shoulder. Theo kept his head down as Rupert swept inside.

Sammy came up beside him. 'Come on,' she said.

'Wait. I've just seen Rupert. We better not run into him.'

He tried to count slowly to twenty in his head. He lost track around twelve, distracted by Sammy's nervous bobbing on the spot.

'Let's go,' he said and then headed into Westminster Hall.

It wasn't much warmer inside than out. The air was musty and cool, like cave air. The hall looked like a great empty church, with stone floors and walls. At the far end, steps led up to a massive stained-glass window. The soaring arched timber-framed roof reminded Theo of an upside down ark.

A warden asked where they were going and directed them into the next corridor, to wait for their turn in the gallery. They hurried across the flagstones. Theo's palms were beginning to sweat. He recognised a few faces – people who worked with his dad. Any one of them might notice him and ask what on earth he was doing there.

The entrance to the corridor off Central Lobby was guarded by police. They wouldn't be able to get to the hidden corridor if they didn't get past them. Sammy had devised a plan for this at lunchtime. It had made Theo nervous just listening to it. Now they were here, his whole body seemed to be shaking in anticipation. There were so many ways it could go wrong.

'Hold on,' Theo said, as they reached the top of the dais in Westminster Hall. The door to St Stephen's Hall was directly ahead of them. They weren't moving that fast, but he suddenly felt out of breath. 'Just wait a second.'

Sammy watched him with concern, while he clutched his sides, trying to get his breath back.

'It'll be all right,' Sammy said. 'If anyone gets into trouble, it will be me.'

'That doesn't make me feel any better.'

'Well it should. If something goes wrong, you just slip away and go home. No one will ever know you had anything to do with this.'

Theo considered this for a moment. She was right. He could get out any time. He could turn back now. But Sammy was offering to get herself into trouble, to take all the blame. Theo knew, deep down, that if he got into trouble his dad would find a way to hush it up. He would be grounded for the rest of his life, but he would still have a life. Sammy had no one to protect her like that.

'This is a bad idea, you shouldn't be doing this. I should be the one to do it,' he said.

'We've been over this. Someone might recognise you. It's got to be me.'

Theo shook his head. 'I don't like it.'

'Get over it.'

Sammy walked towards the door into St Stephen's Hall. She picked up the pace, pushing through the door. Theo had to jog to keep up. On the other side of it, he could see Sammy up ahead, running full pelt now.

'Help!' she shouted. 'Help! He's got a gun!'

People turned to stare. Even though he was prepared for this moment, Theo felt his mood shift with the atmosphere in the hall. A hum of electricity seemed to vibrate through the air. It was fear. And it was contagious.

Suddenly people were running, shouting. A woman bumped into Theo in her rush to get out the way he had come.

Theo could feel his heart pounding in his head and his feet and his stomach. He ran against the stream of people, straight ahead, out of St Stephen's Hall and into Central Lobby. The corridor with the hidden passageway was just ahead.

The police at the entrance were speaking into their walkie-talkies.

Theo slowed. He walked calmly straight past Sammy, who was doing a very good performance of hyperventilating. One of the two police officers on the corridor jogged over to her, as others joined from other directions.

'There was a man, with a gun,' Sammy said between gasps.

The remaining police officer on the entrance to the corridor was trying to hold back civilians who had just arrived. He didn't notice Theo getting closer.

'There he is!' Sammy suddenly exclaimed, pointing back down St Stephen's Hall.

For just a second, everybody looked that way.

Theo slipped past the police officer. Nobody took any notice of him. He scanned the walls. He didn't have more than thirty seconds before the chaos would die down and somebody would take charge. They were bound to see him then.

Like St Stephen's Hall, the wall was lined with statues. The opening had to be here. It must be easy enough to open. The thief had done it within seconds. He searched as quickly as he could. The statutes were all men in robes, carrying scrolls; or men in armour with shields and swords. Theo's eye was caught by a woman – the only one in the corridor. Her plaque read 'Elizabeth Fry'. Just behind her, tucked out of sight, there was what looked like a cupboard door, only half his height. No wonder no one had found it before. With the statue directly in front, it would be impossible to open the door more than a slither.

Theo hooked his finger through the tiny key hole and pulled. The door scraped along the floor. It opened just a fraction. He kept pulling until it was wide enough for him to look through.

He couldn't see anything in the gloom. He could only smell damp stone and dust. This must be it.

He looked back for Sammy. He couldn't see her. Just a cluster of police officers. No one was looking his way.

Holding the door open as wide as possible, he squeezed inside. Now he just needed to wait for Sammy. He had no idea how she was going to get away. He wished he had some of the gas canisters the thief had used, but then, he thought, he would never have got them through the x-ray machines at the palace entrance.

Tentatively, Theo peered out of his hiding place.

Sammy was still in Central Lobby. There were two police officers with her and one member of palace staff. Any moment now, Bob Piggott would be there. Theo had a feeling he wouldn't be quite so convinced by Sammy's story as the others. And he was pretty certain she had been forced to give them a false name by now, which Bob would discover immediately. Theo had to get her away.

He wracked his brains. He wanted a distraction, so that Sammy could slip away. He had nothing with him that would help. An idea flashed through his mind and he shoved it away, too afraid to consider it. But he had no time. Any moment now Sammy was going to be found out. Was it a crime to lie to the police? Was it wasting police time or something?

He shook himself. There was no time. It was the only idea he had and he would have to make it work.

Theo shrugged out of his school blazer and pulled his jumper over his head. He smoothed his hair back down and steeled himself for just a second.

He peeked back out at the corridor. The palace staff member had disappeared; there were only two people left with Sammy. Good. Just two police officers – a man and a woman. No one was looking his way. He closed his eyes and imagined he was his dad. When he opened them again, he was ready.

He plunged out, drawing himself to his full height.

'What the bloody hell is going on here?' he boomed, drawing the attention of the police officers. The volume of his voice echoing off the almost-empty chamber shocked even him, but he tried not to let his alarm show. 'I'm Theo Duncan, I'm working for my dad, William Duncan, and he wants to know what on earth is happening.'

The male police officer put up a placatory hand. 'Sir,

everything is under control.'

Theo wondered at the man calling him 'sir'. He didn't seem to know he was only a teenager.

'It doesn't look it.' Theo carried on walking into St Stephen's Hall, drawing the gaze of the two adults with him. The man ran to stop him.

'You can't go down there,' he said, desperate to stop Theo.

'Is this the direction the shooter went?' Theo asked, dodging around the man. The woman had followed them now.

Theo didn't dare look over his shoulder. He prayed silently that Sammy was making a run for it.

'We don't know there's a shooter yet, sir.'

'What the hell do you know?' Theo said. A little voice in his head was very worried about how rude he was being. But apart from the crippling fear of being called out at any moment, he was almost enjoying himself. It was quite freeing saying whatever he wanted.

Both of the officers tried to tell him what had happened. At one point he thought the woman was going to look back to Sammy, so he diverted them with a barrage of abuse about how angry his father was and how he would want to speak to their superiors.

Finally, he ran out of steam and turned to get away.

'She's gone!' the woman exclaimed, turning to look at Theo with suspicion.

'This is a shambles!' Theo shouted. 'I don't have time to deal with your incompetence. I've got better things to do. Find that shooter,' he shot over his shoulder as he strode back down the corridor towards the hidden door.

Sneaking Past Security

He kept looking back as he approached the statue of Elizabeth Fry. The two officers looked thoroughly lost. Four police officers poured in from the door ahead of him, heading right his way.

'Over there,' Theo said, still booming as authoritatively as he could. 'They need all the help they can get.'

He dawdled as the police officers rushed past him. Finally, the coast was clear and he slipped inside the hidden door.

Sammy squealed and wrapped her arms tightly around him. 'You did it, Theo! You did it.'

'We did it,' Theo said, extracting himself. Hastily, he closed the door, shutting out the sound of running feet on the other side.

'I didn't know you had it in you.'

'I knew you could do it,' he said.

CHAPTER TWENTY-SIX

In the Bowels of the Palace

'How did you get rid of that palace official?' Theo asked, now certain that Sammy had somehow engineered it.

'Said I was diabetic and having a sugar crash. He went to get me a chocolate bar.'

Theo shook his head. 'I would never be able to pull that off.'

'You just did.'

He let that sink in for a minute. He really had. For the time being at least. No doubt his dad was being told at that moment what had happened. How long would it be before they realised it was him and Sammy behind it all? It didn't matter. No one was going to find him, not in here. He just had to hope that they found the mace. Surely he wouldn't be in trouble then.

He looked around at the corridor they were in. There was no light – no windows – just a dim dusk at the other end of the corridor where the shadows weren't so thick.

Theo didn't dare turn his phone on to see by.

'Let's use my phone.' Sammy seemed to guess his thoughts.

In the Bowels of the Palace

As the phone turned on, it lit up Sammy's face. Even in that eerie light, she didn't look scary. Wisps of hair that had escaped from her ponytail fell gently around her face. She had a look of concentration as she turned on her torch that was somehow as heart-warming as those videos of cats and dogs that were lifelong friends.

She gasped. 'Look!' she said. She shone the torch on the wall, close to.

There was a statue protruding out. In the dark she must have thought she saw an actual person. She moved the torchlight over the space, picking out other forms. There were six statues in all – three men, three women – all dressed in medieval clothes, opposite one another. The men were knights in armour, two standing, one kneeling with his head bent. The one kneeling seemed to be kneeling to the woman opposite, whose hand was outstretched as if she were blessing him across the divide.

'Beautiful,' Sammy breathed.

The stonework wasn't very different from that on the other side of the door – grey slabs that looked like they had been there for hundreds of years. But here there was a thick layer of dust over everything. They could see it in the air, floating past the beam of light from the phone. Where the walls met the ceiling there were thick cobwebs.

There must have been a leak from somewhere above, because the ceiling was stained with damp patches and Theo could smell it. It reminded him of a flooded mine they had visited in the Peak District on a family holiday. They had gone on a boat through the underground tunnels. It had been very claustrophobic. Despite the large, empty space, Theo felt the same feeling again – that he was pressed in on all sides, no way out.

'Let's find the mace,' he said, suppressing a shiver, 'they probably left it right by the door.'

With only one light between them, they had to huddle together to search. They shone the light along the walls either side of them for the full length of the corridor. They kneeled at the bottom of each statue, checking the recesses of their plinths to make sure nothing was hidden there. Theo ran his fingers over the statues; the cool stone was reassuringly real in that forgotten chamber. Very quickly his hands were thick with dust that smeared stickily with his sweat.

There was nothing there. The mace was huge; they were hardly likely to miss it.

As she reached the door at the other end of the corridor, Sammy waited for him. She shone the phone light in his face as he straightened back up from his search of the floor.

'It's not here,' she said.

'I know,' Theo replied, feeling irritable.

'Maybe they didn't put it in here,' Sammy said. Theo said nothing. 'It looks like we're the only people who have come in here for centuries.'

'It's got to be here.'

He leant on the door handle of the door for support. It was strangely dry after the damp dust of the walls.

'Wait a moment,' he said and guided the phone in Sammy's hand towards the door handle. He bent to look closer. The handle had been wiped clean before he had touched it. Someone had used it.

His eyes locked with Sammy's. She had seen it too.

In the Bowels of the Palace

'All right,' she said.

He turned the handle and with a soft creak the door swung open to reveal a set of stairs disappearing down into the dark.

'Where do you think it goes?' Sammy whispered.

'Dunno,' Theo whispered back. He didn't know why they were whispering. He couldn't hear any police now. There wasn't a hint of the commotion that might still be going on in the rest of the palace.

But the darkness down the stairs was so thick it was like a black hole. Theo was afraid his voice would disappear down into it and never come back. He wondered whether they should turn back. They had found the hiding place, he was sure of it. He didn't need to find the actual mace. He only needed to go back and tell someone – Bob Piggott probably, he would be the best person – where the hidden passageway was. It should be the police, really, who came to recover the mace.

From out of the gloom a deep clang reverberated through the air – the sound of metal on metal. The hairs on the back of Theo's neck lifted. Perhaps the thief was down there. They might be moving the mace at that very moment.

He could sense Sammy was waiting for him to make a decision. She would probably keep going. She wasn't afraid of anything. But she knew he was. She would let him decide whether they should keep going.

Theo took a step onto the first stair.

Sammy's hand shot out and held him back. 'Do you think it's safe? The stairs might be rotten or something.'

'The thief did it, didn't he?'

In the Bowels of the Palace

Theo moved on to the next step. He went slowly, getting both feet on one step before testing his weight on the next. Sammy followed, only one step behind. The stairs creaked, but they felt sound.

At the bottom they found themselves in a service tunnel, with pipes as thick as great tree trunks running along the walls and ceiling. They must have carried the palace's hot water, because the heat was oppressive.

'Are you OK?' Theo asked, feeling suddenly as if he should check. He thought of the knight in the last room, kneeling to his companion. He would have checked.

Sammy nodded. 'Let's keep going.' She sounded braver than he felt and this solidified his resolve.

Just as he was about to set off, there was a crash up ahead.

Sammy jumped and grabbed Theo's arm. His heart leapt against his ribcage.

'What was that?' she said, her eyes wide in the torchlight.

'I don't know.'

They listened in silence, but there were no other sounds. It occurred to Theo that if they could hear someone else down there, then that someone might hear them too. His own breathing sounded loud in his ears. He tried to keep it as shallow as possible.

His heart returning to a more normal speed, Theo began creeping down the tunnel. The water in the pipes made a distant whispering sound, as though ghosts were trying to speak to them from a far-gone age. He was clammy with heat, sweat prickling under his collar. The air felt thick and heavy. He wanted to cough the dust out of his throat, but he didn't dare make a sound.

In the Bowels of the Palace

Out of the darkness, Sammy's hand found his and he took it gratefully. He was relieved to discover that her palm was as sweaty as his. She swept the light left and right in front of their feet, checking for any sign of the mace. But the floor was empty.

Just up ahead there was another staircase, stretching up above their heads. Theo hurried towards it. He didn't like the tunnel. The corridor had at least been guarded by the ladies and knights. The tunnel was too empty.

They shuffled one step at a time up the staircase, still clutching fearfully at one another.

'Theo!' Sammy said.

At the same time Theo hit his head against something above him. 'Ow!'

'There's a door there,' Sammy continued.

'Thanks.' He rubbed the sore spot on the top of his head.

There was a trapdoor over the top of the staircase. He let go of Sammy's hand and pushed gently against it. There was something on top of the door. Theo felt its weight sliding away as he opened. He let the door close again.

'The thief might be up there,' he whispered. 'When I open the door, whatever is on there is going to topple off and, if he's there, he's going to know that we're here.'

Sammy looked frightened, but the gleam of mischief was back in her eye. 'We're going to catch him.'

'Only if he doesn't have enough time to get away. Are you ready?'

Sammy nodded.

Theo pushed with all his might against the trapdoor. It flipped open and, with a loud crash, landed on the floor of the room above.

In the Bowels of the Palace

As Theo climbed upwards, he realised it wasn't a room, so much as a cupboard. There were paint brushes, stacks of masking tape, used scraps of sandpaper. Several paint pots, which must have been resting on the trapdoor, had been turned on their sides.

Theo threw himself against the door, Sammy hot at his heels. It burst open and they both tumbled out on to the floor. Theo found himself staring at a pair of familiar, dirty old trainers.

'I thought it would be you.'

Theo looked up. 'I didn't think it would be you,' he said.

CHAPTER TWENTY-SEVEN

A Treacherous Thief

Theo clambered to his feet. They were in a high-ceilinged room hung with plastic sheets. Paint-stained dust sheets flapped over doorways into adjoining rooms to the right and left. Metal scaffolding lined the walls, discarded overalls were piled in one corner. The space was cold and naked, like a corpse.

Rupert Spencer was wearing tracksuit bottoms and an old t-shirt. At his feet was the sports bag Theo had seen him with earlier. He realised it was the same one he had seen in Rupert's office on the day of the theft. Sweat was pricking from Rupert's forehead. There was a mark on his shoulder where the strap of the sports bag had dug in.

It couldn't be. Theo couldn't understand. Rupert couldn't be the thief. It was his job to get MPs to vote with the government. He remembered the photos on Felix's hard drive. With a sinking feeling, he realised they might not be photos of Rupert persuading MPs to vote with the government. They could be photos of him persuading people to vote against it.

A Treacherous Thief

He searched through his memory for any clue, any indication that it had been Rupert. He drew a blank.

'But I thought it was Trevor,' was all Theo could think to say. 'Trevor Thompson.'

'What teacher's pet Thompson? He's been secretly campaigning to persuade the Lords to put the Bill through. Sucking up to Duncan, just like always.'

Thinking of their conversation at Montgomery a few days before, Theo said, 'My dad doesn't even know that Thompson is in favour of the Bill.'

'When it goes through, he'll make sure he gets the credit.'

Theo couldn't understand it at all. To hear him, it sounded like Rupert and Trevor had been at school together – teacher's pet Thompson sounded like a school nickname – but that couldn't be. Trevor was so much older.

'It was you,' Theo said. 'You took the mace.'

Rupert laughed. Disturbingly he seemed genuinely amused.

Theo thought quickly. 'You were there straight after the theft. You hid the mace in the passageway and then came out this way and ran back round to be one of the first on the scene. You must have retrieved the clothes you had worn later, then you left them in your office.' His eyes fell on the sports bag. When he had last seen it, it had been with a paint-smeared t-shirt. He looked around at the fresh paint on the walls. Too late, he remembered Hannah in the pub saying that Rupert had never done his own DIY. How had he missed it? 'Where I nearly sat on them. *You* told me Thompson didn't want the Bill to go through. You deliberately sent me on a wild goose chase.' And with that, Theo's heart plummeted. Because if Rupert had known to distract him, he must have known that Theo was investigating the theft. He had just admitted as much; he had known it would be them to find him. Had others realised? Had he so miserably failed to hide his efforts? 'How did you know?' Theo croaked. 'How did you know I was investigating the theft?'

'I told you it was my job to think like the opposition. I must say it was obvious from the start. Wanting a tour days after the theft, your friend disappearing as soon as you arrived. It wasn't very subtle, I'm afraid to say.' Rupert took a confident step towards them. Theo took one step back. Why wasn't Rupert backing down? They had him cornered, shouldn't he be worried?

'You were on the phone to Felix. I saw you answer the phone that day outside my dad's office.'

'What are you talking about?' Rupert looked annoyed and Theo started to feel nervous about what he might do. He remembered Rupert at Gommers, grabbing that bully by the scruff of his neck. He was holding himself in the same manner now, standing tall, firm. He looked powerful. Theo realised he didn't know what Rupert might do, what he was capable of. He was frightened of him. Of course Rupert wouldn't back down in the face of two frightened school children.

'Felix wanted a peerage in exchange for helping you. Did you think you could persuade my dad to give him one?'

'Of course. He's done it for others when I've told him to.'

'That wasn't very clever,' Sammy said. 'You're in trouble now, because Felix has been collecting evidence on you. Everyone is going to know it was you.'

A Treacherous Thief

She had a good point, but Theo wished she hadn't said it. Rupert looked angrier now and Theo was strangely alert to the fact that no one knew where they were. He tried to shuffle in front of Sammy.

'I'm in trouble. What about you? What on earth will your father say, Theo?' He moved towards them again and Theo tried discreetly to move away. 'It's your word against mine that I took the mace. I could say you did it. Leave you here, to be found with the mace. All this chaos, caused by the Prime Minister's own son. The papers will be full of it. His head will be on the chopping block after this.'

'We've caught you in the act, you won't get away with it,' Sammy spat.

Rupert smirked. 'Who would believe you over me? I'm going to walk straight out of here and no one will be any the wiser.'

Theo could see that he was right. Who would believe them if they said that Rupert had been the thief? He had to keep Rupert talking, to give himself time to think. He had to keep him there as long as possible. Could Sammy get away? Get help?

'Why did you do it?' Theo asked.

'Haven't you worked that out? I thought you were doing so well. Not many people overestimate your abilities, I imagine. This must be a new experience for you.'

Theo had that familiar squeezing feeling in his chest, compressing the breath out of him. He pushed against it. He couldn't afford to hesitate now.

'You... you want to stop the Reform Bill from going through.'

Rupert inched towards them and Theo inched away.

'Of course, I told you the first time we met that was why the thief took the mace.'

'You told me you wanted it to go through.'

'Never trust a politician, Theo. Hasn't your father taught you that by now?'

They traced an invisible circle between them. Theo kept Sammy behind him, shuffling her along with him as he moved.

'But how could you do this? You *stole* the mace.'

'I didn't. It never left the palace. There's no crime in that.'

'Oh come off it,' Sammy said.

Theo angled himself further in front of her. He wished he hadn't brought her with him. What a stupid idea! He should never have put her in danger.

'You're a hypocrite,' Theo said. He spied the two doorways leading from the room. If they could just get through one of them. He shoved Sammy a little towards one. 'Everything you told me about how politicians should vote with their conscience. It was all rubbish. You're the worst of the lot. You pretended to be on my dad's side and all the time you were lying. You never believed in any of it.'

'I never voted for this. I fought for what I believe in – this great institution. The House of Lords goes back to the medieval period, when a council of bishops and noblemen advised the king. That's survived all this time and now your father is trampling all over it. Your father, who believes in none of these reforms. Have you ever asked him, Theo, whether he agrees with the reforms he's campaigning for?'

'Why would he create this Bill if he doesn't agree with it?'

'For the same reason every other politician does. For the votes.'

Theo remembered the conversation he had overheard between his dad and Chris Elliot. He had been so interested in Chris and whether he was the thief, he hadn't thought about what his dad had said at the time. He had said if they didn't put the Reform Bill through they would lose the next election.

Theo's stomach dropped. Was his dad a hypocrite?

'You know it really, don't you, Theo? Your father is a phoney. He believes in the tradition of this palace as much as I do, but he's too much of a coward to fight for it. I told him we should stand firm. The country needs leadership. If we had campaigned to protect the House of Lords, those sheep would have followed us on polling day.

'Tell me, Theo, who do you think is worse: the man who does something criminal to stand up for what he believes in or the man who gives up his principles just to be a good law-abiding citizen?'

They had come full circle – the doorways within a few steps. He needed to distract Rupert long enough to get to one.

'I believe in fighting for your principles out in the open, campaigning and changing people's minds, not getting your own way by… by stealth and… breaking the law.' The fire Theo had felt the first time he and Rupert had discussed this came back tenfold.

'A boy's answer. You're still so naïve.'

'He's not,' Sammy shouted. 'He's right and you're just old and bitter, because nobody agrees with you. You knew there was no way you could win by playing fair.'

'Keep your voice down, you stupid girl.' Rupert advanced towards them.

'Run!' Theo shouted and Sammy shot off.

Theo instinctively went the opposite direction, hoping to draw Rupert with him.

He swept through the dust sheet covering the doorway ahead. He choked on dust that fell into his eyes. There were footsteps behind him, following him.

'Theo!' Rupert said, his voice menacing.

Theo spotted paint tins on the floor. He snatched them up. From the weight of them he could tell they were empty – not much of a weapon, but the best he had. He threw one at Rupert, who ducked.

He ran faster, dodging a builder's table. The door at the other end of the room was closed. Was it locked?

Theo stopped and threw another paint tin at Rupert. Still looking behind him, he tripped and went crashing to the ground. He expected hands around his neck at any moment, but none came.

He wiped his eyes and sat up. He could hear soft footsteps somewhere, but the room was empty.

Rupert had gone after Sammy.

Theo winced as he levered himself up from his knees. He crept back to the doorway. He pulled the dust sheet back just a fraction and looked through. The room beyond was empty.

'You can't run for ever.' Rupert's voice floated through the deserted rooms.

Theo heard tins rolling, something falling to the floor.

He crept back into the first room, towards the doorway to the next room. His heart was thumping. He calculated

A Treacherous Thief

his chances. He was tall, but Rupert was taller. He played rugby, badly. Rupert looked like he was in good shape. The odds weren't good. But he had no choice, he couldn't let Rupert hurt Sammy. He had to distract him long enough for Sammy to get away, back through the trapdoor.

There was a commotion in the next room – banging. Rupert might have got hold of Sammy. If he had, she wasn't making a sound. Theo didn't want to imagine what that might mean.

He found a gap in the dust sheet and looked into the next room. He put a hand over his mouth to muffle his gasp.

The room, more like a hall, was cavernous. And it went even deeper than its ceiling was high, because there was a gaping hole stretching the width of the floor. Floorboards jutted across the hole like the last remaining teeth in a skull. The abyss beneath was black, only the occasional glint of steel giving any hint that there was a bottom to it. As Theo's eyes adjusted to the gloom he picked out the shapes of the palace's pipes. It was like it had been turned inside out, its guts opened to the light.

Across the hole, a builder's steel ladder stretched from one side of it to the other.

Sammy was on her hands and knees trying to cross it.

Rupert waited at this end of it, watching her. Theo didn't know what for. Was he too scared to cross it? Then he knelt down and rattled the ladder. Sammy whimpered and clung on; Theo could see her quivering. He wanted to call to her – she couldn't see him – to reassure her. But his only advantage now was the element of surprise.

Theo's palms were sweating and he could feel sweat

A Treacherous Thief

creeping down his forehead. There was no time to hesitate. He had to stop Rupert before he hurt Sammy.

He looked behind him and caught sight of a piece of wooden scaffolding lying on the floor. It had a metal bracket on the end. Theo put that end in his hand. He didn't want to do Rupert any serious damage. He crept into the room where Rupert was still watching Sammy's slow progress across the makeshift bridge.

As he crept up behind him, he thought of what his dad would say if he injured a Cabinet Minister. *We can't afford to make mistakes.* What if he really hurt Rupert? What if he didn't wake up after he hit him? He didn't know if he could hurt an unarmed man who had his back turned.

Sweat was dripping into his eyes, stinging. He blinked and tried to focus. The edges of his vision blurred.

Rupert was so intent on Sammy, he didn't even look round.

Theo raised the plank over his head.

There were footsteps behind him.

With a flourish, Bob Piggott pulled back the dust sheet from the door. 'It's over now, Minister,' he said.

CHAPTER TWENTY-EIGHT

Justice Through Valour

PC Shah followed Bob out of the cupboard Theo and Sammy had come through. Behind him came a man and a woman in plain clothes, who had the look of police officers – short hair, sensible shoes. They put Rupert in handcuffs, unzipped his sports bag and found the mace inside it.

Sammy was coaxed back from the ladder, clearly shaken. PC Shah took them into a room where the renovations were mostly finished and found them a couple of chairs to sit on. He left them with the woman in plain clothes and returned with two cups of tea and a blanket for Sammy. Theo assumed Bob Piggott had stayed with Rupert, because neither of them reappeared.

'What have you got yourselves mixed up in, eh?' PC Shah said, not unkindly.

'We were the ones who actually solved it though, weren't we?' The colour was returning to Sammy's cheeks and with it her defiance.

'Let's wait for your dad to get here and then you can tell us everything,' the plain clothes officer said. She had a very quiet but authoritative voice. She was a head shorter than Theo, about forty years old, with mousey-brown hair and a forgettable face. She was in every way average and unremarkable.

'My dad's coming?' Theo asked.

She nodded without taking her eyes from him and he found he had to look away.

'Good,' Sammy said, getting fired up. 'He'll listen to us.'

Theo didn't feel quite so confident. He thought of everything they had done – causing the diversion, going through a secret passageway they hadn't told anyone about, tracking down a thief on their own. His dad had expressly told him not to get involved and he had ignored him. He hoped finding the mace was enough to redeem himself.

He drank his tea in silence while PC Shah and Sammy argued about who had technically succeeded in apprehending the thief.

When his dad arrived, he didn't follow the officers through the trapdoor in the cupboard. He came through the entrance to the rest of the House, which was meant to be sealed off for the renovations. He swept in wearing his perfect neat suit and a deep frown.

'Theo, your mother has been worried sick!'

'Prime Minister, if I may,' the plainclothes officer began, 'I believe Theo and Sammy have vital information about the theft of the mace. I just need to take their statements and then they're free to go home.'

'Of course,' Theo's dad said. He rubbed at his neck and Theo knew then how worried he was. He only did that when things were really bad.

'PC Shah, I think Mr Piggott would benefit from your

assistance next door,' the plainclothes officer said. PC Shah took the hint and skulked out. 'Sammy, perhaps you could tell us what happened.'

Theo was relieved he hadn't been called on. He was starting to feel sick. He didn't think he could explain anything and he only half-listened while Sammy told them what they had done. He didn't dare look at his dad. He watched Sammy and tried to ignore the flickers of his dad's alarm and anger that caught his eye.

When Sammy had finished, his dad was rocking on his heels.

'You mean to tell me that you're responsible for the all that commotion earlier? You created that scene so that you could come down here and catch a criminal. You're a teenager, Theo, what the hell were you thinking?' his dad shouted.

'But we caught him!' Theo shouted, feeling the full injustice of his dad's anger. 'No one else found that hidden door. Just us!'

'And now look at the problems that's caused. He's in my own party, he's the Chief Whip, for god's sake. Do you know what the press would say about this?' His dad collected himself and lowered his voice. 'You should have come to me, dealt with this quietly.'

'I did come to you. You told me not to get involved.'

His dad turned away as if he hadn't spoken. 'I want to speak to Spencer now,' he said to the plainclothes officer.

'Right this way,' she said and they walked out.

'What does he mean, dealt with this quietly? The press will find out it was Spencer when he's charged with the theft,' Sammy whispered to him.

'Dunno.'

PC Shah came back in and Sammy fell silent.

They could clearly hear his dad speaking in the next room. His voice echoed around the cavernous space.

'When Felix warned me about you, I didn't believe him,' Theo's dad said. Theo couldn't believe what he was hearing. Whose side was Felix on? 'I should have listened. I suppose your dad put you up to this.'

'You know he's right. You're just too much of a coward to admit it,' Rupert replied.

Theo wondered who on earth Rupert's dad was. Why had he never suspected him, even done a brief search into his background?

'There'll be a reshuffle and you'll be out of the Cabinet. I'm going to banish you to the furthest wildernesses of government, so far from the thick of it you'll never worm your way back in.'

'You won't be in power for ever, Will. Once you're gone, I'll find my way back.'

There was an ominous silence.

'I left my son with you. I trusted you.'

If Rupert replied, his words were too quiet to catch.

'Get him out of here.' His dad strode back into the room. 'Theo, Sammy, come with me.'

The children followed him out in silence. He took them back into the main House, with its familiar corridors.

Theo wanted to ask what was going to happen to Rupert but didn't dare speak.

'How long will he be in prison?' Sammy said, trotting to keep up with Theo and his dad's wide strides.

'He's not going to prison.'

'What?' Theo and Sammy said in unison.

His dad stopped suddenly. He hesitated for a fraction of a second then he opened the nearest door on to an office. Several people working at computers looked up in surprise.

'Out,' his dad said, and they all left.

Theo's dad closed the door behind them.

'Rupert isn't going to prison because no one is going to find out what's he done.'

'But—' Sammy started and Will Duncan silenced her with a glance.

'You aren't to tell anyone what happened here tonight. You aren't to tell anyone that Rupert stole the mace and you aren't to tell anyone how it was found. My team and I will come up with some story, heaven only knows what. And neither of you will contradict it.' He pointed from one to the other, emphasising every word. 'God knows how many laws you've broken, but I'll make it all go away. No one need ever know what you did here, as long as you never reveal what really happened to that mace.'

Theo was dumbfounded. Was his dad seriously threatening them?

'Is that understood?' Will asked in a tone that made it clear any dissent was futile.

'Yes,' Theo mumbled.

'Perfectly,' Sammy said. Theo could tell she was seething.

'Your mother has come to collect you, Samira. As far as she knows, you went missing inside the palace this evening. We found you and Theo hiding out in one of the offices. And that's what you're going to tell her.'

Sammy's eyes glittered with rage. She didn't contradict him.

'Go,' Will said, opening the office door for them again. The staff were nowhere to be seen.

Justice Through Valour

*

After they had dropped Sammy off with Karminder, Theo's dad took him home in his government car. Theo was furious. They would never have found out that Rupert was the thief if it weren't for him and Sammy. He had never anticipated a situation in which his dad wouldn't want to know who the culprit was. Wasn't the family motto Justice through Valour? Where was the justice in this? Or, for that matter, the valour? Rupert had got off scot free as far as Theo could tell, because his dad didn't have the courage to face the consequences of prosecuting him.

'You're not to speak to Samira again,' his dad said, his voice quiet.

'What?'

His dad turned to face him. 'You heard me. I don't want you hanging around with her. This was totally unlike you, Theo. You've never been a rule breaker. This isn't you. She's led you astray and I don't like it. So you're not to speak to her any more. She isn't to come to dinner again and you're not to go to hers.'

'This was all my idea,' Theo spat.

'I don't believe you.'

Theo was shaking. There were a thousand things he wanted to say, but he knew none of them would change his dad's mind.

'Your actions have consequences, Theo,' his dad said, turning to look out of the window. 'You need to learn that.'

Theo looked out of his own window. The great black obelisk of the Cenotaph blurred as his eyes filled with tears he refused to allow to fall.

CHAPTER TWENTY-NINE

An Unexpected Offer

At lunchtime the next day, Theo sat on his own on a bench in the playground. He was reading the free newspaper they gave out on the tube; someone had left it on the seat. It was full of the discovery of the mace in the secret passageway, which 'Palace officials had finally located', and the fact that the House of Lords Reform Bill had passed the vote at its second reading with a tiny majority of two.

Theo read about the plans for the Bill to go into committee with interest. He knew almost nothing about the committee process and after reading the article, he suspected he knew even less. Except that it wasn't going to happen until after the summer recess. He still had some time to read up on what it all meant, then.

There was also a disturbing account of an unidentified lone gunman who had been in the palace the evening before. The newspaper was reporting it as if it had actually happened.

> The Prime Minister has denied reports that a gunman opened fire in the Houses of Parliament, saying it was a

An Unexpected Offer

> false alarm. However, several witnesses claim to have seen a man matching an as yet unverified description of the gunman at the scene. No witnesses who were present at the shooting itself have come forward.

Theo felt a stab of guilt. That was his fault. But how could witnesses possibly have seen someone matching a description of the gunman? If the police spoke to them, they would quickly work out that there hadn't been a gunman. Anyway, he was sure his dad must have told the police what really happened, even if the press didn't know.

He had seen one brief mention online that there were rumours of a Cabinet reshuffle, but the newspaper hadn't picked it up. There was too much interest in speculation about who the thief was to bother wasting valuable column inches on a humdrum reshuffle.

Theo remembered the conversation between his dad and Rupert the day before. There had been something about Rupert's dad. What was it? Theo took out his phone and typed Rupert's name into a search bar.

He found Rupert's dad straight away – Soames Spencer. He was a former Foreign Secretary, now a member of the House of Lords. So that was why Rupert was against the reform. His dad had put him up to it. Theo read on and discovered that Soames Spencer had also been a member of the Montgomery Pack, with Trevor Thompson. They had been at school together. He hadn't been completely wrong about the connection with the Montgomery Pack; it just turned out it wasn't Thompson. That must be why Rupert had used Thompson's school nickname. He suspected Thompson wasn't so much part of the Montgomery Pack as constantly on the edges of it.

An Unexpected Offer

Theo flicked through the newspaper, landing on a headline: 'Government scraps plans to slash school meal vouchers.' His eyes flicked over the very short piece. It only told him that the government had finally given in to the opposition to the plans. He sat back feeling stunned. He had almost forgotten his conversation with his dad about it. Was that why they had changed their plans? Couldn't be. His dad had been so angry with him, there was no way he had listened.

His eye caught someone approaching from the door to the school building. He looked up. It was Sammy and another girl – was her name Heather? Her hair was cut in a pixie crop and, like Sammy, she had holes in her jumper sleeves.

The girls were arm in arm, laughing about something, and heading straight his way. Theo closed the newspaper and put it down beside them.

As they drew level with him, Sammy looked at him askance. Her mouth turned up in a closed, forced smile, but she carried on walking.

Theo watched her retreating back as the two girls made for the cafeteria.

Theo was one of the last to leave the school grounds at the end of the day. He had packed his bag slowly at the end of class, trudged down the stairs and loitered on the landing. He didn't want to get home. The atmosphere was unbearable. But he wasn't allowed to go anywhere else either – not even the library.

His head down, watching his feet slap the stairs up to the street, Theo didn't notice Erin straight away.

An Unexpected Offer

'Theo,' she called. 'Fancy talking about the theft of the mace now?'

'No thanks,' Theo said, but he stopped anyway. It was something to do, to put off the moment when he had to get home. Harry was chatting to one of her friends a few paces away, studiously ignoring him.

'I would love to find out who you think took the mace. I've got my suspicions, but I bet you could confirm them.'

'You know I can't talk to you about it.'

'And yet here we are, talking about it,' she said, smiling. Theo shrugged. 'Is there anything you want to tell me about Chris Elliot?'

'Chris didn't steal the mace,' Theo said, a little too quickly.

'I didn't say he did.' She waited for him to go on and Theo thought it was probably time to go, whether he wanted to or not. He hitched his backpack higher on his shoulders. 'I just wondered if Chris might have been in Clapham on the morning of the theft?'

Theo couldn't help his surprise from registering on his face.

'So you know about Clapham and his sister, I'm guessing?' Erin probed.

'You're not going to report it, are you?'

Erin watched him for a moment. 'No, you're all right. His secret's safe with me. At least until it becomes politically relevant.'

Theo figured that was the best he could hope for. 'You're not as bad as you seem.'

'Well, thank you,' Erin said, hamming up her Irish accent. 'You're not so bad yourself. I'm quite impressed actually. I have a hunch you had a lot more to do with this mace

An Unexpected Offer

business than your dad wants to let on.'

'I've got to get home for dinner.'

'If you ever want to take up a career in journalism, I'll show you the ropes.'

'See you later, Erin,' Theo said, walking away. He couldn't help smiling a little to himself as he went.

'Who was that?' Harry asked with disdain.

'Nobody,' Theo said.

CHAPTER THIRTY

A Game of Tennis

That night, when Theo's dad arrived home, Theo found him in the kitchen, where he was talking to his mum. His dad had barely looked at him, much less spoken to him, since he had arrived back from the palace the evening before. His parents fell silent. Theo wondered if it would always be this awkward now.

'Theo, can we have a word?' his dad said, not quite meeting his gaze. He looked shifty, almost as if he felt guilty for something.

Theo nodded and they went into his dad's study together. The last time they had been in there, they had argued about him investigating the theft of the mace. Theo wondered if he was going to be told off again.

He took the seat on the sofa and his dad sat next to him, uncomfortably close. He waited for his dad to speak. He looked like a professor who had failed to solve a particularly troublesome formula – hunched and wan.

'I want to apologise for everything that happened yesterday and for the last few weeks, really.' Theo looked up in

A Game of Tennis

surprise. His dad was twisting the ring on his little finger, not meeting his eye. 'I'm sorry I didn't listen to you about the mace. And I'm sorry you got caught up in that fiasco yesterday.'

Theo stifled his surprise. The day before his dad had blamed him for the fiasco.

'You do understand why I did what I did, don't you? You understand that nobody – *nobody* – can know that Rupert was the thief.'

Theo turned away. He caught sight of his dad's Red Box on the desk. He remembered how eager he had once been to look inside it. He had no interest in it now. Not now he knew that the government secrets people knew existed were just decoys. The real secrets were the ones the government wouldn't even admit to having.

He couldn't quite keep the bitterness out of his voice as he answered. 'I'm not going to tell anyone.'

'But you must understand why.' His dad had become very animated and there was a wild look in his eye. 'If it was known that someone who worked for me, who was in my own Cabinet, was responsible for the theft, it would be the end of my career. I wouldn't just be made to give up my job as Prime Minister, I might never work in politics again. And I have so much left to do, Theo, so many plans that I haven't seen through yet. You understand that, don't you?'

Theo wasn't sure that he did. 'But Rupert committed a crime. He's getting away with it.'

'He won't get away with it. I've made sure his career will suffer. And there would be no justice in me losing my job over it. Would that be fair?'

Theo shrugged.

A Game of Tennis

'In future, you must leave it to me to solve these problems. You know you shouldn't have got involved.'

Theo bristled. They wouldn't have found the mace without him.

'Felix was on Rupert's trail, he would have got him eventually.'

That brought Theo up short. 'Felix knew it was Rupert?'

'He warned me about him. He thought Rupert was trying to swing the vote the other way. I told Felix to get me the evidence.' Theo thought of the conversation he had overheard Felix having with Rupert. He could have been trying to investigate Rupert. But what if it was a double bluff? He still wasn't sure that he trusted him. 'Perhaps I should have listened to him sooner. But we had it in hand. You have to promise me you won't do anything like this again.'

It cost Theo too much to speak. He nodded in silence.

'I've dropped the cuts in school meal vouchers,' his dad said. 'You were right about that. I should have listened to you. And for the record, I do care about children in poverty. That's why it's so important that I keep my job, so that I can help solve these problems.'

Theo felt incomprehensibly lighter. He hadn't realised before how much the issue had been bothering him. He could tell his dad meant it – that he did care. But Theo thought he was a bit deluded, believing he was part of the solution. It was his idea to make the cuts. It seemed better not to get into that now.

'How can I make it up to you?' his dad said.

His dad grasped his knee and his ring dug into Theo. Theo looked down at it. He didn't want to have to ask for his. He was supposed to deserve it. His dad was supposed to know.

A Game of Tennis

He looked up and saw that his dad had seen him looking at the ring. A strange look passed across his face. Then his dad let go of him and looked away. He started twisting the ring around his finger again. Theo wondered if his dad knew what he wanted, what he had been thinking. If he did, he hadn't offered it to him. He still didn't think Theo deserved the ring. Theo clenched his jaw. He wasn't going to be forced to ask.

'There is something actually.' He hesitated. He wanted to remember exactly what he had planned to say. 'I'm not going to do rugby any more.' He had rehearsed these words in his head. He didn't want to ask for permission. He wanted his dad to know, he was giving up, no matter what he thought. His parents couldn't drag him out of the house every Saturday morning and if they did, they couldn't make him run around a field for two hours. So he wouldn't. 'I'm rubbish at it. And I hate it. I want to do tennis instead.'

His dad stiffened. He didn't seem pleased, but slowly he said, 'All right. Your mum and I will look into a tennis instructor for you.'

They nodded stiffly to one another and Theo left.

He went back to his room and closed the door softly. He wanted to call Sammy, but he didn't know if she was speaking to him. Perhaps her mum had banned her from speaking to him as well. Maybe that was why she hadn't come over at lunchtime. He didn't want to get her into trouble. And he didn't know what his parents would do if they found out he was still speaking to her. He was already grounded until the summer holiday. Maybe they would make him stay at home all summer as well.

He checked the time. He only had a few minutes before

A Game of Tennis

he had to check in his phone for the night with his mum.

He decided he didn't care what trouble he got into with his parents. Sammy was his friend. He didn't want to stop speaking to her. The question was, did she want to speak to him? There was only one way to find out.

The phone slipped against his sweaty palms as he lifted it to his ear. What would he do if she wouldn't speak to him? Was he prepared to leave her alone?

The phone went quiet after only two rings. With a sinking feeling, he realised she must have rejected his call. But it didn't go to voicemail. In fact, there was no sound on the other end.

'Hello?' Theo said.

'I'm not supposed to be talking to you,' Sammy whispered.

His heart flooded with relief. 'Me too. But I've got an idea. I've been thinking, I don't think Rupert is going to give up. It doesn't matter that my dad has sent him to Coventry—'

'I didn't know that, what's he doing there?'

'No, he hasn't gone to Coventry,' Theo went on in a furiously fast whisper. 'It's an expression. It just means he's in trouble. But I still think he's going to try to stop the Bill from going through and you know where it goes next?'

'Into committee,' Sammy said.

Theo felt a thrill of victory. She had looked that up too.

'Exactly. He's going to cause as much trouble as possible. So I think we need to be there to stop him.' Theo instinctively checked the door behind him. It was still firmly shut.

'How?'

A Game of Tennis

'Work experience next year. We'll go to work for an MP in the Houses of Parliament.'

'That is genius.'

'It is quite clever,' Theo said, sitting down on his bed. He was glad she couldn't see his cheeks turning red. 'Meet tomorrow lunchtime in the library?'

'Nope,' she said and his heart sunk. For a moment he had thought their friendship would go on as before. 'We've got Citizenship tomorrow morning. See you there.'

She hung up.

Theo lay back on his bed, a giant grin all over his face.

Body in the Thames

Join Theo and Sammy on their next adventure, *Body in the Thames*.

While Theo and Sammy grapple with work experience inside Parliament, Westminster is shaken by the discovery of a body in the Thames. All signs point to murder. Journalist Erin Connelly is convinced the death is connected to rumours of MPs planning to break away from Will Duncan's party.

With security heightened, Sammy and Theo must be especially clever to evade detection as they work with Erin, question MPs and search the Palace of Westminster for clues.

The duo have one vital piece of evidence the police don't have. But can they gather enough evidence to bring the murderer to justice before Will's party tears itself apart and the murderer strikes again?

The next instalment in the Westminster Mysteries series is available now from all good book retailers.

Glossary

Aide
Someone who works for an MP, helping them answer their emails from voters and manage their calendar.

Bill (parliamentary)
A draft of an Act of Parliament which has not yet been approved by MPs. MPs must debate the Bill and vote to approve it before it can be turned into an Act and become law.

Cabinet Minister
The most senior MPs who are chosen by the Prime Minister to run each government department, such as Education or Health.

Civil service
The unelected organisation whose officials do a lot of government work – researching possible new laws and implementing those that Parliament votes through.

Coalition
An agreement between political parties that they will run the country together. Occurs after a hung parliament.

Glossary

Constituency
A voting area in the UK. People who live in each one can vote in a general election for one MP to represent them in the House of Commons. Whoever gets the most votes becomes the MP for that constituency until the next election. Each constituency has what is called one 'seat' in the House of Commons.

House of Commons
A chamber in the Houses of Parliament where elected MPs debate and discuss possible new laws and other subjects that are important to the country. They pass some Bills into law.

House of Lords
The other chamber, sometimes called the 'other place', in the Houses of Parliament where unelected senior people – Lords – debate and discuss possible new laws and other subjects that are important to the country. They can seek to change the proposed laws and delay them from being passed.

Hung parliament
An election result in which no single political party has a majority of seats in the House of Commons. A minority government could form, but they will find it difficult to pass any laws because the opposition parties outnumber them and could out-vote them. The other alternative is a coalition.

Manifesto
A document created by a political party before an election to tell voters what they plan to do (their policies) if they get elected.

Glossary

Member of Parliament (MP)
A person voted for by the majority of the people who vote in a constituency to represent them in Parliament.

Recess
The time when Parliament is closed for a break and MPs either have time off or work in their constituencies.

Shadow Cabinet
Similar to the government's main Cabinet, but the Shadow Cabinet is formed of opposition MPs. For example, the opposition party will choose someone to act as Shadow Foreign Secretary.

Special advisor (spad)
Someone chosen by a Minister, from outside the civil service, to work for them. They usually advice on particular topics, such as speaking to the press.

Whip
An MP who works for the senior members of their political party to ensure that others from their party vote the way the party wants in the House of Commons. Some say they use fair means or foul to achieve their aims.

A full glossary of more terms used in the book can be found at www.sarahlustig.com/extended-glossary.

Acknowledgements

Many people helped in the writing and development of this book. Without them, it would never have seen the light of day.

Thank you to Nick Hawkins, Conservative MP 1992–2005 and former Shadow Solicitor-General among many other roles, for taking me round the palace and checking my manuscript for accuracy. Any remaining errors are my own.

Thank you to my early readers, Sarah Green, Elliot James-English and Sze Kiu Yeung, for your helpful insights and comments.

Thank you to Antonia Prescott for your honest feedback and encouragement.

Thank you to my cover designer, Jacqui Crawford, and my illustrator, Katie Melrose. You made my cover dreams come true.

And thank you to my family and friends for your endless support and encouragement. I couldn't do it without you.

About the Author

Sarah Lustig grew up in London and went to school in Westminster, with politicians' children. Her experiences at school and interest in politics inspired the idea for the book. *Mystery in the Palace of Westminster* is Sarah's debut novel. She has been a book editor for over 15 years and now lives in Buckinghamshire.

To find out more, go to www.sarahlustig.com. There you can sign up to the Westminster Mysteries Readers Club. You will receive exclusive offers, updates about the series and free sneak previews, including an extended epilogue for *Mystery in the Palace of Westminster*.

Sarah would love to know what you thought of *Mystery in the Palace of Westminster*. Why not write a review? You can submit a review on Goodreads, Amazon or your preferred bookseller's website. Sarah can't wait to read your comments!